CW00482038

The

Alan Edward Roberts was born in Liverpool, England in 1973. He is a graduate of The Arts Institute of Bournemouth and Coventry University. He founded Yeehah Theatre Productions and went on to write and stage seven plays at various venues across England, including London, between 1997 and 1999. He currently lives and works as a professional copywriter in North Devon, England. He is also a music historian that has edited 'Megablast – The Top 100 UK Rap Records (1987-1993)' for author Mark McDonald of The Mail on Sunday. 'The Magpie' is his first novel.

Set in Times New Roman & Century Gothic – 11pt
Edited by Samantha Thomas, Jayne Miller & Joanna Gibbs
Synopsis by Samantha Thomas
Typeset by Hanna Lambert
Cover image OVERREVS by Mark McDonald, courtesy of
@getmarktodoit
Author photo by Andy Rous
Printed and bound in Great Britain by Clays Ltd, Elcograf S.p.A
English to Polish excerpt - translation by Ula Markowicz
Steven Taylor – https://federation-design.co.uk

ISBN: 978-1-9160833-0-1

First Edition

Road Song Books (UK)
www.roadsongbooks.com

April 2019

THE MAGPIE

ROAD SONG BOOKS
UK

"I was born the day she first kissed me and I died the day she left."

'In a Lonely Place' – Humphrey Bogart

For my family, for my friends – new, old and future.

One

1994 - Johnny

You Know More About Me Than I Know About You

Up there, on the ancient mountainside, hordes of mosqui-
toes floated in daily on the warm air currents, buoyed up
from the mangrove islands in the river delta. They collected,
unnoticed around the stagnant remnants of rain ponds and
old stockman's wells, as was their sacrament. Drawn in by
the scent of sweat, a feathery-legged specimen attempted to
ally itself to the thick skin of Johnny Pearce's neck. Reclined
in the front seat of his police rover, he could easily hear
their low-watt siren calls - he made short work of the thirsty
insect, devastating it with a well-aimed slap. As the stinging
sensation from the kill subsided he inspected the remains of
the mosquito compacted at the apex of his fingertips.

If he asked himself why he always picked this spot to park
up, he wouldn't have had an answer. Introspection wasn't his
forte. Solitude gets a lot of bad press but even though he'd
spend a lot of his spare time alone staring out at the empty
views around these parts, he didn't feel lonely - that was just
the design.

You couldn't see the city lights from up here behind the
mountain's head at night. And on a bright day there was little
else to dazzle your eye beyond the endless carpet of parched
green tree canopies. Yet Johnny could easily differentiate the
regions moving through the east to the western limits - from
Hogan's Pocket, Stamper's Bluff, The Kerrigans, across to

Miracle Head - all he had to do was tease the thread of The German Road out from the pale khaki melee with his eye and watch it snake out to the horizon. The old named road was little more than a track and it could only be comfortably traversed by the hardiest of utes these days. He had been planning a solo trek out to The Kerrigans for some time; it was a good 30-40 kilometres off but still within his capabilities if he made responsible preparations and took the right gear along. The Kerrigans were elevated enough so that he could see the whole range from his slouched position behind the steering wheel.

His son, Glenn, was getting out of the clink in few days and he wanted to be out of the way when he got back into town. Let him have a crack at Pete first, he thought.

As the sky darkened, Johnny could hear a distant farmstead dog as it hollered at nothing else except the passing of another dying day.

Two

1994 - The Chorus

Ain't No Grave Can Hold Me In

"I've got Johnny Pearce's eulogy right here. I'll read it to you if you like."

*

"That Glenn stood in the graveyard and he read this hateful piece. Bold as an All Black centre-forward, he pretty much damned the bugger to hell. Spat at the coffin, caused a right old fucking brawl too."

"Yeah, I know, I was there."

*

"Announced to us all that we were burying a 'bad man' and no tears were to be shed."

Three

1988 to 1991 - Glenn

This Is A Love Song

Around the time we all started at North Dewie High, I would sit out on the porch and watch as the girls came wandering down Burston Street in their royal blue school uniforms. My eyes would always search Nicole out from my other school-mates. Her skin was so pale: too pale when compared to the other girls round here. They were all tanned, healthy - olive skinned or coffee brown like Indians, even the blondes. Later on, I got up enough pluck to follow them along at a distance on my BMX, slowly coasting down the middle of the street. Me and my mate, Crusty, would try diligently to find a way into their conversations, so now and then we'd get tossed a bone - often a question about one of our sports dick classmates or to flog some chips off us.

I couldn't get her on her own to begin with. These girls ran in packs - using each other for protection; how were we to line up the shot with so many of them around at all times? What did they talk about, sat around in recess plaiting each other's hair or sharing cigarettes at Mully's? They inhabited a hive mind - no room for interloping boys just yet. We weren't able to crack into those circles for years.

Some girls peak early, breaking rank, just to show off to the others. The road most travelled often involved a dramatic show of 'going' with some alpha-wannabe or the strongest available jock in the field. First to flower, first to fall, they say.

Nicole probably picked me simply because her she thought her time was right and the once firm female bonds around her were beginning to strain: the friendships regularly breached by us boys. She wasn't the first to skip the fence, but she was far from the last, and she didn't make a break to impress the other 'ants' either. Maybe Nicole wanted to scratch a subversive itch, buck the trend just a little bit by homing in on someone a little weird like me. I wasn't a himbo, so I avoided sports and popular choices in general, I'd sit in the music room mastering my chords on the guitar, or I thrashed at drums. Whatever it was that drew her in, I got caught up, ensnared in the tricky spider's web that is first love - back when all us teens were experts at longing. To begin with, people took the piss, then she just became a part of our social landscape – not once did my mates ask questions. That's because we didn't talk that way - nobody round here did.

II

Nicole was the first girl I ever 'went down the road' with. For the first month or so she wouldn't let me put it inside. She would just ride my crotch fully clothed, put on a record and rubbed herself off against me. I just wanted to rip her fucking clothes off, not spoof in my pants like a loser. She'd become coy and would leap up off the bed to change the record every time my fingers ventured beyond the elastic of her pants. She wouldn't let the needle play the dead space so all this fucking dry humping shit didn't lead to all that much. Flock of Seagulls, The Blue Nile, Tangerine Dream, Daryl Braithwaite: they all lent their variable talents to the soundtrack of our first few rooting sessions. Beyond the musical choices, I still get a jolt even now when I catch the scent of someone wearing her fragrance, one popular with girls back then. I still don't know what it is yet I'm a slave to the portals that stir me back into those moments and all it takes is a trigger and I'll be lost. At my work desk, I'll get spotted staring out of a window and a colleague will always ask me if I'm OK, but I'm a 1000 kilometres away and nearly 30 years off in the past.

Even in a state of arousal, Nicole's areolas had no pigmentation and were as white as flour dough. A solitary freckle broke the illusion of uncanny blankness on each of her breasts - I've never encountered a woman with such an anomalous bodily quirk since. Up to that point, I'd only seen boobs in the mags that other kids used to cart into school with them - stolen from their dad's or older brothers; it was the only point of reference most of us young dickheads had.

The first time Nicole let me go down on her she made me stop for a minute to explain that she thought she might be a bit ripe on account of working hard that day at the RSL café. Undaunted, I went ahead anyway. I remember there was some purple lint in her pubic hair. There was no odour - I didn't taste anything at all.

Four

1994 - The Chorus

The Past Is A River, Not A Boulder

"All I can tell you is that he'd run Roo Stamper's heeler down on the way back into town. Didn't kill it outright. Took it out to the vet. A real lucky guess that the Doc was still in the surgery that late. Well not so lucky for Mr Dog."

"It was a bitch, dog was a girl."

*

"I advised that Glenn to turn around, get back in his car and piss off back to where he came from. I mean there was no love lost between him and anybody that knew him after what he'd done. Dog needed to be put down. Impact of the car had broken the poor bugger's back and yet he'd carried its near dead carcass into my surgery, bleeding everywhere. Thing was limp, I don't know why he didn't put it out of its misery back out on the road."

*

"It's hind quarters had been flattened into the bitumen."

*

"He should've fucked it with a rock. Killed the bastard. Nicest thing he could've have done, but."

*

"I think that Glenn kid wanted to show us all what he'd done. Like a fucked up calling card saying, "Look fellas, I'm back," or something. Maybe."

*

"Ill blood bears ill."

"Right."

Five

Mid 1980s - Glenn

The Decedents

Me, Crusty and Robbie Diaz used to fuck about with the cane toads. We'd get a catapult and fire stones at them. They were so soft, the stones used to fly straight through them like a bullet. They'd lie, dying in the sun on their backs like this, fingers and palms stretched out in parched agony, and then we came and we stamped them flat into the road - kicking their fetid skins into the overflows. Crusty said he'd gotten the idea from a horror film he'd seen. There were so many of the bastards. I never had much of a taste for it... it was just something us boys did.

Robbie once came up with a really stupid idea for a cockroach killer that he was planning to sell by mail order - it was an ice lolly stick with the letter 'A' written at one end and 'B' at the other. The instructions simply said, 'Hold Point 'A' between finger and thumb. And line Point 'B' up above the offending cockroach's head. Pull and release = dead fucking cockroach.' Like everything else, it got talked out of existence.

Crusty was always the one trying to knock the giant electrified bat corpses down from the power lines with bricks, stones, harsh words and sticks. All blackened with their putrefied eyes bulging, clenched talons, lolling half-eaten tongues: a cloud of busy flies. "That one looks like your sister, ay."

Sometimes we'd try to disturb the dormant rays in the cool river shallows near the town bridge by dropping rocks and stuff off the side. We pinned one down there on the riverbed once, but it wasn't long before other things came along and ate him.

Six

1991 - Glenn

The Long Day Closes

I got on well with Dean Wexler pretty much straight from the off. He had a thing for Japanese cars and he had 20 or so of them sat in a large semi-circle around his tatty Queenslander, some in pieces. I think he grew up in Germany as a boy because his approximation of the Australian accent had a strange inflection. He had an odd European-accented English with a light Aussie twist, so that he'd end sentences like someone from around here would, with an 'ay' or a 'but'. "Ay boy, time for a smoko, ay."

Some time ago, decades in fact, he changed his name to Dean from something exotic, s'all I knew about his past.

Dean seemed wary, almost afraid of my dad and I never knew why. My old man was one of the lads and Dean, although he stayed out of trouble, wasn't in that same circle. If you didn't try to cosy up to my father - whether he was in his role as the senior police officer for the region or in his personal life - you were viewed as suspect: a nobody, and you'd watch your way or else. There was always an 'edge' there whenever he was mentioned in convo but I never saw them within a mile of one another, and I never found out their connection.

None of my friends made an effort with their girlfriends' olds, but somehow I hit it off with Dean. Monosyllabic and as weathered as rust - it was a quiet sort of worship. Somewhere along the line, he began to teach me a bit about small engine repair, in lieu of meaningful conversations or the interrogations most of us might have expected from this kind of dynamic. It followed that I got interested in Japanese cars too. Those bastards weren't built to last decades in their native country but they did in some parts of Oz like the hot parts where constant damp weather wasn't an issue, instead they endured. After a period, Dean fixed up a Datsun Sunny 120Y for me. It was a real 'dog' that was in need of constant repair. I don't think I ever left Dewie in it, and if she ever broke down she was towed across town back to Dean's and fixed up all over again - spit and Sellotape.

He wasn't an official mechanic, he was an accountant and did people's books in a buggered old shed out amongst the wrecks, but if you'd owned a Datsun or a Toyota he'd help you out for a few bucks. Type of guy he was. He always looked like he knew everything too.

"What's for tea, Deano?"

Dean would pull on his rollie and exhale smoke before saying whatever came next, "I don't know, mate," over emphasizing the 't' in mate. Even if he didn't know the answer, he would tell you that he didn't know it like it was the answer you were looking for.

Of all the people to have come and gone throughout my life: best friends, lovers, mates, acquaintances, store assistants you see every day, when it comes to draw down, Dean is the person I'll be found sat with at the end. I'd pick him.

"We're all his sheep, mate..." he'd often say and I don't know

why. I don't think he believed in Jesus or anything other than the business end of his tool kit. Perhaps he was talking about the Devil.

II

Dean drops the bonnet down on the sleepy wreck of a rusty blue Toyota Corolla. A startled bird explodes from its nearby roost into the torn russet sky; it casts a look of self-righteous disgust back over its shoulder/wing.

"She is very fucked," he whinges as he throws his greasy rag down into the dust and I watch him go indoors, slamming yet another door shut. The fly screen gets caught in a stiff waft of hot air blowing. A freight train blares its horn as it hammers through the new night.

I stand in amongst the Japanese hatchbacks and look up at Nicole's bedroom window. A television flickers its glow onto her ceiling.

Seven

1994 - The Chorus

No Bad Deeds, Just Deeds

"Dewhurst Speedway, remember when that place was good?"

*

"We used to go down there as kids with the 'olds'. Used to love watching the vintage cars pelt round those sharp bends. Screaming our lungs out over the engines."

*

"There was a category for juniors. All the old fellas used to compete as there was a leader board for them too. You see them propping up the bar down the Crown Hotel by the river nowadays, talking shit about the good old, bad old days and having punch-ups."

"The racecourse touts, bookies, crooks, cowies, cockies and derros."

*

"Besides being this place for families to come on the weekend to watch the junior heats, the Speedway was also this kind of dodgy place where people of low character met up."

*

"The place became a well-known neutral spot for people to do pick ups. Money, drugs, contraband, stolen shit. Its bad rep killed it off in the end, families kept their kids away.

Local sponsors pulled out. Fucking shame."

*

"People still pull in there to beat an old personal best around the track but there's nothing official, it's mostly closed up like the drive-in. Anyway, the circuit's gone to wrack and ruin, full of potholes; the wet saw to that."

*

"Remember that fucking rat bag Kerry Spencer?"

*

"Kerry was there for going on two years and the bastard never worked a stroke, fucking bludger. He was from Auckland, a Kiwi. Probably back there now. But he was just concerned about creaming money off the top of the place... getting the most money for the least work."

"Isn't that what we all want?"

*

"Yeah that Kerry used to fuck all over the place. Messing with the younger sorts that used to go up to the speed track to get free smokes and booze off the drivers. Johnny Pearce told me one night they'd got called out because Kerry had gotten chained up to his stove by some teenagers – he got some posh girl pregnant. All this boiling water."

"I heard it was vegetable oil."

"Yeah well Johnny and Pete Wilson turned up in the nick of time 'cos he was going to get burned by it."

*

"The cooker was jerry rigged so if someone opened the door the fat would fly off the stove and all over Spencer."

"Not how I heard it mate."

"Well, that's how it happened."

"Way I heard it, he got dowsed in warm water."

*

"He called out. Johnny heard him hollering and they worked out how to get in without going through the door."

"How exactly? He lived on the first floor, remember?"

"Right. Yes he did."

II

1992 - John, Pete and Kerry

What Really Happened

On the afternoon in question, I got a call from Jack Lüven, who lives along Webber Road that runs down the back of the Speedway. There was a big old fire raging and he said there were nothing but kids and dogs out there playing music and making one unholy hell of a racket. Could we take a look, as Kerry Spencer the manager, was nowhere to be seen?

As it was a weekend in February there was nothing too untoward about kids on the loose. But this Spencer owed me some 'blind eye cash' so myself and the only other cop I really trusted, Senior Police Constable Pete Wilson, went out to see him

We didn't put the blues on as we drove up. But as soon as the fit little buggers saw us they scarpered any which way man invented. Jack Lüven was waiting for us pointing up at the crazed track-side shack on stilts Spencer stayed in. He was sweating, and looked put out which was unusual for him 'cos he was a staunched, one-word-a-day type bloke who didn't speak to say nothing.

*

Johnny -   *"Spit it out, Jack. What is it?"*

Jack -   *"He's shouting something about being chained to the cooker. And his front door being fucked."*

Johnny -   *"That makes about as much sense to me as your dress sense."*

Jack -   *"Well go up yourself, he's in hysterics. You know these Kiwis."*

Johnny -   *"Sensitive."*

Anyway we go up the steps and we hear him hollering, crying all sorts but he's babbling. Pete checks the door out. Down on all fours, he says he can see that Kerry's sat on the floor and that he can hear something cooking on the stove. Pete gets up, then tries the door... we hear an almighty scream as Kerry's shouts his mouth off. Nothing's happening inside his shitty hovel, except we see he's been chained to the cooker and that there's a pan that had boiled dry teetering at the edge of the hob. A piece of string had been tied to the pan's handle and the other end to the door knob - except the twits did it, somehow, without working out the door opened inwards. We were clearly dealing with a new order of intelligence.

Johnny -   *"How's it going mate, you alright?"*

Kerry -   *"Fucking kids chained me up."*

Pete -   *"Is this to do with Fallon?"*

Kerry -   *"Who?"*

Pete went and whacked him with a spatula covered in old baked beans plucked from the god-awful squalor.

It was like a proper douchebag's museum in there too: adhesive wood wall-paneling, surf company logo stickers on the windows, a ratty copy of Stephen King's 'It', rap tapes, and a sun bleached poster of the pulchritudinous Farrah Fawcett in hot pants and a yellow tee were amongst its exhibition pieces. The salty smell of feet, farts, Old Spice and two-stroke enhanced by the heat off the hob set the scene flawlessly. You get the picture surely.

Kerry -   *"She's 17. You wouldn't have turned it down."*

Johnny -   *"Shall we leave him chained up Pete?"*

Pete -   *"I've not noted the call, so we could."*

Johnny -   *"You got our money, Kerry?"*

Kerry -   *"Is that what this is about?"*

Johnny -   *"Well you're either with us or you owe us,
               mate."*

Pete -   *"Won't be water in the pan next time either, just
               so you know."*

Johnny -   *"You've got until Monday or you're going back
               to the land of the long white cloud mate or
               worse."*

Pete -   *"Aotea Roa!"*

*Pete stuck his tongue out like a Maori for effect, before
turning the hob off. Funny as fuck it was.*

Kerry -   *"Fucking Australians."*

Pete -   *"Watch it mate, no Australia, no Russell Crowe."*

*Anyway, we left the mongrel there for the night. Bright and
early the following Monday, made him pay up.*

Eight

1994 - Gully

Dead But Never Still

The Pioneer Valley Cemetery is still situated way beyond the city limits, as if Dewhurst had never grown as big as the founders had envisioned.

Everybody was there. From the first settlers to the ashes of a stillborn that died last Thursday.

Crouched at a bend in the Pioneer River, every monsoon season would inspire the flow of the river to encroach onto the cemetery by a few more metres each time before retreating again a few weeks later. The incursive waters would spirit the bones of about five people away whenever it happened, pushing the hapless dead out into the Pacific Ocean to seek not one, but several ever-rotating resting places.

Whilst in the bath the other day, cemetery sexton Gully Green calculated that with the current rate of river intrusion, it would be Johnny Pearce's turn to be washed away in 115 years, give or take.

Nine

1994 - The Chorus

Take This Waltz

"His car was found up on the mountain. He'd been on leave for two days, yet no one had seen him about the city."

"Those police cars got tracking wotsits in them, but."

"Devices."

"You what?"

"Devices, tracking devices."

"S'what I just said, mate."

*

"No one I've spoke to can remember whether Johnny's police rover was up there for the full two days."

"Unlocked apparently."

"Minor detail."

*

"The car park up there has been the lover's lane around here long before my grandfather's day so the presence of a police car up there may well have stopped people from pulling in. I'd certainly think twice about it."

*

"Technically the turn around up there is called Blue Jay Bend."

*

"Poofters mainly. S'how it all turned out anyway. Hardly any normal couples go up there these days."

*

"Not too many people would murder a police cop around here. Mind you Johnny Pearce had a fair amount of enemies. He wasn't one of those cops that would turn the other way like you tend to find this far out, not unless it suited him. He could be a fucking brute too if you got on the wrong side of him. No, he didn't want friends that 'fulla', he wanted subjects."

*

"Johnny Pearce had a regular room he'd book down at the '501 Motel' at City Limits where he'd take Shorty, Fatso or another one of those old boilers every now and again."

*

"I go up to Blue Jay Bend regularly to meet other men for sex. It's been a regular haunt for decades. All I'll say on the matter of Johnny Pearce is that sometimes you'd be very surprised who'd show up come sundown. It's a small city."

Ten

1994 - Bert

You Can Hear The Whistle Blow

A new cop came to town, Maltese bloke called Marcos Vella. Didn't last long, under a year. Looked like the fella who played Paulie in the Rocky movies. He told his oppos that he wanted a tracker. The closest thing they got to traditional native search and rescue around here is me. And it's only because I own a bit of the land going out towards The Kerrigans that they asked me to pitch in.

'Cause I'm a black fella everyone assumes I can track, but I don't have tribal ancestry. Ignorant fuckers.

Two days no word, and the empty police car. It's all they had. I suggested that those police folk need to go shake some trees down in the city. Maybe Motel 501 and I got told to shut the fuck up and mind me Ps and Qs.

Eleven

1994 - The Radio

You Better Sit Still

"This morning the body reported found in remote bush land 1 kilometre west of The German Road near Hogan's Pocket was identified as that of Police Sgt. John Pearce.

The circumstances behind the respected senior police officer's death are not known at this point.

For further news bulletins stay tuned in to 4DW. Dewhurst's number one choice for news."

"4DW. The people's ch-ch-ch-choice."

Twelve

1934

Don't Marry The One You Love

In 1934, the 50 metre long metal steamer, Verity II, floundered
on a reef 2 kilometres due south of Dewhurst at the estuary
of the Pioneer River and there she's sat ever since and all the
while.

A heavy sea.

The passenger ship had left Cairns bound for Sydney, to
meet with the SS Strathnaver bound for the UK and Europe;
she had lost her bearings. Now wedged into the only rocks
around, the vessel stands upright on her keel to be battered by
the surf at low tide and to act as a break at high tide. Nothing
remains of her paddle wheels or the housing on her deck; the
woodwork was stole away by the sea long ago. Like a true
beauty she's beyond all reach. Treacherous tides mean there's
no one willing to risk their own craft to go scuba diving
or wild surfing about her. Wreck baggers have to settle for
close ups through long-range lenses and view her from some
difficult spots along the shoreline.

The man-made debris and waves along the mouth of the
estuary have, over time, created a hefty sub aqua sand bar
that prevents large boats from getting up river. Since the city
hasn't used a dredger in over 50 years the river remains too
shallow even for the smallest of boats. Along with a marina
and deep water dock, a jetty was built north-ways up the coast

a short distance, beyond the mangrove islands that populate much of the delta.

It was so long ago. Only four people can remember the day when the Verity II came to blows on the rocks. One of them was Val Burton from Yalbaroo. In fact, his future wife, Amanda had been aboard. That's how they met. He'd been on one of the rescue boats when the coast guard was alerted after the crew of the floundering vessel had fired a very gun.

And there the Verity II waits, guarding the watery entrance to the city. The mangroves still whisper to her. The fish sooth her battle wounds.

II

"There may be two doors in this room, but there's only one way out."

These were just some of the last words able sea-man Chan Bishop had time to assemble in his mind as he cartwheeled his broken boned dance across the sea floor. The thick, heavy water had already pushed the air from his lungs in a stream of blinding bubbles hours ago.

Bishop was facing backwards now, as the shock of the new overtook him; the fast underwater drift made his arms and legs stream out behind him. Then he stopped moving. Vertically set, his feet hovered centimetres above the sandy bed before he was moved downwards - it felt to him like he was being placed in position by a gigantic hand, almost as if he were a child's figurine.

"Don't try to understand this," thought Bishop.

The battered sailor had never felt less thirsty. The exquisite tenderness from the gentle spin of a bubble of air against the roof of his mouth cavity, Chan's life now, an unfinished letter, his feet touch nothing, and his legs kick - he propels himself upwards through the complement of sea water above his head. Breaking the surface he roars, *"Help meeeee! Help!"*

Don't release this stranger's hand.

The rough fingertips, the knots in their hands yank him clear of the choppy surface and haul him into the lifeboat. Chan lies spluttering like a landed barramundi. *"I'm alive,"* he gasps, spitting blood and seawater. Not one tooth remained inside his head.

"Alive, alive oh," says a voice as cold as the slab.

"Throw him back, he's too small," says another.

Bishop hears the flapping of a small flag caught in the sea wind. Or was it the wings of an angel?

Thirteen

1994 - The Chorus

The Abyssal Plains

"It was like a fucking movie. They got some Abo bloke to track for 'em."

"A Cry In The Dark."

"It wasn't an Abo, it was Bert, fella owns the land back up there."

"Yeah Black Bert."

"He's a TSI though."

"Can't tell the fucking difference. Who can?"

"Yeah well, classical racism aside, he owns all the space back there and up to the hills. Fucking miles of it. Nothing but trees and rocks."

*

"He's got a zucchini farm up there at Hogan's Pocket. I've worked a few seasons for him when I was a kid. Best payer around. And seeing as he best knew the area the cops asked him to assist with the search and rescue."

*

"I imagine Pete and them never go out there."

"Four foot from a road or a bed is those cops' limit."

*

"I think he got 'tooken'."

"By what? A fucking bunyip?"

"His son. Glenn."

"He didn't get to town until just before the funeral, but."

"He could've got here early? Lived out in the bush, asked for a meet up at that gay spot on the hill and knocked him off."

"What do you mean, 'knocked him off' you nong. Are you serious?"

"Fucking bashed him, dickhead."

"You think he's coming back to get even, do ya? Who with? It should be one of us that go and pay him a fucking visit for what happened to Nicole."

*

"I wasn't even living here back then. I was in Mt Isa down the mines. I never knew what happened, really."

*

"People don't talk about it. Nicole's gone. Glenn was gone for a bit. And now Johnny Pearce is dead."

"Thanks for the recap, where's Glenn staying?"

"At Dean Wexler's."

"He still going?"

"Second round of chemo down and he's still up there. Always on his veranda, looking out for her."

"Yet she's not coming home is she but"

"What the fuck do you know about it?"

*

"We located Police Sgt. John Pearce's body at the base of a grand old handkerchief tree about 19 kilometres east of where his police vehicle was found parked. He was in a state of undress inside a bivvy, and was discovered undisturbed in a peaceful state of final rest. Also noted at the scene was a book, 'The Great Australian Loneliness' by Ernestine Hill. Never read it. I'll leave that one to the SOCO analysts to suggest any correlation. There was a fire pit that had been used to warm some soup, and two empty stubbies of VB."

*

"He'd just gone out into the bush to die."

"But why? You can't just turn your heart off."

"You get that from a Charlie Pride record?"

"Leave it out."

*

"When the post-mortem came back, there was nothing to be found."

*

"Circumstances were that he died of natural causes. His funeral's in four days time."

*

"There are some poisons that are undetectable."

"He wasn't poisoned."

"But it was suicide, right?"

"No. He went out into the middle of nowhere. Made a camp, fell asleep."

"Never woke up."

"And he never woke up."

"Fucking weird. Unsolved mystery."

"Except it's not is it."

"How'd you mean?"

"We know how he died. He died from natural causes like that cop Vella reported."

*

"Yes, to put it quite simply, he died in his sleep. That's the

official outcome and no further investigation was ever required."

*

"I still don't buy it, he got done in by someone."

"Think what you like. The likes of us will never know what happened anyway."

"So you're saying there was foul play."

"No, not exactly."

"Well for starters, why'd you reckon Pete Wilson did a runner?"

"He went back to England."

"Well yeah we all know that, but why?"

"He's a Pom."

"I'd get more sense out my cat than you."

"Well his parents were ten pound Poms. He came out here as a boy."

"I know but why did he fuck off, that's what I'm asking you?"

"I only know bits and pieces, ay? What do you know about it?"

*

"Well, he was hardly Mr Squeaky-Clean was he? Him and Pearce were up to all sorts. Some say extortion, and you must have heard about how they kept their arrest record so low right."

"Yeah, kind of."

"Wilson was a fucking dog mate. And Pearce held the leash, supposedly, you'd phone and report some violence and pray it wasn't Wilson show up or he'd fucking go to work on you himself."

"Yeah, that's what I heard too. You hear about that Sheila from Coles."

"Yes."

"What I'm saying is, is that certain people may want to get even with Wilson, now Pearce has cocked his clogs."

"Right."

"Right."

Fourteen

1994 - Sarah

For Every Kiss You Give Me, I'll Give You Three

Roo Stamper's dog, Sarah, knew a thing or two about pain. Flashes of a memory ricocheted around her brain from time to time like a small bird made of knives; a blitz of refracting images flickering on by, like a broken zoetrope. The memory contained that arsehole venomous snake that had been coiled around the tree at the top of her patch. Its sharp face had dropped from the sky and nabbed her - she'd never forgotten it. She pictured from a distance her own furry torso, rigid, wracked in pain falling sideways, like a toppled ornament to the floor.

She'd still bound into the stockade at the rear of her master's garden for months after her recovery, barking or yowling to announce her bold presence. The sneaky serpent was never there though. Mr Snake Face was a long time gone, slinking around in the moist and pungent undergrowth looking for mice, rats and cats to swallow up. Licking on his ancient lips.

This particular night had plans for Roo Stamper's hound it seemed. Tonight she'd bite a man, then die by another's hands.

This dying dog would clamp her dying jaw down on Glenn's left hand in the web between his thumb and fingers as if she were trying to squeeze her way through a very small gap in a hedge. Then she passed out from the terrible weight of pain.

The river stops running.

Glenn lifted her sleeping body off the road, his own blood mixed with hers forever. He caught a glimpse of the nametag around the dog's neck, 'Sarah.'

"Sorry Sarah."

The dog accepted the apology. She didn't want to die in anger tonight.

Fifteen

1922

Without Intent

Notes from Irish historian James Cooper-Greene's book, 'The Other Australian'

The dead of the Jubeira people are buried; the graves piled high with brushwood to keep dingoes from exhuming them. In many cases a body is trussed, heels touching the thighs, with the big toes tied together to prevent them walking with 'evil intent'. The face is turned in the direction from which the tribe has come, the mouth filled with small stones, and the space about the mound cleared of tracks and fire-swept so that their ghosts cannot follow.

II

1870

Captain Stamper's journal

The Pioneer River's source originates from a spring 45 kilometres inland, high up in some formidable green hill ranges (now known as Eungella National Park). First discovered by men serving under Captain Stamper, circa 1870; he remarked in his diaries at the way the land curiously abetted the water's course as it thundered along, choosing the path of least resistance, a convoluted fast-flowing furtherance with a series of insidious grades, tilts and meanders before eventually blending with the profound Pacific Ocean.

The crystal fresh river water still pushes its way out into the choppy seawaters, flushing its coolness out for a few extra, embattled nautical miles. On the other side of the world on a much huger scale, the same natural process occurs as the Congo River's might expels its own contents some 400 miles out into the Atlantic; an accomplishment known only to cetaceans and smart fish.

III

Captain Stamper's diaries were donated to Dewhurst City Library by his great grandson, Lionel Stamper in 1977 after they were rediscovered in a chest found in a spare bedroom at the ancestral home. Each book was wrapped in vinegar paper; this was due to a forgotten marine captain's superstition to protect the readers from any lingering curses. The diaries being found caused quite a stir when they were unearthed and later shared with the public.

Ambrose Stamper's demise is now a cautionary tale among Australians with an interest in the country's early history. Despite being a strong leader, explorer and a respected man upon the high seas, Ambrose Stamper became better known for his mysterious death; it cast a penumbra full of auguries that would overhang all the good he achieved in life.

Echoing the world famous death of Prime Minister Harold Holt in 1967, one bright day the morning watch reported seeing their captain wade chest deep into the sea before disappearing from view beneath the beating waves. The observers said that Stamper never faltered as he set himself forth on his terminal trajectory. Stamper's last diary entry is as thus: 'The ocean is a fisher of men. Something deep inside it calls to me...'

Sixteen

1994 - The Chorus

Crazy For You

"Needless to say after Johnny Pearce's police rover was found up at Blue Jay Bend it got real quiet up there."

"Is that that spot up on the mountainside?"

"Don't be coy you old perv, you know full well where it is... Is that the spot up on the mountainside? Listen to yourself."

*

"No one been cruising up there for a bit, people went to ground."

*

"Wives across town must have thought it was Christmas."

*

"That Maltese cop was up there all the time, snooping about, disturbing fellas, and none of us wanted to get questioned."

*

"A couple of fellas got dobbed in years back and the paper ran a name and shame. Some bloke counter-sued said there was nothing to prove. Story died a death."

*

"The police tended to turn a blind eye to the goings on up

there as long as it stayed reasonably near to the right side of the law."

*

"Story of Johnny Pearce's death hung around for ages though. Yet, that cop, Vella filed it as unsuspicious in under four days."

"S'a bit quick. Four days."

"If there's nothing to prove, why take a long time over it?"

"It should take longer though, ay."

*

"Some of us would see Vella down at Motel 501 too, in the Palm Club when he was off-duty. When I saw him last, he was just sat watching the karaoke. Mr Madonna let me in but he said I was too drunk for anything but beer."

"That pushy bottom queen still there?"

"Lyp-synching to 'Crazy For You' on stage every night. Crazy for steroids more like. Made me do a sketch of him."

"You mean a drawing. You any good?"

"I was in school, you know. But it was all flashing disco lights, shit pencils and he fucking gut punched me, said I'd got his beard wrong. He still stuck it on his locker up there. One of the bar tenders told me."

"Tough love."

"Rubber glove, more like."

"You were there alone?"

*"Yeah, it was like four in the morning. Nowhere else serves
drink that late, you know that."*

"So Vella was down there."

*"He wasn't on duty, I told you. He even got up and sang.
Some sad song, 'Sylvia's Mother' by that old crew."*

"Doctor Hook."

*"Yeah, well, a few of the girls and dolly mixtures gave him
a clap, then he bowed, wiped his eyes of tears and threw
the microphone on the floor like it was a lolly wrapper. Mr
Madonna was furious, it's lucky he's a cop right. Vella then
goes back to his spot at the bar and just has drink after drink,
staring like a goldfish at whoever was up singing their lungs
out."*

"What a dork."

*"Yeah, well anyway, I saw Vella later that night, just sat in his
car out front watching the palm tree blink on and off. Doing
the same thing, just all googly-eyed and that."*

Seventeen

1990 - Glenn

All Things Bright And Beautiful

*An early date with Nicole was to see 'The Fly 2' at Dewhurst
Hoyts 1-2-3 and a pizza at Mona's. Back in the day, Mum
wouldn't order pizzas there because they let their cats lounge
on the food prep benches, I never saw any, but. We drove out
in one of her dad's Datsuns to Hunters Beach and ate our
food in virtual silence. She'd not been bothered by the film yet
I'd been a bit put out by some of it. Was a black old night and
you could hear the ocean waves pulverizing the cliffs below
the pull-in. A car tore out of one of the parking spots, all
squeal and peel, just as I switched off the engine.*

*Nicole just raised her eyebrows at me, "Fucking rev heads.
Small dicks." Then she wiggled one of her pinkies like this.*

*

*Swearing seemed to relax her yet it put me on a razor's edge.
People swear all the time but I couldn't understand why I
felt scandalized, almost disappointed - high up on the plinth
where I put her, now there was clay on her shoes. Her eyes
softened and she was looking at me and me alone. This was
exactly where I wanted to be, with her, square and centre. To
be the only thing on her mind, to be summoned to someone for
reasons I never had been before. To be seen as someone other
than a son, a team mate, a dork - all that. This was it, the
pinnacle of my young life. I wasn't thinking about the carnal
ox waiting to crash the walls down but the devastating weight*

of infatuation - it felt like a desert's worth of insects, reptiles and animals were all holding their breath. They'd stopped grazing, undulating and dreaming to watch and wait. As the seconds smoldered and burned out, I turned my head away from her to look out towards the ocean. I could just about see the white crests of waves out there in the deathly night sea beyond the windscreen. I'd be safer out there.

She asked me if I was crying. I told her that I wasn't even though I was."

*

Unseen by Glenn or Nicole, the other darkened cars at Hunters Beach pull-in also held their own vigil; marijuana smoke billowed out of the windows of one as a hot-boxing session came to a heavy-footed ending; another vehicle moved around on its suspension like a nesting bird, a feint mimic of the movements of its occupants. It didn't cross anyone's minds that this is where their parents had probably parked and theirs before that. How many of the cookie-cutter locals had been conceived up here beneath those crosswise currents of wind and stars? The natural cycle had worn too thin; it was flat at both ends.

*

The pizza stank the car out so we wound the windows down. Without saying much she moved over to my side of the car and sat astride me. Her breath was terrible but then so was mine.

*

Dean would have a pop at me a few days later for spoofing in the foot well of the car, all over the rubber carpet by the pedals. I didn't bother to correct him, to say that it had been

Nicole who'd spat it there... As she dropped me at mine later that same night - she steamed up the driver's side window with her pizza breath and drew an ejaculating cock onto the glass with her finger before speeding off down the hill in a fit of laughter. The next time I saw her, the time Dean had a go at me, Nicole was working slightly late at the RSL but it was OK for me to wait in her room.

"I've nothing I want to hide from you," she hummed down the phone making the handset vibrate through my fingers.

The bedroom was to the rear of the house on the first floor, next door to the kitchen. The remainder of a half-eaten hamburger from Slack Macs sat on her dressing table, I watched as a path way of ants made its way across it, fastidiously ferrying crumbs and salt crystals away to their secret lair. I moved her idle copy of Stephen King's 'It' into their path, sweeping some on to the carpet so as not to squash them. The soldiers made short work of the obstacle in their path; they acted as if the fat book were nothing and marched up and over it, maintaining their course. My attention flicked to her collection of records and tapes - I found a Polaroid of her tucked inside a gatefold hits compilation, 'Chart Topping Dynamite 1987.' In the photo she was sat on the stairs that went down to the garden of car wrecks; she was wearing a light blue singlet and a patterned brown skirt. Dean stands above her, leaning on the rail smoking a cigarette. The words, 'me an Dad in the back' are scribbled down on its grubby reverse. I put it into my school bag and tried not to forget I'd hidden it there.

I recognised her looped handwriting on a sheet of foolscap where she'd copied down Judith Wright's poem, 'The Train

Journey', the source book itself spread-eagled, face up on the bed next to where she'd laid her school uniform out on the bed. Stood in the mirror I pictured myself with her body. I ran my hands down my sides. When she arrived later I decided that I'd ask her if I could wear it, try it on. I somehow knew it would be OK. That she wouldn't tell anyone.

Eighteen

1994 - Gully

The Recently Entombed

The turnout was pretty big at Johnny's funeral; a lot of familiar faces turned up. Yet there were some conspicuous absences as well, like Pete Wilson - Roo Stamper informed me that he'd bagged a load of dough up and gone to Papua New Guinea. How the fuck would Roo know that, the little pussy? Fucking Papua New Guinea. Others reckon he went back to England, I couldn't give a fuck, as long as he never comes back.

Glenn Pearce's tirade was a showstopper. He showed up, may as well have rode into the churchyard on a black horse, he spouted his piece and then had to be dragged off after spitting on the coffin - fucking oath, he brought hell with him.

At first nobody recognised him, looking all sharp, filled out, nice suit, clean shaven, not like the long haired, skinny kid who'd gotten slung in jail three, four years ago. Many thought he was better off staying away, starting over somewhere new. But I'm glad he came back - show some of these arseholes that the past never rests.

A few of the fellas gave him a right sorting out. Smashed his hand up, bashed him about. That young cop, Brett, broke it up, made Dean take him to city hospital.

II

I watch all the funerals out here. Sometimes people get angsty to see me there, as if they're holding me up from doing my job, but I won't start in filling the hole until the very last person has passed back out through the gates and out of earshot distance of my shovelling. In the odd case, it can take hours for a family to leave, for a congregation to disperse, but nope, I'm happy for them to take their time. A few hours is nothing compared to an eternity after all...

On the day of an interment, I'll often review my thoughts up there by the cenotaph, at the top of ANZAC Road - I'll remember the recently entombed, if I knew them in life. I'll also go on to wonder who I'll be burying this time next month. A pointless wonder, but I do it nonetheless.

III

Gully Green sucks noisily on a green hardboiled lolly; the only other sound in the light-polluted night was the ceaseless shrill opus by unseen cicadas and grasshoppers. Just who was it that was responsible for the baton movement? Nobody heard their songs anymore; it's what stands in for the silence up north in the tropics.

Focusing his gaze on the twinkling suburbs below, Gully picks out the speeding headlights of a car moving from the east across the city suburbs via Nebo Road. Like a bead on a thread, he follows the distant car until it disappears behind a rise on the north side of Sandergrove. There was a high chance he'd bury everybody in that car one day - a dubious claim. Another pointless, lonely thought he pushes away.

Nineteen

1994 - Pete

And The Magpie Lifted The Sky With A Stick
- part one

Former Senior Police Constable Pete Wilson had a disturbed
sleep. He was dreaming of half-seen wallabies gamboling
about a remote beauty spot in England called The Roaches.
He'd learned somewhere down the line, that during World
War II, five yellow-footed wallabies broke out of a private
zoo and journeyed to a remote grit stone outcrop in the Peak
District National Park; an unforgiving wasteland high above
the punctured, wheezy towns of Mansfield, Matlock or Belper.
The Roaches also resembled parts of Australia with its red
soil, sandstone and those yellow rocks that reflected sunlight.
Pete pondered (for way too long) whether or not creatures,
like wallabies, could inherit memories from their ancestors,
was that even the right term? He doesn't know.

The population of wallabies on The Roaches had thrived
and today there was supposed to be about 50 or so hopping
about up there. When he was a very small boy, he'd gone on
holiday and come face to face with two of them eating heather
down in a thorny gully. One of them was a female with a joey
peeking out its pouch - or that's how he'd always picture the
encounter in his memory. He couldn't have been up there at
the break of day without his parents but he recalls an icy nip
in the morning air and deep patches of fog, dew on the grass
and weeds.

When Pete looked back up to the rock elevation nearby he thought he caught a glimpse of Johnny Pearce looking out across the valley - he was fanning himself with the brim of his ubiquitous police-issue Akubra. Ghosts love a view.

Anything was possible up here though, fast asleep, hurtling at 500mph+ through the clouds, sat on the back of a gravity-defying rocket-propelled envelope of metal, processed air and flaming fuel. Waking with a start, an ugly air stewardess was gently shaking him to ask if he'd move his leg out of the aisle for her.

Was that a wallaby crouched out there on the wing? Clouds spin past.

This must be how the world ends.

Twenty

1994 - Glenn

Do You Still Have That Photograph?

The Motel 501 was an institution in the annals of Dewhurst's
cultural history. It might still be open for business - Glenn
hadn't thought to check all these years later.

Squatting roadside a few hundred metres inside city limits, it
was/is also home to the Palm Club, lovingly nicknamed the
'Hairy Palm Club' by the men-folk around that way. Built
in the early 1960s to resemble American interstate motels, it
had high hopes of being a friendly and clean place for long
distance drivers and young families to rest and recuperate
on the way north. Sometime in the 70s the highway was
diverted, changing its fortunes forever as the road ended up
bypassing the whole site. Motel 501 was left to dominate
a kind of lollipop-on-a-stick shaped island at a dead-ended
section of road on the way to nowhere but a chain link fence
and a pile of farted out condoms. The horseshoe of single-
level, flat-roofed, portico walkway embellished hotel rooms
resembled a soiled cheerleader: all grubby knees, smeared
make up and hair that had been dyed too often, sad, smelly,
all used up and bruised. The only thing it had in its favour was
that the sun always set behind the clapped out edifice; travellers who turned in for the night were blinded by its glare,
obscuring their vision, so once they found their way into
reception it was all over for them. Dupes check-in but they
don't check out.

The once dreamy pastel colours of the Palm Club had
become an advert for late night booze, pop music 20 years
past its sell-by-date, bad sex with half-baked business men
with bloated animal faces; dead-behind-the-eyes wives who
squash in a quick genital work-out with their physical fitness
instructor between the kindergarten run and a trip to the
Soak-O-Mat; and strippers who should have been harpooned
out of kindness. Years pass, it's the 90s and nothing ever
changes but the cars that pull in.

II

Glenn and Ed

"I used to know you didn't I?"

"Hey Ed, how's it?"

"When'd you get out then, loser?"

"About a week ago."

*"I heard about what you did at your dad's funeral. Fucking
spitting on coffins. Teach you that in jail did they?"*

Glenn can smell the cardboard, wooden, tropical wet smell
that permeated everything: the carpet, Ed's clothes, the walls.
Nothing ever gets completely free of that mildly mouldy, deep
earthy odour in Dewhurst: the damp. Rich or poor round here,
you stank. Ed shifts in his red leather chair and reaches for a
smoke.

"Not talking Glenn? What do you want anyway?"

"I need something."

"Well they do say, always ask a busy man a favour."

The only busy thing about 501's reception area is the wallpaper – a bad day if The Triffids turned up, Glenn thinks. The figurine of a perpetually revolving Hawaiian hula girl wiggles her booty and it's pure lunacy that its movements are the primer for an erection. He shakes his head at his own 'sadness' and luckily it coincides with Ed shaking his packet of cigarettes at him, the ends of which jostle for selection.

"Since when have I smoked?"

"So what do you want?"

Ed slides the pen out from behind his ear and runs its length across his tongue. The back end of the pen is a lighter. The sight of it makes Glenn tut, unimpressed at the gadget as his potty friend fires up his cigarette. Inhaling deeply. At one point he would have summoned up some mock awe and banter at the dappy uncoolness of the device. Portrait of a shabby motel manager as suave British spy.

"So? What?"

"I'm with Dean and, he's too ill. I tried to arrange home help for him but… He just soldiers on and I'm under his feet. He don't say as much. I can just feel it. Also, I just need something to do."

Ed goes onto offer him bar work and the keys to his cousin Kenny's holiday apartment. Resourceful and convenient, with no catches, except for the actual thought of working the bar in the Palm Club, he feels lightly grateful.

"Anyway, give us A$15 bucks now and you can have a room here for the night. Dickhead's rates." Ed tips him a wink and gives it a click sound for effect. And slams a room key on the desktop.

"As Ice T once said "Today is a good day.""

"That was Ice Cube."

"No he's the one that said "Life ain't nothin' but bitches and money!""

"He said both."

"You sure?"

"Positive. S'all they played in the clink. Fucking Eazy E and 2Pac."

"Right, anyway it's shit in there mate, you're gonna hate it, but at least you get to see some tits."

Ed nods towards the bar across the parking lot. He throws the cigarette through an adjacent window and shotguns a plastic bottle of water. The bottle follows the cigarette on a similar trajectory outside. *"You remember Steve Sedona, Mr Madonna? Yeah, well that prick's the bar manager these days. I give you a week, tops. You won't last longer, nobody does."*

"Thanks."

Ed holds his gaze; the bilious, fat master of the sonorous, and well-rehearsed cut downs decides to be serious for once.

"Anything for you, Glenn. Your being here will remind some of those fuckers that what happened back then isn't going away. They're all complicit - sheep wankers. Fucking cunts the lot of 'em."

Glenn heads out in to the lot. The blinking red and green neon palm tree in the car park creaks in the vacuum facing out into the blackness of the Queensland bush. Its plastic sounds like it's on the verge of cracking and splintering, yet at the end of each wet season there it stands, still. Glenn wonders if anybody has ever tried to hang themselves from its boughs before.

Twenty One

1994 - Glenn

I Fall For The Same Face Time And Again

A car pulls into the almost empty lot outside his window.
Loose gravel shifts under tyres, followed by rushed footsteps
in high-heels. Then there's a '1-2-3' scuff of a smoke being
stubbed out underfoot. The green, red, green, red of the neon
lights penetrate the thick curtains at their frayed edges. Glenn
was delivered back in time to a conversation he'd had in
jail with some old fart about how expensive those kind of
coloured lights were to buy or even hire, maintain, replace
and repair. One of the better exchanges he'd enjoyed in the
clink.

The hired sexual help was the humorous, sincere nurse who'd
bandaged his hand at Dewhurst General after the barney he'd
had with Roo Stamper and his boy band prick handlers - it
was the same hand the ill-fated Sarah had bitten too.

"Cop this Skimmee," Roo had said as he handed his jacket
over to one of his cock-jugglers. *"Can't get it dirty."*

*

*Then he swings at me. Misses but then before I can get a
punch in, all his mates pile in kicking me and pushing me until
I fall back to Earth. The congregation just stood watching.*

*Jack Lüven shouts, "Kick him in the fucking nuts."
At some late stage I pass out. On waking up in the back*

of Dean's car he tells me the damage. He's no doctor so someone must have told him what to say as he sounds like he's repeating something he's heard, verbatim.

Roo was put in the cooler for the night until his old man came and demanded his release.

Twenty Two

1994 - Johnny

X Marks The Spot

Johnny Pearce had noted three cars making their way back down the half-sealed road from Blue Jay Bend as he waited at the pull-in near the mouth of the car park. All lone men - each one of the occupants avoided his gaze, or even looking in the direction of the police rover. Dirty fuckers.

Johnny dug a map out of the glove box, and unfolded it across the steering wheel. He traced a route with a fingertip to a place defaced with a red 'x'.

"Walking through the jungle, X marks the spot."

Another car left the car park but this one had an elderly couple inside with a 'Westie'. For once someone who was genuinely up here to take in the view, he mused. With that he swiped the map onto the passenger seat and drove into the car park, persuading his rover to stop under the cool shelter of some skeletal trees by some long abandoned wells where stockmen would let their horses stop for a drink.

Staring around the lot for life, Johnny's eyes focussed on something he wished he could 'unsee.' At the edge of the car park, someone had repurposed one of the boundary posts and carved the wood down into a 3.5 foot varnished cock; there was a soiled John Doe rolled over its knob end. He spat out the window. Johnny had to admit that there was a fair degree

of craftsmanship gone into shaping this wooden phallus. I
need a good carpenter to help me with my fire moat at home -
shame this bloke didn't take credit for his work, he thought.

Johnny got out of the rover walked over to it, and pushed
hard on it with his foot but it was embedded deep into the
ground like it should be (when it was a boundary post). The
day's moving on, but first things first. Johnny returned to the
rover and retrieved his small axe from the trunk. With his
first swipe, the hardy bell end flew into the air and landed
on the roof of one of the last remaining perv mobiles at the
turnaround. He swung again and again until there was no
trace of the beautifully rendered dong except for its discern-
ibly splintered base mere centimetres tall.

A youngish fella about Glenn's age sidled out of the bush,
stopped and looked at Johnny with the axe and pieces of
the chopped up cock on the ground all around him. The guy
smiled at him.

"Up here for the fishing are you mate?"

"Could say that," the young perv replied.

The young fella wiped sweat off his face with the inside of the
t-shirt he was wearing.

"If I see you up here again son, I'll fucking book you."

"Right, sorry."

The young perv got into the car with the wooden knob end on
the roof. Clearly unnoticed, it rolled off as he drove away.

Almost immediately, Johnny spotted another man doing up his trousers in the distance. He replaced the small axe in the trunk of the rover and retrieved his bivvy bag and rucksack for the walk he'd been planning for weeks. He scooped up the unfolded map from driver's side seat with a laboured sigh.

"X marks the spot."

Twenty Three

1991 - Anonymous

Sade Dis Monne

One of the stranger fellas that used to drive up there to Blue Jay Bend was this old guy. Looked like he was older than the mountain itself. Could've been a real life vampire, but he wasn't, obviously. This weirdo was known amongst the regulars as 'The Grand Old of Duke of York' because it was thought that he'd had ten thousand men, so fucking witty. He was never short of company; always had someone sat in his car out there at the edge of the car park, his sound system playing that infernal 'Sadeness' by Enigma. You could hear bass from the Alpine speakers about half a kilometre away, even above its noisy V8 engine.

After some of us blokes had conducted our business up on the hill, we'd exchange the odd pleasantry as we got dressed and cleaned up; so if this freak was up there, he was always the talking point. Funny thing is, is that nobody admitted to ever being with him, yet, as I just said, the Duke always had someone with him. The Duke's custom-enhanced black saloon had never been seen by any of us around the city, not in the daylight, parked on a drive way or at one of the city malls. It was an utter mystery. It's like this old dude didn't exist beyond the peripheries of the mountain. Then one day he stopped coming.

Sade dis monne. Qu'est ce tu vas chercher?

Twenty Four

1994 - Glenn and The Nurse

I Wear These Chains I Forged In Life

Glenn can tell that she's come straight from another job as
she asks if she can spruce up first. A bit later on, he sees dried
semen on her back as he's fucking her from behind. She
has a tattoo at the base of her spine of a man with a fat face
smoking a cigar, smiling. Is it a trick of the light that the eyes
change shape and the cigar wiggles up and down in time with
their movements? He noticed as she undressed, that there
were light stretch marks on her stomach but she doesn't talk
about her kids. Why would she? She just talks filth and coaxes
him until she's full to the brim. As he comes to a natural halt,
he wishes he could swim all the way in like a frog up a rising
river.

"Thanks sister."

She detaches, then rolls onto her back and tips Glenn a wink.
Holding her hand out, he compliments her for her bandage
dressing of his fingers and hand, and gives her an extra five
bucks. She stands and counts the money then gives him a
mock curtsey. She throws the spare fiver down on to the bed
sheets.

*"Put it towards your next go. And by the way, you don't call
nurses 'sister' unless they happen to be nuns as well."*

"What do you call a nurse who's a prostitute?"

"Anything you want baby. Anything you want."

"Fuck me, you're corny."

Green. Red. Green. Red go the lights.

II

In the closing hours of the night, an old drunk wearing a lumberjack shirt, combat shorts, long socks and Jesus sandals, weaves his way across the car lot. He cocks his leg and deploys a fart so good and lengthy he wished his mates had been there to hear it. He loved making his pals laugh with his endless supply of guffs. A rare moment of introspection presents itself for him. But it's too late, the shadows at the end of the lot are long and dark. Within seconds fart man has all but vanished into them.

III

"I love you too, feel free to call anytime."

Beeeeeeeeeep.

Twenty Five

1991 - Pete and Nicole

Where There Is No Vision, The People Perish

They drove fast through the sugar cane. A tape of
'Downbound Train' by Bruce Springsteen was played loud.
Tonight, Pete Wilson would try the handle on an unlocked
door. Nicole was sat with her back against the passenger
door of his white convertible, short strawberry blonde hair
blowing. She yawned, but he could tell she was chipper. This
girl was an enigma. She had a boyfriend, Johnny's son, yet
here she was and he couldn't detect anything else but the early
signs of her undoing.

"You like The Boss do ya, Nicole?

"Sure."

"Ever played the 'Bruce Game'?"

"No."

"No?"

"What's the 'Bruce Game'?"

*"Well you put on any one of his LPs and you take a shotgun of
beer and take something off, you know, like your socks, each
time he says railroad track, or county line, state trooper and
so on."*

"Like strip poker."

"Yeah, like strip poker, but with better, simpler rules."

"I see."

"It's a simple version for people that just want to fuck rather than fart about all night until they're all too pissed to even stand up."

"I gotcha."

"I know."

The tape goes silent.

Nicole avoids his gaze, smiling out at the blackness ahead. The corners of her mouth moisten.

The next song, 'I'm on Fire', weaves its way in and as the cassette slowly spools onwards, the car slows down. Bruce's train whistle-like yodelling gets taken over by the sound of the evening insects and toads in the yonder cane. On some future page, the tape clicks off and the stars go out. The wooden door in Pete's mind's eye gently blows wide open. He always pictures a door.

Twenty Six

1994 - Dean

If Suddenly, You Do Not Exist

Dean Wexler flicked a caterpillar off his seat up on the first floor veranda and sat down. From there, he could see to the bottom of Manuel Street. Not that his place was on the way to anywhere, but if a car was coming up the slope he could pretty much deduce who it was after darkness fell by the shape of the headlights, the sound of the engine. He sparked up the tip of his dead cigarette. But the end of his finger and the fag flamed up due to some remnants of engine oil soaked onto both, *"Shit in the bedroom."*

'Hey Hey It's Saturday' is on his telly. Sports pundit Ronnie Vaughton is in the process of being duffed-up by the mascot for the Paramatta Eels for reasons too stupid to get worked up about. The in-studio audience roars with laughter as Vaughton loses his rag for real.

Australia just wants to see you smile.

Twenty Seven

1994 - Johnny

The Wandering Sheep

The rough hands of spirits shake Johnny Pearce awake. The air is cold and all he can see are the dying embers of his campfire in the early hours of the morning. The pages of his book flutter quietly on their spine. He doesn't see anybody but he can hear breathing. Then a voice whispers in his ear so closely he can feel his hair bristle.

"Well, well, well, the magpie awakens."

Johnny doesn't have time to recognise his own voice. It's too late for that.

Twenty Eight

1991 - Glenn

Until The Sun Grows Too Cold To Touch

Glenn turns on the car radio. Home is a short drive away. He toys with the idea of leaving the city, even for a day, but the distance to the next place is too great. Where would he go? The road sign by Dewhurst Showgrounds is oppressive and not at all persuasive.

Bruce Highway South   *Bruce Highway North*

Rockhampton 336 km ← → *Townsville 390 km*

Stay in jail, miss a go.

'In The Air Tonight' by Phil Collins fades into 'Drive' by The Cars - the music of shitheads.

"You are listening to 4DW, giving you all the hits, all n-n-n-night"

"Dewhurst's number one choice!"

The only fucking choice.

Twenty Nine

1994 - Vella

Follow Me Down

"You ever had an attachment so deep you'd throw away your life for it?"

Were these words he'd once heard in a film, or read in a book? Vella wondered. The words coiled around in his head, his voice quietly intones each syllable in a whisper. He imagines the passage projected on to the sidewall of the motel he can see through the car windscreen; whisky breath baking the enclosed space inside the police rover. Vella can't say where he's heard it before. Perhaps he heard a king utter it to his first son as he lay dying - a prelude to a last confession - an introduction to a closed off room - a dead man's lie / secret. The nearby neon palm tree blinks green, red, green. Is it Morse code for, *"Let's go get a room and fuck like rattle snakes?"*

Nobody knows or has ever stopped long enough to notice. All the sailors, except for the mock ones, left town decades ago.

This approach to sleep is short - the descent, treacherous. As he dreams about the endless passage of time, he is in flight, a low pathway across the top of a limitless canopy of trees all pressed together sprouting upwards towards the sun, the sound of a crackling fire.

When he awakens the following morning from his nocturnal

magic show he sees a green silhouette of the out spread tangled branches and tree leaves branded into the backs of his eyelids whenever he blinks. His mind is in the grip of the incorporeal.

Thirty

1991 - Glenn

The Spectre At The Barbecue

Baked beans, Impulse deodorant and toilet tissue were just some of the odours that slapped his nostrils silly whenever Glenn walked into her bedroom. This time, Nicole smiled and whispered that her dad had turned in for the night. He often slept in a hammock he'd hitched up amongst the car wrecks below with little more than a light mosquito net to offer protection. She turned around and wriggled out of her jeans. It was all he could do not to fall on her, kissing every inch of her. He dropped to his knees behind her, slowly pulling her cotton knickers down. Gently biting her buttocks in several places. Her dog, Bets, began to scratch at the bedroom door, whimpering as she tries to get in.

"Glenn, take care of Bets?" She smiles. *"You're still dressed. She probably needs a crap."*

Down in Dean's junkyard garden, Bets disappears into the small maze of new and old wrecks. A procession of lost dreams, scenes from an auto-killing, money down the drain. The blank-faced headlights peered out through the peach and cobalt night air, each vehicle a revenant from an endless flow of thick, hot days squandered. He can hear Dean snoring gently in his hammock, strung between a 1970s Holden and a Japanese camper van. The dog is somewhere in the metal-strewn undergrowth scratching at the ground. As he walks about the semi circle of wrecks he hears the sleepy, bassy drone of a bee swarm but he can't see its whereabouts.

Bets is a curious mix of Alsatian and dingo. Her coat sandy coloured, her puzzled furry face and ears, so brown. She's a good dog, but she never gets walked, so her days are like weeks - her animal boredom never dissipating.

Glenn prizes the badge from off the trunk of an electric blue Renault 12 and pockets it. You don't see many French cars in North Queensland, or French people.

Thirty One

1984 - Johnny and Glenn

Product Of Australia

"See this fork, Son?"

"Yes Dad."

"Product of Australia."

"Oh."

"Only Aussies could make you a fork like this. Strong, sharp, endurable."

"Where was my fork made, Dad?"

"Brisbane, Glenn."

"How'd you know?

"Factory bought."

"What's Brisbane like?"

"It's big. We went there to see the footie when you were tiny. You won't remember."

"To see the Cockroaches and the Cane Toads."

"Yes that's right. One of the State of Origin games."

"And that's when you bought the forks."

"Yes, yes it was. They were a present for your mother."

Thirty Two

1988 - Glenn

Social Mediocrity

We put the 'Tit Hills' on the local map. There were some younger kids who lived on our street, Bradley Little and his brother Robbie, a miniature skate punk we called Little Bob. One deadly afternoon when we were all fucking about doing wheelies and stunts on our bikes, Brad says, "Wanna go up the Tit Hills?"

Now we knew everywhere within cycling distance but we'd never heard of any place called the Tit Hills.

Glenn -   *"Ah yeah, where's that?"*

Little Bob - *"Bucky Road."*

Robbie -   *"What the fuck are the Tit Hills?"*

Bradley -   *"We'll show you."*

Glenn -   *"What are yers on about?"*

Little Bob - *"We'll show you, it's not that far."*

Robbie -   *"You're giving me the shits. Tell me what they are…"*

Crusty -   *"I'm gonna fucking lump yers if we don't get some fucking answers..."*

Bradley -   *"OK, OK. Well you know the humped back hills where the road goes up, down and back up again on Bucasia up the back there?"*

Little Bob -   *"You go up through there where he's pointing?"*

Bradley -   *"Duh!"*

Robbie -   *"Will you shut up. So go on, the bit of the road that goes up and down. Yeah we know it."*

Little Bob -   *"We drew a nip on top of both hills. So now it's the tit hills."*

Glenn -   *"Get snickered."*

Crusty -   *"You're a bunch of dickheads. Lamest thing I've heard all fucking week."*

Robbie -   *"Let's go and look."*

*

To this day, people still call 'em the Tit Hills and someone will go back periodically and spray paint a circle at the crest of each of the two rises along there. Us Aussies love championing our own mediocrity, just like Dad and the dining set. It got back to Dad that kids had been fucking with the road markings, but he couldn't give a fuck; the spoils of losers and dags.

Thirty Three

1987-1988 - Glenn

The Bisley Boy (Or Girl)

*At Dewie High we had this intense teacher called Phil Ball.
Everybody's had them, those teachers that rail against all the
conventions and rules alongside you as if they were one of
the kids. I'm not talking about the 'try-hards' or the fucking
fakes that wanted to be down, I'm talking about the teachers
that had their own agenda, their own need to shout and to
stamp. The ones that wanted to act up and shake a few of us
out of our stupor along the way, to make us wantonly question
everything around us. Mr Ball didn't get all that much respect
from any of us at the time, some of the lads called him 'Phil
My Ball Bag' but I kind of liked him so I didn't bother with the
name slinging. With the benefit of 25 years' hindsight I can
see he was a livewire, fighting against his personal boredom,
small town traps, no friends, no outlets - his 'lot' in life. In
his lessons, he'd always wrap things up with something a
little bit weird for us all to mull over - a conspiracy theory or
an urban myth.*

*He'd always be tapping a chalk stick on the blackboard to
get our attention, I can recollect his high pitched 'ermmmm'
noise he made to clear his throat; the greasy black hair that
he'd flick out of his eyes with a jerk of the head; his stinky BO
ingrained teacher's jacket, and his massive chin. He was in
his 20s and hadn't been qualified all that long before moving
to Queensland from Canberra. Skinny in adulthood he once
asked our class to guess the weight he was born. I'm guessing*

he was either fucking huge or very light but nobody even pitched in a guess. People just cowed him by throwing insults about his mother and the fact they wish he'd never been born. Quietly he turned to his blackboard and wrote the words, 'Man, woman, birth, infinity…'

I fancy that he was trying to fight back his tears before he walked out of the room. It's not for us to know why that particular day of cruelty got to him, we were shit to him every day. After that lesson, he was gone for the rest of the semester but was back with a vengeance after the summer.

II

"Braaaaaaaaaaaaaaaaam Stohhhhhhkerrrrr!" (tap) ! (tap) ! (tap) ! (swipe) !

*

Ladies and gentleman – please note the spelling. Last year, we had a girl called Helen Bright who wrote an excellent essay worthy of an 'A' except she chose to spell the poor Irishman's name as Bram Stroker."

The class erupts into fits and gales, and kids pulling the 'spasmo' face.

"Paahhhhh!"

"What a dork!"

"Eroooooowwwww!"

"Bum stroker more like!"

"Ok, shut up. Pipe down. I said shut up! OK Bram Stoker, most famous for inventing the vampire legend as we know it, and for writing the novel Dracula. Yet, unbeknownst to the majority of us, he concocted a most delicious myth for his long-forgotten other book, 'Famous Imposters.' Our man Stoker had many readers of his day believing the following myth was true. It doesn't stand up to any direct scrutiny but it's still an amazing flight of fancy. Yahnundasis what is it?"

"Can I go for a shit please sir?"

"That's no language for a young lady now is it? Try asking me again."

"C'I go the dunny?"

"(Tuts.) Yes, you may go to the bathroom. Hurry back."

"The story goes that in 1542, Henry VIII was on his way to a hunt at Berkeley in England, and left his nine-year-old daughter, Elizabeth, at Overcourt, a royal hunting lodge in Bisley, somewhere in Oxfordshire. This was so that she would be safe from the plague that was prevalent at the time. Unfortunately for Elizabeth and her temporary guardians, the princess succumbed and died, but the courtiers, ever fearful of their royal master, devised a cunning plan to evade his wrath. A substitute for the princess had to be found before the king returned, but alas, no girl who closely resembled the recently deceased Elizabeth could be located. So they opted for a 'plan B' and found a red-headed boy in the village instead. The male substitute must have been very convincing because history tells us that Elizabeth I went on to be a great queen, reigning for 45 years.

So what 'evidence' does Stoker bring for us to bear? A few 100 years later, the then Vicar of Bisley told his family that during renovations at Overcourt, an old stone coffin containing the skeleton of a girl of about nine, dressed in Tudor clothing had been found. Point two: his book also tells us that Queen Elizabeth never married which, in an age when royal marriages were created for alliances, was very unusual. Three: she was completely bald, covering her shiny bonce with a fine selection of orange wigs."

"Same as Crusty's mum."

"Suck my kneecaps Newman."

"Can I continue? Moving on. Point three or is that four? She had left explicit instructions that no post-mortem should be carried out on her body on the occasion of her death. Hmmm. And five: nobody knows where the Queen was buried. The event and location was a secret and remains so forever and ever."

"It's bullshit sir!"

"Well obviously, and put your hand up if you want to say something in my class room."

"How come Henry VIII or none of the kingsmen and them spotted the switcheroo...?"

"See? It doesn't stand up does it. The arguments are too strong, the evidence is too weak. But if it was true, if it really did happen this way, and besides a complicit few, those who knew the secret, Elizabeth I fooled the world, what does this

riddle say to you? What does it prove? What does this vital allegory ask of us all?"

"Who cares?"

"It ask us this, if nobody is looking for you, are you still missing?"

*

When he asked us this, the room had pretty much been cleared, his voice drowned out by clattering chairs and the stampede of junior primates heading for the lunch hall.

When I had a lesson in the same room later, the maths teacher pulled down the cascading blackboard to reveal the question, "If nobody is looking for you, are you still missing?" written bold by our troubled teacher, presumably after the lesson.

Without reading it, our dead maths teacher rubbed it out with a cloth. No great legacies were ever written down in chalk.

*

Returning after summer break one year, we all went back and Phil Ball had gone without a trace. No mention was made of him at the assembly and his replacement was cagey about his whereabouts. I went through his desk and found a copy of Bram Stoker's 'Famous Imposters' so I took it. I've never read it but I come across it from time to time when tidying my bookshelf at home.

Teachers leave. Pupils move on. Schools fall down.

Thirty Four

1994 - Dean

I Will Love You With All My Heart

And still Dean waits, on his porch, every evening. But he knows she'll never come back. Still, he can't help but inch forward in his outdoor Ezee-chair and crane his neck each time a car turns the corner at the bottom of the rise.

Thirty Five

1994 - Bert

Always Here And There

Where does all this sand come from? Black Bert blew the lightly ingrained red dust from the framed photograph he was holding, and replaced it on his mantelpiece. It gets everywhere, he thought. The shadows were long in his lounge and the reflections of light through the windows around the room drained all colour from his vision. Bert's place was a long way from the sea but the warm ocean thermals were constantly welcomed in, like lost brothers, blowing through his veranda doors, permanently open except for through the wet.

No workers that day, his pickers had done a royal job yesterday so he'd given them a shift off. Some needed the money and had a whinge but he wouldn't work these kids every single day, they needed to rest sometime. See the place. Journey all around the world some of them and ended up stuck in a fucking field with their arse in the air picking fruit and veggies. Well, not today. Bert reached in his back pocket for his foam stubby cooler and walked to the fridge - pulled out a VB.

"Couldn't you hear the phone Bert?" His lodger, Will poked his head through the window.

"Who is it?"

"Cops. They need you for a missing person's."

"They tell you that much?"

"They thought I was you."

"They still on the phone?"

"Yeah."

"You're fucking useless. Which phone?"

"Out in the old hangar."

Bert takes a sup of his beer and puts his thongs on. He didn't know the phone out there still worked. Guess he knew now.

"OK Will, tell 'em I'll be a few minutes."

That beer's good he thought, taking a second swig.

Thirty Six

1992 - The Chorus

Bottle It In

"My mum said that Nicole is experienced."

*

"People say she fucked a lot of people, but it's not true."

*

"She was in love with that Pommie cop... She didn't know what she was doing. Girl was playing with fire. Why she get involved with that brute when she had Glenn?"

"Thing is, Glenn, never knew until later the full extent of it."

*

"Glenn didn't know 'cos he was always up at her place fixing cars with her Dad."

*

"She fucked everyone. She did so much fucking, she had no time to put her knickers back on."

"No she didn't. She was playful, but it was just the cop and Glenn, anyone else said they went up her is a fucking liar, and I'll call 'em on it."

*

"I think she loved Glenn though, but his head was up his arse. When I saw them at Canelands Mall, they looked like any

young couple in love."

*

"She just had an itch. And Glenn wasn't there to scratch it all the time."

*

"She was fucking that Pommie police guy, Wilson. Johnny Pearce's pitbull. He'd take her out in that big white fanny magnet of his, deep into the cane fields."

*

"Glenn found out and beat her the fuck up. Beat her so bad, he got sent to PMRF for years. Her name was dragged through the mud and she just fled. Not so that I'd know. It's just what I've been told."

*

"I saw her at the Greyhound terminal getting on to a bus to Sydney."

*

"I heard she flew to the west coast on a plane."

*

"Probably a hooker by now."

*

"Fucking a lot of people isn't a crime. She was discreet. It's the fellas that weren't, shouting it all over the place."

*

"Yeah, I fucked loads of girls when I was a young fella. You don't

hear me screeching me fucking head 'awf' about it do ya?"

*

"Who didn't have a high sex-drive at her age? I fucked loads of boys when I was in college, I was terrible. I still see some of them now, about town with their families. We still say hello. Why was she any different? One rule for boys, another for girls? Idiots."

*

"He fucking almost killed her. Left her out in the cane. Lucky the cops found her."

*

"I saw Glenn down at her house wearing a dress. Putting stuff out on the washing line."

"They don't have a washing line."

Thirty Seven

1960s and 1980s - Gully

So Cold The Night

Me and my dad would sea swim together most days. It was our thing; my brother, Michael was afraid of the ocean and he'd hardly ever set foot on the beach, so we left him to do his own stuff.

I can't remember learning how to swim, it would seem that every one in town woke up Australian one morning, and we were all naturals.

My dad's routine would start with him paddling out about 50 yards then he'd turn to swim parallel to the beach and go as far as he could. I would follow a few yards behind him and slightly nearer to the shoreline, every time I came up for a breath I'd see the wake from his illusionary propeller feet up ahead.

I'd go out with him throughout my school years and then I stopped joining him for some reason. He'd go most mornings, checking the tide times for when he could get the best out of his 30-minute swim before he went to work. This routine he stuck to up until he was too old and weak to continue.

Is the sea the purest expression of the human heart, a canvas, the big green blind, the very idea of oblivion at our core?

After he died, we scattered his ashes across where the ocean

*spills on to the boulders at the end of the jetty. The local
fishermen duly cleared their rods and tackle out of our way
so that we could have the area to ourselves. The remains
were carried apart quickly as the waters ebbed. A man born
to water, I recall his neat jack knife dive off the high board at
our local swimming pool up at one of the trailer parks on the
edge of town.*

*Dad was in the hospital a long time at the end, but somehow
we knew his days were in the low numbers - his prolonged
sleep patterns, slow breathing, cold hands.*

*At the end, I drove all the way down south to spend a few
weeks in Bateman's Bay. When I was back there, I took a trip
to an out-of-town beach with an estranged friend of mine,
Bernie. We drove about 60 kilometres up the coast to go for
a sea swim; we knew the spot from our teenage years. On the
way back home, we had a near miss. Coming down the track
from the beach to the highway, this tree shed a big old branch
in front of us - missing us by less than a metre or so. It's
perhaps overly symbolic and goofy to mention but my father
passed away at roughly the same time we encountered the
falling branch. I commented on the coincidence to my brother,
when I saw him later, but he had nothing to say.*

*I went for a run at the beach at Bateman's the evening
following Dad's passing, and surveyed his favourite swimming
spot. I walked into the waves and floated on my back, letting
the gently swirling mass of salt water buoy me up.*

*I read somewhere that almost every Australian rite of passage
occurs on or near the beach. It's where we test our physical
limits, have our first sexual experiences, it's the location of*

our adulterous slips, and it's the place we ultimately retire to whilst waiting for whatever comes next. It's where many of us mourn the passing of our parent's too.

My dad had lived his whole life poised at the edge of this huge dry country. He'd never been beyond the 'Back o' Bourke' and he wouldn't venture further than Canberra his whole life even when the world was at war. With the land at his back and sea to his chest, all that was gone now.

By contrast, he loved to read all those old books about the empty spaces: the plains, hill ranges and deserts at the heart of Australia. He once told me how the land could cast spells over a man, ones so potent you could lose your way in a space no larger than a phone box. These days, I pick over the same books like Arthur Groom's 'I Saw a Strange Land' or Ernestine Hill's 'The Great Australian Loneliness' so that I might be able to tap into that same mind space. When we were out on our walks together he'd often gaze off into the nothingness as if searching for something far out on the horizon. I'd ask what he was looking at, as I couldn't see a thing - his reply was simple, he'd say, "The land."

Thirty Eight

1991 - Glenn

The Time Machine

Sitting at the kitchen table, the dim, yellow light bulb poised unfeasibly low over the gingham-patterned tablecloth.

Glenn watches her fingers trace the highway inland and out of Dewhurst on the map. Within seconds she's in Charters Towers, Mt Isa, Katherine, Darwin. Time travel must work this way.

Next, she draws an invisible outline of a love heart somewhere in the Simpson Desert.

She chuckles under her breath.

Glenn wonders if he would be able to replay these few throwaway/important moments with clarity for the rest of his life.

Why can't he summon the ability to gift her a smile? The gravity of the moment hangs there yet he doesn't have the courage to slowly reach out across the wide Australian map and take her hand in his. Stroke the length of her hand idly with the tip of a finger. Just once. Had he seen it in a pop video?

This is what we all do, right? He thinks.

The molecules change in the air, the charge fizzles out. The electric and amazing contents under pressure of the situation, where every light touch counts, when nothing has become familiar or worn out, there's nothing else like this. Yet this odd alchemy of teenage love longing is squandered needlessly as the seconds slip away; can she rescue him?

Nicole's fingers become a tip-toe that steps up his forearm like a ladder... *"Walking through the jungle, X marks the spot...!"*

Man overboard.

Thirty Nine

1994 - The Chorus

If You're Born To Hang, You'll Never Drown

"Can you name a Bruce song about a woman who leaves town on the Greyhound?"

"Nope. Don't listen to his stuff."

"Why?"

"It's fucking dull. Imagine if we wrote songs about going around in 'utes' and drinking too much Budweiser and old divorced women driving tractors. That's life. Don't want to hear it in a song."

"But you do like love songs."

"I suppose."

"Bruce writes about love."

Forty

1994 - Gully

In Many A Darkened Room

*Edward Hopper was my favourite painter as I was growing
up. I still love his stuff now.*

*It's not what he paints, I find, it's what he leaves out. His
compositions make you wonder as to what lies behind that
door, that closed blind or wooden shutter, what's in that
shared whisper. It's the suggestion, the mood. As I look
closer, all sound drains away and I'll be able to sense a
different set of noises, small and isolated emanating from the
painted scene itself. I begin to tune into the grass blowing,
a disembodied train whistle, or the bell at a distant level
crossing. Arriving at his paintings in my well-thumbed,
worn-out Phaidon Press book of reprints, I get the feeling that
I've reached each composition a moment late or minutes too
early to see the action. The conversation is already over, the
room vacated, the lover's touch evaporated.*

II

It had been about six weeks since Gully had last gone near his
easel with any purpose. Glenn Pearce had come back to town
stirring up old memories for everybody and you could sense
it in the air that people were waiting for something else to
happen after the war at that brute Johnny's funeral. Everyone
he met was on edge, ready to jump up to confront him for the
smallest thing - this was one touchy city these days.

Pure association brings more then one face back to him.
The one he'll dwell on now is Glenn's girlfriend Nicole, the
shorthaired girl with the lop-sided smile. If she'd have been
born in Paris she'd have been an artist's muse, what you'd call
an ingénue, except she was born here. Doomed to be mauled
by uncultured fucking animals. She'd sat for him in his studio
a few years back. He catches himself calling it a studio when
it was really just a corner of the cemetery storeroom with a
north facing sloped glass ceiling. One side of the shelves were
for his paints and oils, waiting patiently in the green hued
gloom - upright, like a row of sleeping sentinels awaiting
redeployment. The other side was for his hill range of flower
stands, Astroturf cuts, mounts for reefs, boxes of Oasis and
other funeral props. Gully knew exactly where Nicole's
portrait was, sat on its side with other unfinished epics. She'd
promised to come back another afternoon but he could tell she
was too restless to remain posed for long. He was lucky to get
her for that initial hour.

III

Gully smoked rollies sat on the bonnet of his car at the top of
Anzac Road most evenings to watch the sunset – he loved the
magic hour as it was the most painterly part of the day. The
Unknown Soldier looked out for his appearance most nights
and Gully imagined that the statue, may one day, even be
so bold as to enquire what he got up to on the nights he was
absent. Sometimes magpies would attempt to make a nest in
the dimple of the statue's digger hat but it was too exposed to
the winds for their efforts to come to much. He'd sometimes
watch them in the early evening flying around with twigs in
their beaks. But it was all folly.

The burbling of the magpies was his favourite sound to wake up to - a warm first encounter for a new yet empty day. When he was a young fella, Michael had speculated that it was koala bears making the warbling bird call. His brother had been the first to call him Gully. Short for gullible - this was because he fell for everything, believing anything anybody cared to tell him.

He thinks again of Nicole's portrait in his store at the far end of the cemetery. He imagines himself working late at night by gas lamp chasing her likeness down with his brushes. The portrait seems to call to him, imploring him to finish what he started three years earlier. Gully acknowledges the need, the unpaid debt to this girl's memory - neither dead nor alive, just unfinished. This lost beauty was the spectre at the barbecue. Her name barely whispered, a cautionary tale for kids old enough to hear it - a flesh noose waiting to make good on its innocent quarry. An evil spirit, coiled, poised to spring out on the beautiful young.

The headlights only stretch so far ahead on the black roads out beyond the city - out there in the sugar cane.

Whilst farm animals watch from behind the fire, atrocious things befell her. They still remember her silhouette, even the ones that have been torn limb from limb, flesh from bone.

Gull pulls on his rollie. Her face in the newspaper cutting, caught in a breeze, whilst nailed to a post in his mind's eye begins to change. Her face changing like a series of passport photos seen through a spinning zoetrope.

Black - pose - black - pose - blackness.

Maybe she's still alive - he realises his lips are moving. But he knew she'd never come back. Dewhurst was full of people that left never to return and without a backward pointed thought. Then he laughed aloud. How can anywhere be full of people that aren't there anymore?

The cicadas mark the pulse of the sleeping city. The night sky is thick with heavy summer and he's again reminded of an Edward Hopper piece - the famous one, 'Nightbirds'. Nobody painted the night like he did. Nobody.

Forty One

1870 - Ambrose

A Most Pointy Reckoning

Notes from Captain Ambrose Stamper's journal

The boomer (male/buck) is the only breed that shows good sport. When hunting with our trusty pack of hounds we were never at a loss to find one. You can generally find a boomer in a high cover of young wattles, and on occasion out in open bush lands.

I recollect one very fine individual who came about ahead of the hounds one afternoon all con el sol del membrillo lit. Looking to see when the coast was clearest, without a second's hesitation he shot away from the dogs. With little effort this specimen gave us the longest run I've ever experienced. He ran 14 miles by my calculation. He would have beaten us had he not accidentally turned out on to a small land spit jutting out into the sea, shutting his only route to freedom firmly closed behind him. So when we pressed him, this fellow was forced to try to swim across the arm of the sea. The boomer had almost made it halfway but was forced back by strong waves and currents. After he came back ashore he was fatigued and swiftly killed by the pack.

We found another boomer later in the day by following his tracks in the sand - a big chap, the gap between each jump was nearly fifteen foot. When a male is forced it is likely to take to water to limit the fronts it has to defend. In these situations it will usually take several dogs to kill him, for the boomer will stand, waiting for them in the shallows as they swim up on the attack. What he then does, is he grabs the dogs and holds them under the water with his forefeet until it is they instead who have met their maker. This buck was very bold and they generally are when faced with certain death. In cases where he cannot make it to water, he will place his back against a tree where, again, he cannot be ambushed from the rear. This way even the best hunting dog will find in him the most formidable of opponents.

Forty Two

1991 - Glenn

Youth Is Beauty

Unbeknownst to anybody that wasn't in the know already,
the Dewhurst Speedway was on its way out. Even though it
was no longer making any money, the fences were falling
down and nobody even bothered to buy tickets at the booth
anymore, races still happened. They were mainly populated
by the kids of those who had made it their weekend home
during their own spells of youth. Many were involved behind
the scenes, pulling the cars to the track behind their suped-up
utes, or commentating, wreck recovery and other bits about
the place. But nothing could save the free-fall plummet the
manager Kerry Spencer had put the track into. With his lack
of interest and seedy ambitions elsewhere it seemed to be
doomed. Ripped, torn, sun-faded film posters of the Tom
Cruise flooperoo car wank flick, 'Days of Thunder' were
pasted everywhere from the dunnies to the bodegas to the tree
trunks to the cash room. Show me heaven.

II

The red dust and dirt flies up from under the spinning
wheels. Glenn looked for Nicole each time he tore around
the speedway. The young driver would catch glimpses before
being slammed off course by one of the other stock cars.

Forty Three

1991 - The Chorus

A Storm-Swept Plain

"Always needed to be reasserting his position as top dog, king of the mountain, Deus of Dewhurst, bleach blonde cunt".

*

"Every story has a villain but Roo Stamper was a minor, junior league wannabe. His terrorism never extended beyond the peripheries of the sports field. Touch footie, Aussie Rules, Indoor Cricket, Speedway, he was king for a day - no one else got a look in except for him and his comic book cronies".

*

"In real terms he was a rich cunt pussy, small-town spunker."

*

"When he'd corner you, he'd press his chest into you and twist your nipples really hard. Boy, definitely had unresolved sexuality issues."

*

"Old soft cock Stamper? Yeah I recollect a few run-ins with that mummy's boy. I pulled a sheath on him once outside The Lulls. Fucker pissed all over his shoes. He was a fucking Sheila and he knew it."

*

"If it wasn't for his family's connections. His father's

influence at the Chamber of Commerce and the planning council, that kid would've been a laughing stock. In fact he was, most of us just wafted him away. Stamper wasn't tough. He thought he was, but."

*

"Roo had a deep seated fear of inadequacy as a young man which manifested itself in his tyranny. Once he settled down after university, he became a kind man, he's done a lot for this city, just like his father has and his father before him."

Forty Four

1991 - Glenn

How Long Has John Hughes Been Dead For Now?

Kerry was stood with Nicole and her friend Fallon. That
sleazy Kiwi always had an angle. If he had been uglier, the
girls wouldn't have pissed on him even if he was a toilet. He
had those fading, surfer looks. Easy blues eyes, crinkled dirty
blonde hair down to his shoulders, and a band of freckles
across his crooked roman nose. He reminded Glenn of a jaded
TV star from Home and Away. This prize guy had the ability
to coax barely legal girls into his dirty bed with all kinds of
lines no older girl would even consider falling for even if
they were dying for it. To sleep with this bag of shit was like
a local rite of passage for some of the Dewie High girls and,
boy, did he know it.

Two more laps and there were only two other cars left in the
race. The wrecks or conk-outs were all rolled to one side
on the bank. The drivers in a huddle, all pointed fingers and
screwed up red faces. Skids Yahnundasis' ute, with the tyres
nailed to the front, was primed to push their wrecks off the
track any minute. The next revolution's glance over revealed
a solitary Fallon and no Kerry, no Nicole. At that point he
got rear-ended and his Toyota flew up the bank and out of
the race. The engine farting black smoke. Glenn climbs out
the car and scans the crowd. He sees Kerry at the top of the
staircase that led up to his squalid apartment. He waves in
Glenn's direction. And gives him a double thumbs up. He
quickly realizes that the gesticulations are for Roo, who's at

the finishing line nearby. As Glenn removes his helmet, he receives a well-timed 'bird' from the third-division douche-nozzle, Roo, who mouths two words - Fuck you - in his direction.

This must be what it's like to be in a John Hughes movie.

Forty Five

1994 - Glenn

False Lights At The Coast

"Most of you think you're here today to see a good man buried. Well, the man in this coffin was far from goodness. Hell's too good for the cunt."

Turning to the priest he said, still loud enough for the congregation to hear, *"Throw him in Father. That's all I came to say. Bury the fucker deep."*

As he turned to leave someone in the crowd of mourners shouts at his back, *"Fuck off back where you came from."*

"Yeah, fuck off Glenn," adds another with more fetid gusto.

A stubby bottle is thrown. It hits the coffin on its broadside. The priest holds his hands up scurrying in front of the coffin as a second bottle skims the lid, aimed at Glenn.

The cop, Brett Coulson switches on his loud hailer. The crowd of mourners hadn't seemed large enough or even angry enough to need a riot control instrument, but he was glad he'd brought it anyway.

Roo Stamper and his goons got the grab on Glenn, but within minutes most of the mourners rapidly dispersed to the Chan Bishop Hotel for a drink in Johnny's dishonour.

Forty Six

1994 - Dean

The Thrill Is Gone

The dawn came for Dean, as his chilled, now dead body sat
up stiff in the recliner on his veranda. The vanilla-coloured
swathe of sky was slowly sandwiched between two grey
wedges of cloud as the early stages of daytime marched on in.
Magpies warbled their melodic greetings and the neighbourhood cats patrolled the streets and backyards for sport. Bets
had come past, nosing former-Dean's leg to remind him it
was time to eat. His ashtray, balanced on the chair's armrest
clattered to the floor spilling the butts across the mildewed
mat. The mildly perturbed dog sniffed at the contents before
hammering back down the outdoors staircase to look for
untainted grass to eat in the scrapyard.

Dean couldn't remember what was on his mind before his
heart valves opened and closed for one last beat. He wished
he could. He wondered if he'd know where Nicole had
ended up, that she was OK at least. Dean reviews long-faded
memories of Poland, then Germany. A paddle steamer. His
boyhood. An SS officer with crazy-blood shot eyes. He
simultaneously looked to his mind's eye for retained images
of his lost wife, Nicole's mum, Jeanne who left with Nev
Leishmann all those years ago - she left him to bring their
daughter up alone. She'd just gone, no words, just like his
Nicole. Chopped veggies still boiling on the hob, wet washing
on the line, a swinging garden gate in the westerlies.

Forty Seven

1994 - Vella

For Every Good Man, There's Ten Gone Bad

*I think of my sexy wife who is in the process of packing down
our house in Sorrento. Ari has all these friends, so do the
children, they all have their little clubs and now she comes to
this fuck shit hole. Full of palm trees and red faced losers -
drinking beer and farting instead of talking to one other. Beer
drinking chimpanzees in stripey vests. Poor Ari. Poor Luca
and Maria, coming to this suffocating city. Everybody has the
same head, everybody dresses the same, talks the same, likes
the same food, even same songs. This is the land of 'same
head people' tah! I hope next hurricane it blows into the
bloody oceans forever. X'ghala Zobbi!*

Forty Eight

1994 - Glenn

Come Gentle, The Night

The sounds she made during this session were authentic enough to bring him to climax within minutes. Glenn had, by then, ordered the nurse's services three times and she had gotten better and better every time - more into it. Beyond the tattoos she was your regular sort, her upper legs and arse cheeks were uneven with cellulite - which he'd never seen before - to date, the only other girls he'd ever been with were Nicole and that time with Jocasta Bublik. The nurse had an enormously wet pussy that fit around his cock like a glove. Tonight he came all over her stomach. Then he fucked her again from behind, his fingers between her teeth as she gently bit down on them. He wouldn't cum again so quickly, so he asked her to lie down on top of him with her back against his chest; then he pulled himself off between the cheeks of her buttocks whilst she brought herself to climax. In turn, she leaned her head back into him, putting her mouth to his, kissing the tip of his tongue. He didn't kiss her back as she did this. Glenn liked being grazed this way.

Afterwards, Dani congratulated him, *"Good onya sport,"* took a shower and before leaving, she gave him a frequent flyer discount and a lemon flavoured lollipop.

"What do I call you?"

"You ask me that every time."

"I know, and you never say."

"Who do you ask for when you call?"

"The one with the cigar tattoo."

"Ask for The Red Nurse next time."

"What's red about you?"

"You don't know?"

"No."

She tips him a wink.

The rain began to pepper down outside, like a scene from 'Bladerunner' he thought. Now dressed, but not well enough to survive a soaking in the deluge, she offered Glenn a smile as she tucked herself away out the door. Going to the window, he can see The Red Nurse stood under the portico walkway in front of his room eating a chocolate bar.

Forty Nine

1994

My Name Is Not Myrtle Slate

Deep in the mangroves, blindly groping through the shallows
is a ghost that has lost her people. It feels a deep shame. She
hangs on to the fragments of a memory. If she stops thinking
about her former flesh and blood existence for even a second
she'll lose her anchor in this world. Be cast adrift again on
the tides. It's only coincidence that she's back here. Out of the
millions of souls that try to keep a grip, it's an infinitesimal
number that makes it back home or get to stay. She doesn't
know this place but it is her country. But she knows her way
without seeing. This isn't her house. But this is the same
air she once took into her lungs many years ago. The same
breeze, the same sounds. The people slumber an eternity in
the firmament - she was one of them once.

Fifty

1994 - The Chorus

The Black Bird Way

"You needn't look far for evidence that the Australian police force is a racist institution. Not having any real natives to do any bush tracking when they went out searching for Johnny Pearce, they got the only other black fella they could be bothered to look for."

"Black Bert."

"Yeah, Black Bert."

"Not true, they had a search and rescue helicopter out too and it was that which spotted his camp else they'd still be looking."

"The pilot was a black fella too."

"Bullshit."

II

"Fat, White Bert died in 1983, but that's how Black Bert got his name. There are hundreds of Torres Strait Islanders that have made the Dewhurst region their home, and there's probably about 30 fellas called Bert down here as well. Don't know what colour they'd be though. Thing is Fat White Bert

owned a lot of the land to the north of Dewhurst and he shared a border with Black Bert. Both fellas had zucchini plantations back then, so if you happened to be a labourer, a distinction was needed, and a simple one at that. And like we just said, even though Fat White Bert's been dead since 1983, Black Bert's name has stuck. At least that's the way it got explained to me..."

"He knows. We all fucking know. He's probably the one who told yer..."

*

"It's just a name. It's what everyone calls him."

Fifty One

1991 and 1994 - Glenn

Four Tree Trunks of Aspen, Cast Out On The Ocean

*I've lost the art of conversation. I don't like talking as much
as I used to. Maybe I'll start passing people pieces of paper
to save myself some trouble but then there's the question of my
handwriting, which is unreadable. Ever read The New York
Trilogy where the man disappears into a room and all that's
found of him are his glasses? I only wish I had the substance
to be that guy. It'll be different tomorrow. I won't feel this way*

II

1994

Glenn is three-storeys up at Kenny Wood's apartment
watching the sea theatre - the ocean is grey and the sky pallid,
full of movement. A plume of foam emerges from the sway as
the surge below hits a rock break. Through the thick windows
he can't hear anything except his own breathing as the tons
of salt water continuously crash against the marina walls.
The seagulls are pushed around in flight, brave and stupid
souls. The big blind swirls in an unruly mass, a fearsome
swell yet the townsfolk stand along the marina wall like
they're watching television. There's a 55 mph storm coming
in, columns of sea water fold in and slide down their own
formations and these cock muppets are all stood yards away,
silhouetted like ghouls from 'Dawn of the Dead' - stunned
fucking mullet.

A wave could hurl a rock a big as your head out of the surf, could be any of you down there who's got his or her name scribbled down in the 'freak death' column he thought as he watched them all, cooing and laughing as the waves pummeled the concrete dock.

Ed had given him the keys and told him, *"No fucking funny stuff. Definitely, no party girls, yer poof."*

It was patently obvious to him that Ed hadn't been within a mile of the place as he hadn't known the address or even how to find it.

The absent Kenny certainly loved Hollywood movies regardless of quality. There was a cabinet full of Hollywood schlock, like 'The Best of the Best', 'The Salute of The Jugger' and 'Wings of Apache', yet there was nothing approaching anything truly decent. Names like Eric Roberts, Kiefer Sutherland, Lou-Diamond Phillips and Rutger Hauer turned up again and again. The photos on the sideboard of his invisible host portrayed a happy looking fella with dark red hair and brown eyes beaming out. He hadn't seen him around before but he looked kind.

Glenn put on a videocassette to watch. He'd never seen 'Flatliners', so he threw it on. Afterwards, he thought of Dean haunting him the same way Julia Roberts' dad does her in the film. He shrugged the idea off. What did he owe Dean? He wasn't in deficit, or maybe his friend was. Maybe Glenn took more than he gave.

Fifty Two

2009 - Nick

The Freak Accident Express

"A passenger died on the Greyhound bus northbound somewhere between Sarina and Dewhurst earlier today. The driver, Nick Bootman, said that an alarm was raised by other travellers. The dead man is reported to be have been in his early 30s. His identity hasn't been made public by the authorities at this time. The man is thought to have been a foreign national who was backpacking in Queensland and had joined the bus service in Gladstone."

"Stay tuned for the best news around - 4WD! The p-p-p-p-p-PEOPLE'S-people's-ch-ch-choice!"

"Keep your driver, aliver."

"Next up, super listeners, we've got today's installment of 'How Green Was My Cactus' sponsored by Samboy Chips and Mr Big's Sports in George Street, Mackay. We'll be right back, after this word."

Fifty Three

1985 - Johnny and Aggie

This Be The Verse

"Take the boy fishing with you."

"He's fucking useless. Weak handed."

"Then show him what to do. You were taught once John."

"I don't have the patience. He's better here with you. You know I don't get much time off duty. So I don't want to waste my spare time teaching him how to fucking tie his shoelaces, let alone fishing. All this shit"

"He never sees you."

"Too bad, I need me space."

"Fine."

"Yeah, fine is it. Good. Have you finished flapping your lips, cos you've got me running late?"

"Yeah, I've finished alright John."

"Right."

"Well, what are you waiting for? Go. Go out on your boat, by yourself. Fucking prick."

"You shut your fucking mouth. Or I'll shut it for ya."

"You try that's the last thing you get to do. One touch, I told you. I'm off."

"Just like that? You'll go?"

"You get to do it once and live to regret it. That's all it will take. I'll walk and I'll take Glenn with me."

John walks across the kitchen to where Aggie is standing. *"I told you to shut up once already with my mouth."*

The floorboard creaks involuntarily under Glenn's foot. From where he's stood behind the kitchen door in the lounge, he's afraid but poised to confront his dad.

"Glenn? Get your arse in here."

Fifty Four

1969 - Aggie

Sometimes Love Isn't Enough

Aggie Pearce was an English rose; she had light brown hair,
light blue eyes, slightly red cheeks, belying an aversion to
direct sun worship. Freckles dotted her face, a few lingering
in the early creases around her eyes. She didn't laugh easily,
humour was lost on her but that wasn't to say she was stupid.
Certain things could raise her spirits: a kind gesture from
a stranger; a sincere question about her well-being from
unexpected quarters; a thoughtful lover; an old song sang
well; long drives that allowed her to watch the country spin
by through the window: she appreciated art and was drawn
to imaginative and creative men, women and children. Aggie
disliked coarse men, yet she married a policeman because he
seemed to be good with people which betrayed a warm heart,
yet he proved himself to be as hard and as unforgiving as the
dry soil at the core of his country. Like a rock or a pebble, he
was formidable, but there was no centre to him. A stone has
no heart.

Aggie was born in 1948 just outside Liverpool, England, she
was raised and educated to be factory fodder, to work on the
production lines down the Binns Road. Huntley & Palmers
or Dinky Toys, along with all her sisters, but it wasn't to be
a long-term thing. The future, now the distant past, had other
ideas. One fateful day she met a secretary called Kollette on
the bus into the city who told her about a night spot she went
to, where all the new and upcoming bands would play - they

were both just to a bit too young to see The Beatles, The
Escorts, or The Big Three at their local peak. This pair got to
see the next wave. The band-shift nobody remembers.

The course of a life can turn on a dime, or in some cases the
change is a slower one. One Friday evening Aggie caught
the number 10 bus opposite the Eagle & Child in Page Moss
to the centre of Liverpool. Kollette was waiting at the end
of Bold Street for her up by the bombed out church with her
Australian cousin. Aggie had never met anyone from Australia
before. She'd seen something on TV called *They're a Weird
Mob* about an Italian that moves 'down under' to learn the
'ins and outs' of the way of life there. Kangaroos, ANZACs,
gorgeous beaches and dark fellows with spears - that was all
she knew about the place. Kollette's cousin was talkative and
over polite. He was diminutive in stature and he called her
'love' (pronounced *'lav'*) all the time. She only knew him
that one evening, and would never remember his name, it was
something like Peter, Ron or Bill. But the meeting inspired a
curiosity in her. Kollette confessed to having only met him a
few hours earlier that same evening. He'd come over to see
the mother country and his long lost family in Liverpool were
on his route.

After a dance and a bit of laugh, the Australian was gone but
he'd had a fair bit to say for himself. During the evening,
he'd spoken about his town back home, a small place called
Braidwood, which was a farming town that stood in the lea of
a bowl shaped hill that was named after the town's founder, a
doctor. He'd regaled us with a tale of how his sister had met
Mick Jagger who had recently starred in a flick about Ned
Kelly that was shot out his way. His parents owned a stud
farm and the filmmakers had used some of the horses, and

Jagger had ridden one with her for a few kilometers along the
back roads. Just her and the world's most famous rock star, all
alone in the wilds.

The Australian went on to speak about magpies, kookaburras,
the golden skies and the sense of community. Talk drifted
to how come so many of his friends had joined the army to
fight in Vietnam alongside the Americans, and how a rift had
formed in the town because a lot of their fathers had fought in
Europe in the Second World War and before that Gallipoli in
WWI. *"They didn't want to have survived to see their sons die
in the next conflict that came along, whereas others saw that
angle as cowardly and dishonourable."*

The drunker the three of them got, the less conversation was
heard over the music, and when Aggie told the Aussie she
could no longer make out a word he was saying he tugged her
arm and gestured for her to follow him out into the street. But
Aggie stood fast and instead stayed leant against the wall, she
knew not to wander off alone with men she'd just met.

"Stay," she implored, but he shrugged and was soon obscured
by dancers filling the gap on the floor between her and him.
The short Aussie with the aqualine face and a gold tooth was
swallowed up for good. Perhaps he drowned in the press
of people or just set himself adrift in the sea of dancing
Scousers.

Aggie asked her mum if she'd ever met any Australians
before but she told her to 'give over,' going on to explain that
the most exotic man she'd ever met was a Welsh coal miner
called Dai. Her mum had almost married him during the
Second World War. His story remains hanging in the air like

fragrance - Aggie suspects that maybe he'd have hoped for a bit more than to become a comedy punch line to a serious question.

*

Poor Dai, his name sadly echoed his abruptly delivered fate. He took several bullets somewhere on a country road in the Languedoc-Rousillion region of France. Moments before the roadside ambush, Dai had shared a joke and a cigarette with another soldier.

"Taffy goes into a pet shop. Can I buy a bumble-bee please? goes the fella. The shopkeeper, non-plussed goes, I'm sorry boyo, we don't sell 'em. Taffy replies, Yes you do, there's one in the window!"

Bang, bang, bang. At least they went out laughing…

When the guns ceased in their deadly soliloquy, the attacking squad of Germans were annihilated with a pair of allied grenades almost instantly.

Dai's corpse, along with his dead partner-in-mirth, were ferried by some Americans in a jeep to the first church they could find just as the heavens opened. Torrential rain to flush away the blood and eviscerated German teenagers. A young soldier from Bute, Montana who had been tasked with 'owning' the job, received an ordered to note the names of the fallen duo down, so he scribbled them down on a cigarette paper. The British had already taken the duo's ID disks (why were both the circle and the octagon removed?) so when he left the two bodies under a tarpaulin on the church steps he tucked the cigarette paper into one of the Welshman's boots.

The young soldier stepped back, rain dripping from the finial
on the arch at the foot of the steps. Something this elaborately
crafted, how had it survived the shelling? Leaving these
lifeless warriors on the steps didn't seem to him like it was
the right thing to do but nobody was around: no minister, no
army personnel, nothing but a billowing cloud of starlings
making patterns in the grey rain. The church seemed to be
abandoned and locked up. There was a shell crater nearby
and many severely damaged gravestones - smashed teeth in
a suicide jumper's face. As the rain began to gain weight, he
walked away backwards to get a better view of the scene.
Four feet and one beckoning palm lay exposed, from the
black cover. The trooper's buddies who had already returned
to jeep shouted to him, *"Let's hit the fucking road! Come on
Montana!"*

Within three hours, Dai's boots were stolen by a raggedy
brown shape with feverish black fingers.

"Merci, mon cheri, mons fils. Merci."

The creature leant down, folding back the tarpaulin and kissed
the corpses on their bloodied cheeks. The figure stepped
down into the driving rains. The scrumpled up note with the
soldiers' names on blew away, just like the origins of the man
this bedraggled monster once was.

*

Kollette told Aggie that millions of Brits were pissing off
'down under' for good jobs, mainly marrieds but the odd
single could apply to emigrate.

Within two years she was working in a typing pool for a

company at the heart of Sydney. She lived in a boarding house with seven other girls, all from England. She saw an Aborigine dressed up in a businessman's suit doing cartwheels for money by Circular Quay. He had a briefcase and a toy gold watch. One morning she awoke to find the word '*Eternity*' written in chalk on the wall opposite her house in the most beautiful calligraphy.

The Opera House was only a few years old by then but she didn't know anybody that would be interested in seeing a performance there, or would even have that kind of money. There was a mail order initiative where you could apply for a free ticket every month if you could be arsed to jump through all the hoops. So she did, just like the native performer at Circular Quay.

Fifty Five

1873 - Wilfred

No Tale, No Twist

Notes from Acting Captain Wilfred Bloom's journal

One such scouting expedition ended in tragedy for us when we were in a hilly region to the north of the river. We had journeyed past a cluster of low-lying ponds that happened to be breeding grounds for, as yet unspecified, flying insects that loved the taste of human blood. The one obliterated on my arm was at least half the size of my outstretched palm. The men were in agony for days with the pestilent spots and boils they contracted. Moving away from the water's edge we headed into rocky country where our tracker dog caught the scent of a lone kangaroo. We could detect a lot of disturbance as it had beaten a path across a wide patch of thick bush land. We only had one dog, Wilf, with us on this particular outing but it was able and agile enough to follow any animal's scent. However, a full-scale hunt was out of the question without the pack.

On arrival at the crest of a hill, one of my men, Graeme Hawkins, saw movement in the direction we were headed, led by Wilf. Hawkins went down on one knee to take steady aim with his gun, and I gave him the nod to fire at will. He took the shot and all the men cheered as we heard our quarry fall down in the thick jungle area up ahead. The dog set off in the lead without further command to go and check out the spoils. He is used to doing all the hard work when it comes to hunting but on this occasion he was brought along to make sure we found our way back to camp in good order, so this incident was an unexpected bonus for it.

Wilf returned to us with a very bloody snout before we had reached the befallen boomer. A man in the vanguard, Charles Ashley, came down the line asking why I had given the mandate to kill a native woman. I told the man to be silent in no short order. The command was for Hawkins to shoot an animal not a person. It was the dog that had picked up the scent and Hawkins that had seen the woman / animal up ahead. On seeing the woman's corpse, I established that the shot had blown about 10 pounds of flesh clean away from her torso and that she had probably died instantly. Poor lassie.

I subsequently ordered two men, Ashley and Hawkins, to fashion a makeshift stretcher from a tree trunk and to take the body back to the camp where we would give her a proper Christian burial and then convene a meeting to decide how we would account for ourselves to the local tribe: the Jubeira people. By the fall of darkness, the two men had not returned to camp like the rest of us having stayed back to chop a tree down to make the aforementioned stretcher. We sent a boy up the tallest tree at the edge of our camp to see if he could see a campfire. The child shouted down that he could see three from his point of vantage. I decided that I couldn't spare my men to go and find Ashley and Hawkins until daylight. How could I have known which of the camp fires (if any) had been made by the missing men? By morning they were still unaccounted for. I sent out two search parties - one to go along the riverside trail, and one to follow yesterday's route including a fast sweep of the insect-infested ponds.

*Around mid-afternoon, the second team returned with
Hawkins who informed me that Ashley had been killed by a
snake. Hawkins explained that they'd panicked after getting
lost on the way back. Ashley had threatened to leave Hawkins
with the girl's body at one point when they couldn't agree
on the right direction back to camp - as a result a fight had
broken out. Somehow, during the course of the brawl, Ashley
was bitten by a poisonous snake. They made camp, but by first
light Ashley was dead. Hawkins, in his wisdom, explained that
he had therefore rolled both bodies down a steep hill where
they became cut-off deep inside a maze of giant rocks below.
He theorised that both bodies were now out of reach and
impossible to retrieve for a traditional burial. Sensing foul
play, a team of men was mustered and led to the ridge above
the rocks where Hawkins had the left the bodies.*

*Our chaplain led a memorial service for the dead on the ridge
in the sweltering jungle heat below the trees. We were losing
men at a steady rate - ten had died from tropical diseases
since January last.*

*On the map I'd drawn of the region, I pencilled a small 'x'
at each end of the ridge. In between the marks I scribbled
the words, 'Ashley's Ridge.' As I write this, I sincerely hope
that one day the remains of both this native woman and of
my comrade Charles Ashley can be found and given a proper
Christian burial.*

*

*Within a week, Hawkins was dead, having hung himself from
a tree at the seashore. After he was cut down we buried him
outside the walls of the cemetery, the chaplain acknowledged
that no suicides could be interred on consecrated ground. He*

was buried next to our former captain, Ambrose Stamper's empty grave in an alternative area to the rear of the church without fanfare, without love. In God's absence.

Fifty Six

1994 - The Chorus

Errant Mothers, Randy Fathers

"Don't forget, after Jeanne Wexler ran off with that prick Nev Leishmann, no one heard from her again."

"You might not have heard off her but we did... She went out to the country, lived with her folks for a bit. Put Nev to work on the land."

"Who said romance is dead?"

"Had to have been an Australian."

*

"Nev Leishmann worked on the railroad, came in with a gang and stuck around. Don't know how him and Jeanne hooked up..."

"Me neither."

*

"Dean Wexler, met Nev at The Crown Hotel, I think it was one ANZAC day and they was playing two-up... They got along alright. You know Dean, never says too much. But anyway that's how they met. They met playing two-up at the Crown Hotel. Can't remember the years, ay? Time is a thief, a real bastard."

*

"Not sure if Nev stuck around for long up there in the boonies with Jeanne's family, but she fucked off to the city at some point. Only came back to employ some young fellas to run the farm when her olds got too weak to work for themselves."

"Yeah, I wouldn't know if she ever kept in touch with Nicole. She just fucked off, like so many others. One minute they're going about a normal life, then next they've shot through with some fancy fella. Not that Nev was anything to look at, the good lord definitely made his face with the lights off."

*

"You made me miss a girl who never existed."

Fifty Seven

1991 - Glenn

The Things That You Hold In

Dean said he had a surprise for me at the house. He sounded unusually chirpy. "Don't worry, it's a good surprise, Glenn. Don't worry."

Turns out the car he'd been working on and off all summer was for me. It was a wreck for sure but now it was to be my runaround. The half rusty, white Datsun Sunny 120Y sat on the front driveway, soapy water running off it. Nicole was in the back of the car dusting around the interior. She saw me and clambered out. "We know it's not your birthday or anything, but you help Dad so much around here."

I told her that the car was perfect and it was. Dean strolled around the back of the house and came back a moment later carrying an esky full of beers. "Not bad is she?"

II

I remember Nicole would sit on the bonnet of my car reading a book, it would be parked on my driveway or at that short strip of tarmac behind the line of forlorn palm trees at Hunters Beach. She used to wait for me like that whilst I went surfing. Another place we'd park up was opposite the Showgrounds. We'd usually share a box of Red Rooster and watch the American football players training routines, or the occasional tryouts under the over abundant spotlights. She'd

*let me lick the chicken grease off her fingers - a thing I took
to be the norm until I tried to do it to another girl years later.
What a shock it was to find out that young lovers around
the world weren't up to the same thing. I'm reminded of this
every time I go to see a sporting event at our quiet space just
beyond the fence at the Showgrounds. It was here that I'd also
go by myself, just to stare at the lights and listen to shit pop
music on the radio."*

III

*Nicole spent a lot of time with her friends growing up. After
her mum went off with Nev Leishmann, Dean wasn't equipped
to bring a child up so the other families on the street kind of
came together 'unofficially' to help him out. She was always
over at somebody's house having her tea, watching TV, doing
her homework. Dean would often go a whole day and forget
to eat, go for longer without shopping. Dean wasn't being
neglectful, he was just out of step with the whole parenting
thing. Her friend Cody's mum bought Nicole her first bra;
Fallon's mum helped when she had a period and gave her
feminine hygiene advice; the nurse up the street took care of
common colds. It was no big deal; it's just how it was. And
in return (sort of) Dean would look after people's cars. But it
wasn't a straight 'quid pro quo' situation. People just came
together and helped them, no worries. And as Nicole grew up,
she pulled her weight by helping around her friend's houses.
A bit of washing up, hoovering, or an occasional meal.
Spaghetti carbonara was her specialty, but Dean hated white
sauces and mushrooms, so he never got to try it. Strange how
all these annoying details come back so clearly years later,
but who gives a fuck?*

Fifty Eight

1970 - Aggie

Time Without End

"I see this everywhere, this word eternity."

Throughout the neighbourhoods of Sydney she saw the bold calligraphic declaration *'Eternity'* – it was usually on the pavement, sometimes on a wall. The immaculate joined up writing. Whenever she was out walking and happened on an example she'd ask a passerby if they knew what it meant but nobody ever seemed to know. No one had ever been found actually writing the word down. It was a strange phenomenon, almost, she thought. Under the tree dappled streets of Glebe and Balmain, the brick stairways of Woolloomooloo, and the flophouses of Darlinghurst Road, he'd been there, assuming the ghostly scribe was a man. Maybe it was the city itself, but that was a ridiculous thought. Aggie had spent too many of her weekends in the city alone, walking to Circular Quay and back, a long walk across this wonderful, airy city. Of an evening she'd marvel, as the gigantic fruit bats would depart their treetops in the Royal Botanic Gardens, taking to the skies – such an exotic and peculiar sight to see these large airborne creatures mingle with the tall office buildings along Market Street and around the centre of the city.

Today was ANZAC day, and the streets had been lined with soldiers on parade. They were laying wreaths at a huge memorial at the edge of Hyde Park. She watched as families waved flags and children were held aloft to see the columns

of men and women strut past. There was always something
to see in the city, always somewhere to go without getting
harassed. Carrying a reading book she decided that she'd
spend sometime at the waters edge down by Mrs Macquarie's
Chair. She thought about her family fast asleep on the far side
of the planet - a different world.

II

Arthur Stace was a drunk who found God after hearing a
reading by a local preacher called, 'Echoes of Eternity' at a
Sydney Church. He said it made him want to sing eternity
throughout the city streets to spread God's good tidings.
The newly indemnified soul then took to the city with his
waterproof yellow chalk at daybreak to leave his one word
sermon on the pavements and buildings of the city. The man
died over 50 years ago now, yet his legacy lives on. Someone
somewhere must have made it his or her own business to
continue his mission, because Stace died in 1967. Singing the
message of eternity for eternity.

Fifty Nine

1994 - Glenn

The Terminal Bird That Rolls

Dean wrote to me, once, when I was inside to say that he knew I hadn't done it, I hadn't hurt Nicole, and that he was ashamed of himself that he'd never helped me. That he never demanded a proper court case to see justice done and served correctly. Dean had gone on to apologise and concluded his letter by saying that I could live with him when my sentence was up if I could see my way to forgiving him. The rest of the town didn't bother to look any deeper than my sentence.

Sixty

1991 - Glenn

Beauty Is Youth

He looked at himself in Nicole's full-length bedroom mirror. Her pleated school skirt fit him snugly. He smoothed it down feeling his own arse as he did it.

"You better not ladder my tights," she said as she moved in behind him and began to gently nibble his ear lobe, *"I wish I had two uniforms."*

Glenn didn't realise at first because he was fascinated with this new version of himself staring back out of the mirror at him; Nicole had removed all of her clothes except for her pale yellow blouse with a ridiculously stiff collar. She then reached over into a wooden bowl on her dressing table and produced a hair clip.

"Get that hair out of your eyes." She then turned him around and told him that she would be in control from there on in, *"I'll take it from here."*

Sixty One

1994 - Dean

Everything Ends

Dean died. His last breath, already behind him. Yet here he is.

II

Dean gradually becomes aware of the gently drifting snow.
He hasn't seen snow since he left Europe. And he's feeling
the slight cold. It had been snowing that day in Helsinki he
got packed on to a small steam ship to England before he
stowed away, hidden onboard the SS Strathnaver to Sydney,
Australia. How he got to Helsinki alone back then was a
concealed mystery and even now he found himself embroiled
in another one.

Dean makes his way down through the gently sloping
woodland, the branches of the trees and the ground now thick
with snow. A childhood memory comes back to him, and just
then as the thought hits him, an arm reaches up from inside
a snowdrift, the gloved hand shooting up into the firmament
like a firework.

"Help me up - (Pomóż mi wstać)"

*"I am here brother, but I am weak - (Jestem tu bracie, ale
jestem słaby)."* He answers, *"But I will try - (Ale
postaram się)."*

Dean remembers playing this game with his brother who would hide under the snow and lie in wait just to ambush him. Today Piotr was calmer. He was playing gently as if he didn't want to frighten Dean away.

"It's OK I can help myself - (Jest OK, poradzę sobie). " Piotr stands up eyeing Dean with curiosity.

"Artur, my brother, but you are so old now - (Artur bracie, jaki ty już jesteś stary). "

Dean thought, yes, my name is Artur, he'd almost forgotten. Piotr is smiling at him, brushing snow from his coat.

"My little brother is an old man. Like Granpa (Mój młodszy brat jest starym człowiekiem. Niczym Dziadek)...) " Piotr shoves Dean in his shoulder playfully. His smile drops away.

"Who's that? Who have you brought with you? - (Kto to? Kogo ze sobą przyprowadziłeś?) "

Piotr's face is frozen as if he's been caught mid-sentence saying something disparaging about a loved one. He slowly points to a spot behind Dean.

Dean turns but all he sees is falling snow and a woodland full of trees.

"I see nobody, dear Piotr. - (Nie widzę nokogo, drogi Piotrze...) "

"Then what's that sound, brother? - (Więc co to za dźwiek, bracie?) "

Piotr stands staring, his pointing hand lowers to his side. Dean brings to bear the scene but he cannot see anything out there in the snowy woodlands. The only thing moving is the downward, floating snowflakes. They are alone. Yet when he concentrates he can just about make out the gradually deafening chorus of cicadas getting louder, louder, and louder.

Sixty Two

1994 - Glenn

Pam Short's Broken Both Her Legs
And I Wanna Dance With You

The sickly yellow light seeped under the curtains of his room
for the night at Motel 501. Glenn rubbed his eyes and slowly
sat up. He gently puts his hand on Laine's shoulder. Oh fuck,
it's Laine. *"Laine. Laine, you better get going. I've stuff to
sort."*

Laine turns over and lets her eyes adjust.

"Heyyyy Glenn."

"You okay?"

Laine hadn't bothered to get undressed and had slept on top of
the sheets. Her tussled hair everywhere, falling over her face
as she sits up. *"Can you buy me a coffee?"*

*"Sure. But then you have to get off. I've got stuff I need to
sort."*

*"Thanks for last night. I was out of it, and you fucking... well
you were there. You sorted it. Can I smoke in here?"*

"I guess."

Laine sparks up a half-smoked cigarette that she retrieves

from behind her ear. She gives him a look as if to say what's the big deal?

Then she takes a massive lungful down.

"I knew you'd come back to Dewie. Didn't seem right that you'd have done that to Nicole."

Breathing out a stream of smoke that hangs around her.

"S'all anyone wants to talk to me about."

"Well, she was my friend too Glenn."

"More than I was."

"What makes you say that?"

"Look, Laine. You best go."

Laine stands up and gets off the bed, she points the end of her cigarette at him, holding it between her thumb and finger, *"If you've got something to say, mate."*

"It's just this. I'm getting sick of people coming up to me saying, "I knew you didn't do it mate. I knew you weren't capable."

"I see."

"Good, because barely anyone fucking stood up for me back in '91 did they? Only Dean defended me, and he's Nicole's pop. You see where I'm going with this?"

Laine picks up her bags and marches to the door.

"Yes, I do Glenn. And you can stick your coffee up your arse. Fucking prick."

Why'd he stick his neck out for Laine. Fucking always the same. Always mouthing off at some girl or fella late at night and she'd need bailing out. When he'd come back to his crash room at the end of his shift, a few yards from the bar, she was sat outside his door, *"Cheers Glenny, my knight in shining armour, I'll suck your dick for that."*

Fucking Laine. Needs to get back on the tills at Coles and stop haunting the city bars looking for easy marks. Glenn had been working his first shift. Ed had given him his keys and float and told him it should be quiet, and it was deadly until Laine spat at Christine Tork for sneering at something she said. And this was the result of a long drunken conversation about how high your waistband should come up to when wearing jeans. Dewhurst fashionistas got into a brand war. Mel Little or Big Mel was caught in the middle of the girls before Glenn told Laine to go to his room and cool down.

Mel looked amused, *"You'll be sorry you did that."*

"You having a pop Mel?"

"I'm saying, just don't fuck her whatever you do? She's fucking feral."

"Get real."

"Your dick'll fall off."

"Yeah she'd fuck a tree that one," piped in Robbie Diaz from the pokey in the corner.

When he knew Glenn had spotted him he just tipped his cap at his old friend and continued his game. It was the first time he'd seen his so-called good mate Robbie since he'd arrived back. He didn't have much to say when they were kids and now they were grown he seemed to have even less. He was about to go over, shake his hand, whatever, when Mr Madonna bursts into the bar carrying his speakers, *"Hold the fucking doors, you pricks."*

Then came two solid hours of endless Madonna renditions, mainly 'Crazy For You.' He had on a yellow singlet that had the words, *'Pam Short's Broken Both Her Legs and I Wanna Dance With You!!!'* emblazoned on it. He caught Glenn and a punter he'd never seen before laughing at his version of 'Vogue'. It did turn out to be a quiet night except for two young fellas getting thrown out for snorting cola in the toilets. That was Madonna's department, not his.

"Should have joined in," the punter said loudly shortly before he was gut punched and thrown into the derelict kids' sandpit at the side of the Palm Club along with the two lads. The sandpit provided a deliberately soft landing strip for all those La Madonna fucked up, supposedly to lessen the load of any assault charges that may have made their way back to him.

"Fucking comedians, Madonna hates them, so do I," said the hilarious 'Muscle Mary' as he clattered back into the bar.

Sixty Three

1994 - Vella

Remember, The Night

Vella likes this song. He turns up the radio in his police rover. He didn't even know the band was Australian. At the time he'd always thought the song was by Chicago… He bursts into song when the chorus comes on, *"I'm all out of love… what am I without you…?"*

The Maltese detective chuckles to himself, but there's no one around to hear him. The wind picks up and the sugar canes sway begrudgingly. Insects dart around the static headlights of the police rover. He takes one last draw on his short cigarette, stubbing it out in time with the lyrics. The song reaches its climax.

"And that was 'I'm all out of love' by Air Supply, a great Australian band. Before that was Heaven 17's 'Let me go'. Next up, a forgotten soft-rock gem from Sharon O'Neill called 'Smash Palace'."

"All the hits and more on 4WD, the peoples f-f-f-f-first choice."

Vella's already asleep and he remains that way for the next half a dozen songs. Dream baby, dream.

Sixty Four

Forever - Everybody

Just When You Least Expect It,
Just What You Least Expect

Some girls peak before all the others. Some venture out to see if the boys are as fucked up as they are even before some of the others have put away their dollies and teddy bears. Is it safe out there, beyond the shallows of their teenage female friendships? Out through the narrows and onto the shoulders of an unpredictable ocean.

Sixty Five

1994 - Vella

Adulterers Write The Best Love Songs

When did it all go fuck shaped?

Vella is sat at his off-balance kitchen table; freshly prepared
pappardelle pasta, sauce and beef mince stews in a plastic
bowl. A trio of large high-resolution photographs showing
Nicole Wexler's face - two before and one after the assault
sit before him. Her light brown eyes, and the ghost of a smile
in her most recent school photo inspires the black hair on
his short forearms to stand up to attention - a warm breeze
susurrates against the screen door.

Earlier that same evening he'd watched a storm far away from
his veranda. Miniature forks of lightning had stabbed at the
rinsed out orange skies. The storm had no voice, it had been
drowned out by sheer the distance, made up of bush land and
uncoloured hills. The tall wild grass in the yard below had
seemed to kneel down in awe of the sultry air currents, and
now a callous rain was on the way. He always looked forward
to the abstruse petrichor that emanated from the garden
although he never found out the name for its persuasive scent.

Vella hums to himself as he dials his wife who may just be
at their family home in Sorrento. As the call connects, he
remembers the lyrics to the tune he's bombilating.

"Are you singing?"

*"Eyyyy Gina, I'm serenading you my beauty. Even so far
away I am picturing you. I miss you so much I want you to
hear me sing."*
"Why'd you still call me Gina?"

*"You remind me of her. The most beautiful actress in the Milky
Way."*

*"You're hopeless Marcos. What are you working on tonight? I
can hear you playing around with papers."*

*"I am looking at a beautiful face of this girl who was walking
in the footsteps of the whirlwind. The man who died, Pearce,
who I was sent to replace. This girl was his son's girlfriend
sometime back, but she went missing."*

"An old case?"

*"I've talked to you about this. You forgetful wife animal.
Listen, no one cares about this girl who ran away after she
was assaulted. The day after she was badly beaten by her
boyfriend, Pearce's son, she miraculously walks out of the
hospital, after being beaten black and blue. The full extent
of her injuries, unexplored because of no doctors that night.
Some bullshit."*

"Couldn't have been that bad."

*"Photographs were taken by police, but the guy who took
them is the last person to have seen her officially. Video
doesn't show who came to fetch her...she's just seen sat on
a bench at the front of the hospital, then she walks out of the
gates so slow, like a plant. So much pain.*

The boyfriend, never beat her though. A local policeman did it, but the crime was pinned on the boy, Pearce's son."

"That sounds terrible."

"The investigation was so under-manned, is that a word?"

"Under resourced."

"Thank you my sweets. So his father sides with the assailant (who was his police partner) and the boy goes to jail for three years. It gets rushed through, they got a recorded confession, somehow. Boy admitted guilt, I heard the tape but none of it sounds right. It's the shit deal. Case would have gotten thrown out in the city but out here it's kangaroos in the courthouse. I want to clear his name but I don't have any support. And everybody's certain he did these things to this beauty. But everybody's gone. Pearce is dead, his partner Wilson vanished too, only the son is here - fighting with everybody who looks at him. It's cold shit, my flowers. What can I say?"

Vella's eyes fall back to Nicole's school picture - this gamine mystery.

The line goes dead - Ari has stopped listening. She often feigns a lost connection when the truth is that she has no taste for police business. Her depression makes her rude and impatient. Why let yourself be a spectator to such ugliness, she'd demand? Does he tell her these stories to show how safe and good her life is? That these hell-eyed evil men and women are but a heartbeat away?

Vella blows the phone a kiss and kills the flat dial tone.

"And the wonder of it all is that you just don't realise how much I love you." he trills flatly, singing to himself as he tidies his papers away. Ari is more breathtaking than the famous 1960s film star, Gina Lollobrigida, he tells himself. And she is. She really is.

The famously recalcitrant detective pins the picture of Nicole, unscathed, under a red Dewhurst Indoor Cricket League 1988 magnet that came attached to the second-hand fridge when he bought it.

"You look wonderful tonight," he says as he touches the photo absent-mindedly. He then takes the picture back down and looks at her again.

"There's a big difference between being this missing person and someone that's just left town for good, ay. I make a bet that no one's even looked for you have they?"

Sixty Six

1991 - Glenn and Robbie

Mr Black Magic Himself

One of the best spots to escape the city was below the newer bridge which spanned the full and fast Pioneer River. It ferried all those travelling along the Bruce Highway, round to the west of Dewhurst. Most people bypassed the place to get to Airlie Beach in the north or just closer to home if heading south. You only stopped in Dewie if you knew somebody.

Robbie Diaz stands up on the bank as he struggles to get his cigarette lit.

"Surely it's windier if you stand up."

"Nope. You get the chop of the wind directly off the surface. Your dad told me that, that's why they put weights on your fishing line as well as bait. So it goes plop, instead of haring around in the sky."

Robbie dumps himself in a heap on the humpty of scorched grass and dried earth. Searching for a can of beer, he tosses the first one he finds to a patient Glenn.

"She's a bit bloody warm Rob."

"Shut your lips and drink. Christ."

The sky was peach coloured and the air was thick with the

smell of wet asphalt - the odd mosquito buzzed around, chucked in to the mix for bad luck. The sound of speeding cars knifed the stillness here and there. A road gang, out working late, was packing down a diversion of road cones. Orange lights blinked on a parked maintenance van up there on the highway. Voices called out to one another.

The pair said nothing, tired from a day of sea fishing, as the night shadows lengthened and the waters lapped. These were the days when it was OK to be quiet. If you had nothing to say, you didn't advertise it by saying lots. Empty vessels and all that.

Glenn worried about Nicole's whereabouts and tried to put those concerns out of his head until he could talk to her himself. People loved nothing more than a break up. Staring on from the wings, offering venomous advice they were unqualified to give. Johnny had smirked at him when Glenn had asked if he'd seen Nicole with Pete. The old man had just said, *"You keep girls like that on a leash,"* before marching out the back door.

Three days, four nights, no sign – just a succession of near misses and failed meet-ups. But it didn't seem like she was aggressively avoiding him, she just wasn't available.

Glenn noticed the maintenance van pull away. It had left one of the workers behind who was running to catch up. The van would stop, wait and as soon as the hapless guy reached the vehicle, it would lurch off again. This routine continued until they were all out of sight

Everyone's a comedian.

Sixty Seven

1994 - Vella, Jack and Tom

It Exists At Your Next Life

It's the first blistering hot day since Vella touched down in Dewhurst and a rare canvas of grey rain had engulfed the antique city. Slippery brick pavements would ensure that the hospitals would be busy bandaging broken arms and busted faces - it always happened. The local authorities argued that it wasn't worth installing gritty pavements for the sake of the odd freak storm and a single month of bad weather when the wet came.

Vella felt partial to a quick beer; he would have to adjust to the damp heat another day. He had given Brett Coulson the slip while he went for a spot of lunch. Even though he was Brett's commanding officer he still wanted to make a vaguely good impression, or did he? No, he actually didn't give a fuck. Vella had dumped the police rover that he'd inherited off Johnny Pearce RIP at the side of the kerb when he saw the Chan Bishop Hotel ahead of him at the cross roads.

"Pass us those mate, let's have a look."

"Be careful with 'em. They're older than anything else in here."

The barman gingerly hands Vella the plastic human mandible with a full set of manky wooden teeth attached. Each one of them had once been screwed into the fabled seaman Chan

Bishop's jaw. He'd had all his real gnashers knocked out when the rescue boat he was pushing out into the waves all those years and years ago had sharply risen up and shattered his chin. Bishop was knocked out cold by the impact and slipped virtually unnoticed below the messy waves.

Luckily, he was plucked from the jaws of death by some other rescuers on the same mission to save the stricken passengers on the Verity II.

"So these are Chan Bishop's teeth?" Vella unscrews one, an incisor and measures it to his own. *"Big teeth."*

"Look, give us them back. You'll wreck 'em."

"So this guy is the town legend?"

"I don't really know. D'you want another pot?"

"No, net yet. So you don't know anything about Bishop?"

"Like I said - "

"This place has a tiny bit of history yet you don't give any fucks for it. It's a good story. Why not find out more?"

"I'm a barman not a fucking professor mate. Now can I have the jaw and all the teeth back please?"

"I flap my dirty apron at you, impatient."

Vella set the jaw down and the tooth he unscrewed. The barkeep screws the tooth back into the fake mandible and replaces the artefact on a high shelf where it could almost be described to hold court.

"Where's the top row?" asked Vella. The barkeep just wandered off, picks up a rag and begins to dry a glass.

"If you want a drink, just ask?"

"Why so serious?"

Vella doesn't see the diminutive Jack Lüven walk in, although he unleashes a weird 'Lily of the Valley / Mr Clean' pong off about the place as he compresses his lower body onto a bar stool along from him.

"Bishop got buried with a full set of wooden ones. Those were his spares."

"You are fucking my face."

"Nope, I'm not fucking your face, mate. He lived upstairs most of his adult life and after he died they found these ones rolling around in a dresser in his old room. He used to sit right there." Lüven points to a shady spot under the window closest to a door onto the street. *"He used to sit down there, sup cold beer until he fell asleep. Didn't say much on account of you know, his wooden toothy pegs."*

"How'd you know all this?"

"Jack. Jack Lüven."

"I am Marcos."

"I know, you're Johnny Pearce's replacement."

"Correct. Can I buy you a beer?"

"Line it up. Tom get us two pots of XXXX, mate."

"One last question for you, so that's why the pub was named after him."

"You got it. The town needs stories, figureheads, and there's nothing. He's what stands for a local legend in these parts. A bloke with wooden teeth, who lived in a pub, and had to be carried to bed every night 'cos he was too bloody sozzled to get there himself. About sums this place up."

The beer arrives. Vella pays.

"Cheer up, old chum."

The barkeep is a glum sod.

"In answer to the other question you asked," Jack continues. *"Everybody of a certain age knows about Chan Bishop. Even Tom here knows it now. Surprised his old man didn't tell him. But there you go. Nothing's happened here since Stamper's great-great grandfather dropped anchor out in the bay. It's so shit boring here even the dinosaurs avoided it. Cheers..."*

Both men take a long sip of their afternoon beers. *"Ahhhh."*

"Yes, so lovely. So lovely." says Vella, smacking his lips.

Sixty Eight

1994 - Glenn

The Man From Yalbaroo

He's leaving. Glenn has nothing left but old and used up days
that lie in wait just to haunt him on every street corner: the
whispers in the supermarket, unwelcome stares at the Video
rental shop, poison on the city folks' libellous brown tongues.
Time to un-see it all. Time to fabricate a future based on new
foundations.

At the start of the Bruce Highway going north there's a large
layby ideal to hitch lifts from. There's lots of shade beneath
the birch tree canopy. It's long enough for a road train to
comfortably pull in for the night too.

Glenn's got one bag. He's sporting a pea green baseball cap
that sports the words Deere John on it (a weak joke), and the
standard singlet, lumberjack shirt, shorts and thongs combo.
He'll rent a bed in a YHA in Bowen - a passport is all he
needed and he's got one - then he can work picking fruit or
packing. Easy money, cold beers, hot European backpackers;
a bit of hard yakka - no one around to jostle him - a clean
break in dirty clothes.

The weather is turgid, the branches above the layby suddenly
pick up a king sized gust of stuffy wind. Most of the drivers
that pass him give him a smile or an apologetic look. A
friendly teenager pulls over and asks how far he's going
saying that he's only going up to Black's Beach, but that's just

over the way.

"Good luck, mate."

His small blue car kicks up a bit of gravel as the rear wheels spin and he's off.

After a while, a very old white Ford Divisadero slows down nearby where Glenn's stood. There are boxes of fruit on the passenger seat. Yet the driver, a frail geriatric in a ten gallon hat gets out from the drivers' side, *"Can you drive, skip?"* he asks.

Glenn nods. *"If you move the fruit to the back seat, we can go as far as Yalbaroo. Know where that is?"*

Glenn's heard of it. It's about 50 kilometres up the road, but he figured he was helping the bloke out.

"I'll take you home."

"Thanks, young man. The name's Val and my hat is over one hundred years old."

Sixty Nine

1994 - The Chorus

The Way We Were

On the sidewall of the Motel 501 there's a massive faded mural once drawn and painted by local school kids. The frieze depicts a white backpacker standing beside an Aborigine fella. In the background, there's a highway, straight as an arrow, shooting upwards to the horizon illustrated above their heads. The painted desert about them features cartoonish kangaroos, snakes and koala bears. Both characters are smiling; the Aborigine is resting one of his hands on the shoulder of the rather pale pink skinned, blonde male backpacker. He's giving us the thumbs up which is accompanied by a goofy smile compounded by tremendously gappy teeth - must be a Pom.

The mural was created in aid of a long forgotten campaign - a push by the Dewhurst Tourist Board for us locals to engage with anybody passing through the city (like the pictured backpacker). It was 1988 - Australian Year of the Tourist. Big Hollywood-style words spell out the decree: "Give a tourist a hand."

Some time later, some dag had added the word 'job' after 'hand', so nowadays it reads: "Give a tourist a hand job."

The mural is still in the top five things to see in Dewhurst if you are passing through.

You should check it out.

Seventy

1991 - Glenn and Roo

Real Bad Boys Move In Silence

Roo Stamper's sparkly maroon and chrome bejewelled tonner appears over the crest of the hill at the top of Burston Street. The car's pumping the chorus from 'OG Original Gangster' by Ice T. The 'souped-up' flat-bed ute begins to slow down as he draws parallel to where Glenn is walking along the pavement.

Roo bellows over the music, *"Hey, Glenn, how come your girlfriend's got no nipples?"*

"What did you say, fuck wit?"

Roo switches his engine off and begins to get out the car. Glenn feels the world's anger behind the skin on his face and he kicks the door shut. *"Stay down."*

One of the arsehole's legs is now trapped between the tonner's door and the jamb.

Next Glenn reaches in through the open window and grabs Roo by the neck pushing his head back into his seat rest, hard, whilst putting all his weight against the door. Roo's in pain, the door of a tonner is fucking heavy. The defiance is draining from his face.

"Bad move, Roofus."

"Let me go you fucking prick."

"Original Gangster are you, Roo?"

"Fuck off."

"You got something to say about Nicole, have you?"

"It was a fucking joke. Fucking chill."

"Come on then. Fucking throw it, Roo. I'll fuck you up. No qualms."

At that point, a neighbour comes over and manhandles Glenn. *"You know better than this Glenn. Leave the bugger alone."*

Roo pushes the door from inside releasing his leg from its trap. He wrestles himself free, spitting venom. *"Your girlfriend's a fucking whore, mate. Fucking true."*

Red faced with popped tyranny.

And with that, Ice T is fading into the distance in a cloud of stones and shit. The tonner stops for ages at the T-intersection at the end of the street waiting to escape into the busy traffic. By the time Roo turns out into Malcolmson Street, Glenn's disappeared into his driveway - big mouth strikes again.

Oh GEE! Original Gangster.

Seventy One

1991 - Glenn

What If I Remembered Her Wrong?

The Datsun Sunny hops along the Nebo Road. From the
air it adopts the appearance of a mobile yet solitary sweep
of electric light in a sea of blackness. The miles have been
emptied out of the equation.

Crusty is driving for some reason. Maybe Glenn's over
the alcohol limit, or Crusty asked if he could. It wasn't
uncommon for them to share the driving. It's a detail. But it's
definitely the same car that Dean gave Glenn a few weeks
earlier. These boys of 1991 like Hip Hop, even Vanilla Ice,
who was in a film playing at the local cinema a few weeks
earlier. They'd all queued to see *Cool As Ice* with the rest of
town, nobody had that much to say about it afterwards, *"Was
alright."*

Good Hip Hop was hard to come by in the North. Reluctantly,
Glenn had to admit that it had been Roo Stamper who was the
first to be heard playing Public Enemy and Big Daddy Kane
at a stock car meet and he just had to find out what it was. So
much focussed, political anger directed at a government in a
far away country by a band that would never tour this far out.
The boys were playing *'Run's House'* by Run DMC on the old
tape player. It seemed to suit the mood.

Crusty looks in the rear view mirror at Glenn who's now
away in his thoughts again. Looking past his reflection into

the barely visible cane fields, there's nothing out there.

"Is it true you fucked Roo Stamper up today, just 'cos he cussed Nicole?" Crusty aims the question to land on its tip-toes.

"What have you heard?"

"That you gave that fuckwit the limp he's sporting."

"Yeah, I did. He said he'd seen Nicole's tits."

"Mate, she hates that prick. She'd go nowhere near him."

"Yeah, well he said something alright. So I gave him a limp."

"Turn here."

The car turns off the main drag and off towards a house deep behind the rows of sugar cane.

II

"Jocasta wants to suck your cock. The Boobers wants yer mate."

The music was fucking loud - *'Love the one you're with'* / *'I touch myself'* or some other awful shit by The Divinyls. Glenn looks across the hallway through the throng of mouthy kids in their boardies and hooped tops. Bellowing at each other to be heard. In the melee, he spies Jocasta. He knows Robbie's right, she's a good sort now, and if the rumours were true and she really did like him, he could well be dragging her knickers off before sunrise, but he was here to find Nicole.

Glenn hadn't seen or heard from her in nearly five days.
School had been out for a week or so, and Dean had told him
that he hadn't really spoken to her, but he had seen her. There
had been sightings around town, but nobody could really pin
her down to say where or not they'd seen her. It was always
somewhere neutral like Video Ezy, or Mount Pleasant Mall,
Slack Macs or Mully's. It didn't feel good. He felt like he
was losing traction, that he was falling out of favour, and a pit
grew in him large enough to swallow his words, his rationale,
his love.

Tonight, everyone in Dewhurst was at Sapper Smith's
farmhouse behind the sugar for the party.

"Play some fucking dance music," some rev head shouted.
A record skips and hops along the vinyl, and the custodian of
the turntables winds up some fucking dope Chicago House
or Detroit Techno - was it Joey Beltram, JM Silk, Liz Torres,
Inner City?

No sign of Nicole. That prick Kerry is over there, talking
to two girls and a bloke. Why the fuck he hangs around
teenagers is anyone's guess, Glenn wonders - most of them
would be able to peg the answer correctly though. One of the
girls is stroking his left hip. His filthy army issue shorts. He
leans on the wall smoking a cigarette, nodding and saying,
"Right," as the young fella he's with gets into talking about
some footie player for the Wollangong Wallflowers. Glenn
must be staring because Kerry gives him a smile and a nod.
Glenn flips him a quick and discreet bird.

"How's Nicole?"

"Dunno, not seen her."

"She's here mate. Saw her about half an hour ago, out in the barns with some kids. Roo Fuckface and them."

"Yeah?"

"Heard you gave him a limp."

"Is that what you heard?"

"Yeah. You think you're hot shit do you? Son of a cop."

"Fuck off Kerry."

"Yeah well nice seeing you again, mate. Sure we'll talk again -"

Glenn's already turned his back on the loser, and that's when he notices his Mum's old friend Gully Green stood against the wall at the back. Wasn't he too old to be at a kid's party? Leeching energy off us like a vampire.

"The coffin man's here. Bring out your dead." Glenn points Gully out to Robbie and Crusty. *"There's no telling when you'll be next."*

"He manages the best spot in town. People are dying to get in," ventured Crusty before he wanders off.

Seventy Two

1992 - Glenn

**And The Magpie Lifted The Sky With A Stick
- part two**

*PMRF - or Pigs, Monkeys, Rats and Fish. That was the name
of the big jail in Dewhurst. The 'P' stands for prison, that's all
you need to know. I shared a cell with a Torres Strait Islander
for about a year. He was fascinated with native Australian
myths and the creation story. He told me as many as he
remembered and the new ones he discovered. Got a bit boring
at times but it was better than sharing a cell with an arse
rapist or some cunt thug. Someone somewhere was looking
after me (and him maybe), because he was a soft soul - too
gentle for jail. Smiled too much, got bounced about by other
inmates for it as well. His name was Chris Green and I've
not seen him since he got let out some time in '93. He was a
kleptomaniac. Kept on stealing beers from the same bottlo in
the small town he was from upstate: Winton I think. Just got to
the stage where jail was the only cure, but it was no place for
him.*

*The other inmates would take the piss out of him for ordering
children's books from the librarian. But he explained to me
that the only other colour in here was from the lolly wrappers
and, this is probably true, a lot of books about the Aborig-
inal stories were published with bright illustrations. The only
other thing he was into were the Rocky movies and he was
pissed off because he'd been put inside the week Rocky V
had come out at his local drive-in. I told him it was terrible*

*and we gained some mutual trust by way of him making me
recount the plot. At the end he agreed that it did sound pretty
fucking shit.*

"Sounds shit bro."

*Chris went on to say that his old mum had cried for three
days when he got put away. She had said that he was the only
person goofy enough to make the dog laugh, and that he had
to promise her that he'd hide his smile away until he came
back home to them again, in his words, 'one happy day.'*

*All these years later, when I think to look, I search and fail
to find the silly bugger on the internet. I find so many Chris
Greens out there, and at least four that could be him.*

II

One of the myths I remember Chris telling me most vividly
is one told by the Mandelbingu people of Northern Arnhem
Land. When I read it, I hear his young voice.

*"Long, long ago the sky was so close to the earth it shut out
all light. Everyone had to crawl around in darkness until
the magpies decided that it was time to work together, and
by joining forces they could help bring about a new day. In
doing so, they were able to raise the sky slowly using long
sticks. They propped it on low rocks then gradually hefted
it up onto some grand boulders high up above their camp.
As they struggled to lift the sky even higher, it suddenly split
open to reveal the first sunrise. The beauty, light and warmth
delighted the magpies so much that they suddenly burst into
song. As they warbled and trilled at their pristine sky, the*

blanket of darkness broke apart into fragments and drifted away as clouds. That is why every morning we can hear magpies as they still greet the sunrise with their happy call.

Isn't that wonderful Glenny boy? Better than Rocky V, ay?"

Seventy Three

1994 - Glenn

On Paskins Road

Old Val asked me to carry his fruit crates upstairs to his kitchen. He lived in a Queenslander that had the exact same layout as the type of house everybody I ever knew grew up in. I didn't need directions. He offered me a glass of water and I accepted.

We'd arrived at the tiny settlement of Yalbaroo, a wide spot on the Bruce Highway, no shops, just seven or eight bungalows and Val's house up on a slope behind a railroad crossing. The Queenslander was situated at an elevation and from my point of view it gave out an illusion that we were all alone out there in the bush, because all the lower buildings were hidden below the tree canopy and our line of sight.

Inside, the cupboards and doors had been happy slapped with white gloss by somebody who was drunken, old, or very careless. There were hundreds of large cardboard boxes absolutely everywhere, filled with business papers, bundles of reports stapled together inside, bent up lever arch files, the cheap metal clips and locks corroding in the heat. Aside from a threadbare couch and a small TV, the lounge was packed with these boxes. In some places they were stacked right up to the ceiling.

For some reason Val felt compelled to show me around the rest of the house, he confessed to feeling lonely all by himself and that visitors were rare. The old farmer told me that he went to feed the cows old zucchinis once a day. That was his main job besides watching TV and going to Dewhurst every three weeks for supplies. Every single upstairs room was the same - full of these boxes. In Val's bedroom his mattress was laid neatly on more piles of cardboard boxes. He opened a door on to another room with a single bed version of his own sleeping quarters - just boxes. "If you're tired you can lie down, stop a while. You like TV?"

Val didn't explain the boxes, he seemed to live his life around them - the ground floor was full to the ceiling of collapsing towers of the same, miniature cityscapes of unread litera-ture, full of mildew. There was a car on collapsed suspension trapped below this paper avalanche. There was even an old birds nest and evidence of animal activity as the ground floor was open to the elements and was actually little more than a carport. There were rooms back there but you couldn't get near them. Somewhere I could hear water dripping. Fucking mosquitos, the old guy was probably in the process of breeding them in an old toilet somewhere in the compacted darkness. All Val said when we were down there was, "All this holds the upstairs together, I reckon." Waving it away.

We stood looking at it with nothing left to say.

There was a large barn up on the symmetrical green hillock behind the house and a well-kept horse paddock. The cows were seen to be grazing a short way west. I asked who ran the place but he never answered.

"Will you write to me, let me know how you get on. How it all turns out?"

*He wrote his name in full, Valentine Burton and the farm's
address down on an old bus ticket that I never saw again.*

*These days, if ever I drive through Yalbaroo I feather the
brakes so I can snatch a glance at his Queenslander up on
the slope but I don't think I ever manage to catch a sighting.
But then I never stop off to drive up Paskins Road to see if
Val's house with its mountainous box city is still there. I get a
strong feeling that the old fella was close to death when I saw
him that day and that I may have been one of the last people
he'd had a chat with up there. I can't explain it. Sat out there
on his balcony drinking iced water listening to the sounds
of the cows lowing, I remember the distant swish of cars
powering along the highway - the ascent of gear changes.*

Seventy Four

1994 - Glenn and Vella

I Saw Your Photo On The Wall,
I Took The Picture From The Frame

Whenever Glenn left Dewhurst for the wilderness he was
made to wonder, given the overpopulation of the planet, how
he could be the only human being for miles and miles around.
Yet today as he scanned the country he'd already passed
through he spotted a bright red hat descending the adjacent
escarpment.

Vella had come to the bush over prepared with a rather large
rucksack and a big floppy hat with a fly net on it. His kit was
proving cumbersome and he was falling further and further
behind. All Glenn would have to do was steam ahead and he'd
easily lose him. He couldn't see whether Vella had a map, it's
likely he did, but did he know how to read it?

Glenn divined to sit on a rock and wait for him, high above
the tree canopy - the quilt on his father's deathbed. The bony
hillsides, wincing in the hot, bright sunshine, the ground hard
like metal. Low trees lined a winding spectral river that was
now dust and leaf-silenced. Frail grasses, long in the dying.
Hard working ants hollow out the innards of a dead taipan,
crawling in through a dried out eye cavity. The sky was hard
blue. No clouds, no shade up here.

Vella looked up at him all sweaty as he collapsed on to a large
rock, throwing the ruck sack aside, casting his daft hat off

next to where Glenn had perched.

"Wouldn't it have been easier to come and see me down in the city?"

"I agree with you. This was a stupid idea."

The cop rummages for his water. And then takes a swig, spilling a little onto the dry ground.

"Well, as you can tell, I'm hiking out to where Dad was found."

"Yes."

Vella falls silent surveying the bush land below.

"It just goes on forever, doesn't it, like the sea."

"Yes."

"I am from an island. From every part of Malta you can see water. In Melbourne, you are deep in the streets. It's just a city like any other."

It only takes the droplets of drinking water a few short seconds to dry out into the dusty earth at their feet.

"How far you think we've come?"

"About 7 kilometres."

"Phew."

"What's on your Walkman?"

"This? My portable tape player? Chicago, a little Terry Kath."

"Not sure I know their stuff."

"'Tell Me' by Terry Kath is enormous my friend. It is from this film about a desert motorcycle cop who is this little short arse. But the song is about the Earth. About man's arrival on the planet. The glory of Jesus. Of God."

"Yeah?"

"But the film, 'Electra Glide In Blue'. It shows you what people do in small places caught out in the middle of big empty spaces."

Vella offers some water to Glenn.

"Conserve your water. You're gonna need it."

"The film reminds me of this place. What lies beyond the city might as well be outer space. This is like moonwalking. It's like you've all been walled in."

"For a guy of your physique, carrying all that weight you wouldn't have made it out much further."

"Perhaps, perhaps not."

"Hell of a gamble. It's dangerous out here, I'm not just saying it. You can get lost so easily. Dehydrated, bitten by a snake

or a spider. It's like the sea, you've got to be so alert. People don't realise, it's not like the city out here. There's no-one to save you. All over Australia people get caught out everyday because they think it couldn't happen to them."

"But I'm not Australian."

Vella holds Glenn's stare and his face bursts into a toothy grin.

"Why pick today then? So hot to come."

"Because today is when his will gets read out. I wanted to be out of town."

"Your father's?"

"Who else's?"

"No scores to settle?"

"No, no scores to settle. Time to start again."

"So tell me your side of things."

"Re-read the police report, Marcos."

"But I want to know what happened from you. I never knew your father, met him at a police conference in Canberra by chance, however, five years ago perhaps. But I got to know Pete a tiny bit and he's this big shit, we all know. For a police man..." he pats his chest around his heart. *"He was a black heart."*

"Then you'll know what Pete did to Nicole and you'll also know that my dad shielded him from the impact. And that I got sent to Stalag Dewhurst for three years."

"You feel perhaps that your father's death wasn't a natural one?"

"You read the coroner's report. Of course it was."

"OK. I am in no doubt as to how your father died. But I think that you are."

"I don't know you Marcos. I don't know what you want."

"You know. I want your side."

"You tell me what you know on the walk back. Try to keep up, we'll go via The German Road but it's all uphill in that direction."

They stand up. Vella reaches up to Glenn who pulls him up to his feet.

"Thank you. Let me tell you something. In my experience, every time, without exception."

He pauses for dramatic effect, ever the performer and when he's completely sure he has Glenn's eye he says, *"It starts with a girl."*

"What does?"

"Every story."

Seventy Five

1994 - Pete

Last Night's Dream

Pete parked his new Mercedes in the gravel car park at the edge of The Roaches. He was on the other side of the world yet here he was checking whether or not a boyhood memory had been real or not. Sure enough the man in the local village shop had confirmed that he had found the right place but that the wallabies were unsociable and seldom seen, all 50 odd of them.

He slung his bag over his shoulder and strode down through the heather lined paths below into a small valley. Dog shit everywhere. Fucking England. He was never going to get used to this climate again either. The last few weeks had consisted of him staying with his brother, then his sister, and revisiting various old mates and cousins who took him around a procession of sorry threadbare pubs, begging for stories about having barbecues on the beach every day and whether he or not he liked 'The Paul Hogan Show'.

In South Yorkshire, nobody seemed to know anything about life in Oz apart from the rudimentals; Sydney Opera House, koala bears, Christmas on the beach, boomerangs, and fucking 'Crocodile Dundee'. He was preparing lunch for his sister's kids the other day and found himself playing up to it. He'd asked for a knife to cut some cheddar with and when his sister, Lou, presented him with one he went, *"That's not a knife..."* The kids looked at him blankly. His brother-in-law

Michael was a good fella. Basic but kind. Would always say *"Good day mate..."* in the worst Australian accent he'd ever hear, but he was genuine in his line of questions. Comparing cars, whether they had Boddington's Beer in Oz, or what the Australian women were like. But he had said his goodbyes now. They were poor, struggling and pretty stupid in the main and he knew it wouldn't be long before he'd have a falling out with them or unfairly lose his patience. He left Lou a bit of cash to help out towards birthdays and Christmas for the kids. Michael was humble enough to accept the money because it was hard, anyone could see that. The shops were shuttered up at nights and the bottlo had bulletproof glass installed around the display cabinets to protect the forlorn yet hard-faced cashiers. Everybody here wore multi-coloured tracksuits with patterns that reminded him of African kangas, sported greasy hair and caught the bus. The girls dressed up to the nines, plastering make up on and concealer with a butter knife, trying to bag a rich guy at the local clubs. Life here was a different order of complicated and every ten quid was measured out carefully.

The Roaches was deserted. He could just about make a climber out, way up, on one the crags. He was amazed in the light how much this place looked like parts of the interior he'd seen, back home. What the fuck was he doing though? Sniffing around the countryside on the other side of the world looking for wallabies. He shivered, his new shoes had already leaked in water. A mist was drawing in; he could no longer see the inclines up ahead.

Seventy Six

1994 - Glenn

A Heavy Summer

It took Glenn a few seconds to react to Jocasta Bublik's sudden reappearance. There on the concourse of the City Marina, it's like she'd exited through one door in his life under a thick grey cloud and come back through the front door seconds later, a perfect inversion of light.

"Glenn, hi, it's me. Jocasta."

Once he had snapped out of his reverie, all he could muster was a *"How's it?"*

The most direct and zealous of girls had squarely placed herself front and centre in his life, once more; albeit for a short time. Again, the rest of the world had shrunk itself to fit around her. The people they grew up with quietly envied her forthrightness, her fearless ways and sincerity, and in later life they'd also be moved by her kindness.

Most of the boys that Glenn went around with at school were terrified of Jocasta, as she was a very sure of herself; a woman in a growing girl's body more confident and emotionally intelligent than just about anybody they'd ever meet. Her nickname, 'The Boobers' was bestowed upon her to take the edge off her dominion over all things frivolous and trivial, like the boys. Only the dumbest of the rough pricks would try to humiliate her, but they always came off worse, caught out with a withering, emasculating put-down. She left the cartoon beauty queens to do their worst to each other and left the brainy girls to bypass their sexual awakenings in exchange for the dry academic wastes. Sports fit her fine, but it didn't win her heart, because deep down she was lost. But who wasn't? The number of options for a high-school graduate of her high calibre in Dewhurst were about the same number open to somebody with a far lower skill-set. A good set of grades counted for little in a city where the only thing that was respected was hard graft and your family's reputation. There was no room for female ambition, and virtually none for the male equivalent, anyone that shot through and made a run for the big cities like Sydney or Melbourne was seen as a misfit, a snob or gay.

"So what's happening? You're out!"

Standing on the concourse at the City Marina, Glenn realised that they had an audience too. Throngs of people were sat at the pavement café less than a metre to their left, variously, drinking coffee, reading the paper or talking amongst themselves. Some even stopped what they were doing to tune into Jocasta and Glenn's shaky reunion.

"I'm out."

"You want a coffee? I got time. My dollar."

After the pleasantries and small talk ended, her genuine smile faltered, then it dissolved into a sour grimace. She pushed her empty cup and saucer into the centre of the table and went on to light a cigarette. After taking an eternal drag she took an even longer, silent look at Glenn, before exhaling.

"You haven't changed. Still slippery. Vague. Why did you come back here?"

"See Dad. Get square."

"You're an enigma."

"There's no mystery Jocasta. Everything's out in the open."

"Except for Nicole. She just vanished. You don't want to find out where she went?"

"Can we talk about something else?"

"No. Why is it everyone talks about you but not her? She was the one got her life fucked - yet you've come back here to play the victim. I heard what happened at the funeral. Where's Nicole? Do you even give a fuck?"

"I just spent three years in jail."

"Wake up to yourself Glenn. You loved her didn't you? Don't you want to know what happened? None of this is about you anymore, yet too many people think it is. For all we know she's out there in the bush."

"She's not dead."

"Of course she is." As she spoke, the words came out in a slow stream, after locking him into her glare, she fixed her eyes on a point somewhere behind him, further down the concourse.

Almost instantly the past loosened its moorings and her ambush fizzled out. The fuse wet, the throw weak. Jocasta had already decided Glenn wasn't worth it and that her key to the old days had rusted out of neglect, broken, he thought. Yet she only knew part of the story, her opinion was more than likely cast long before the close of play.

Jocasta was a bit a player, her role in the story played out on the margins; yet there were still some cards being held by people in the shadows that even Glenn would never get to speak to; some were still left standing, waiting to deal their hand.

It was then he realised that she had seen a girlfriend and she stood up like a shot from her chair and waved. When he turned to see who it was, it was someone he just about recognised from school but couldn't place. Jocasta put some money on the table and went off to greet her friend without looking back.

"Bye Glenn, you take care."

Glenn took time finishing his coffee, and watched the seagulls get embroiled in their gusts of ocean wind. Banners lassoed to the Marina railings rattling and clinking their shaking pulleys and drawstrings in arrhythmical disharmony. Small yachts jinked on the petulant squared-off acres of seawater.

The days were weighed down with summer back then, and everything was difficult.

Seventy Seven

2014 - Glenn

Ask The Dust

I can still recall every girl I've been with in detail - the places, the positions, the tastes, the talk, the seduction, the bullshit I'm only talking about the ones that I slept with three maybe four times before they moved on. After I left Dewhurst for good, I spent time picking fruit up Bowen way before heading to work here in Brisbane to start my work as a sub for a city paper (long story).

It was mainly the gaps between pay cheques where the girls I knew would evaporate off. Most of the time they fell by the wayside simply because I couldn't afford to get across town to see them; between pay days I could barely even afford to buy them so much as a single beer. You had to move quick else they'd be off with another fella, but they had the same to say for us. Everyone was at it, like a bunch of frogs hopping about across the lily pads. Of course, this was before the internet, mobile phones and so on. It was so easy to lose track of people back then. Mind you, I'm still in touch with one or two; the ones that escaped to where the grass is just as parched. The legend of its greener hue, nothing but a bullshit story.

There's one particular girl I remember, from Canberra called Ally that I've kept in touch via the wonders of Facebook. We've met in person six or seven times over a 15 year period and that's including our two initial dates, yet each time we

*meet for a long session of beers we end up in a clinch and
the penultimate (great word) time it escalated to us getting
a hotel room. This was right before she got married to some
fella or other. The last time we met was the strangest though.
On that occasion she brought her one-year old son, Kit, along
with her and we sat on a bench at the Botanical Gardens in
Brisbane by the river. We shared some genuine laughs and her
company was easy but she'd paint herself into a sad corner
here and there, especially when I wouldn't pick up the bait
and talk about 'us', what could have happened, etcetera.
Call me a weirdo but I felt bad for the baby. It's like he was
complicit, aware of his role in her woe, yet he was still all
smiles and regurgitated food. No way was I going to have his
mother in some city hotel room with him waiting quietly, sat
in his carry-cot nearby, perhaps with his push chair parked
up, pointing at the wall. I couldn't be that cruel to the little
bugger - his brown inquisitive eyes. Kit knew my game but I
wouldn't disappoint him by pawing at his mother, bring his
God low. I spent about an hour with them and headed off into
the more populated regions of the park. "See yer later Ally.
And I'm sorry, but I'm not the one."*

*Later on, when I got to some public toilets in Fortitude Valley,
I physically reminisced about what we'd done to each other
two years earlier in that hotel room. I find it's easier this way.*

*Ask me what I like these days and I'll always tell you that I'm
still quite at home putting my weight down on some generous-
hearted woman, half-heartedly bouncing around a bit and
then rolling off them with a sigh of shame-tempered satisfac-
tion. This time next year I'll still be condemned to be the top
half of a lumpy fucking double-act of damp disappointment - a
horny pantomine horse with commitment issues wrapped in*

a pongy doona. That's my pressure release. All it amounts to these days is little more than letting a vaguely amusing fart escape. It's never anything more than one big fucking dead end, but, and I don't say this lightly either, it's better than 50 years of family jail with a wife and sprogs - I'd sooner trap my knob in a burning car than endure that type of sentence.

Seventy Eight

1994 - Glenn and Uli

Load Bearing Structures

The engine churned. Hydraulics screeched and yawned as the on-truck crane balanced another Japanese hatchback on top of the last upon the rusty flat bed. Some neighbours had even come out of their bougainvillea-clad Queenslanders to watch. Glenn strode over to the controls of the crane looking up at Uli. The short, baldy Pole was smoking a cigarette, it clamped between his lips. The talons of the crane relinquished the Datsun onto the pile, narrowly missing the corner of a second flat bed truck already loaded and ready to go.

"Before you say a word"

Uli speaks over the splutter of the engine.

"Dean told me I could."

"Could what?"

"Have his cars for scrap."

He turns back to the controls of the crane and the grab swings around, away from Glenn to hoist up another car.

Glenn goes off to check on the house. He finds a badly written note tucked into the fly screen. *"Too Glenn, We took Betsy in, knot that you care anyways. Shes our dog now."*

Shit, he thought. The fucking dog. How long had she been
hiding out here with nothing to eat? He goes out to the back
balcony through the kitchen; the whole house is unlocked, full
of midges and God knows what. The mini crane is just about
done on the right-hand side of the lot. Dean's cabin stands
by itself. One of the walls is bowing outwards and in the hot
climate must have gotten soaked through one wet season and
never quite dried out. Cars had propped it up before but now
with no support the whole structure looked like it was about
to come down in a heap. Probably nothing in there but old
paperwork. He'd check later if Uli didn't put his car claw
through it.

It didn't seem right that Dean would get rid of his cars. But
Uli had always helped his friend out in huge ways over the
decades, and vice versa. Glenn wasn't quite sure how but
he thought Uli had something to do with setting Dean up
in Dewhurst, helping him get citizenship when the Australian Government called an amnesty on a certain amount of
illegal immigrants back in the early 1980s. It was one of
Uli's tonners that Glenn had used to drive home to Dewhurst
in when he returned to town from jail. The one he'd used to
accidentally kill Sarah the dog; the one that had spun around
and that he'd also walked away and left mashed up in a grove.
Was it still there? The vet, Alan Dawes was a grumpy old sod
and he was especially peeved when he found out that the poor
dog had belonged to Roo Stamper. Somehow Alan was still in
the vets three hours after surgery hours had ended watching
the TV in the reception area. He was rubbing his neck from
looking up at the television from an awkward position.
'Outback Hell' was on. Glenn had watched a clip whilst
waiting for Alan to make his assessment but it took him years
to find out what the film was and then another few to actually

sit down and watch it as part of a retrospective on 'important' Aussie movies at the Rialto in the centre of Brisbane.

Seventy Nine

1980 - The TV

Village Roadshow Pictures Gives You A Dare

Hey you. Yes you. Have you taken your Sheila to see 'Outback Hell' yet? Well Village Roadshow Pictures in conjunction with Warner Brothers gives you a dare. See it today. Grab on tight and witness nature turn against man. The spiders, the kangaroos, that tree branch. None of them are your friend.

Outback Hell. See the film all your mates are talking about before it's too late and your Sheila goes with somebody else and not you...

Outback Hell starring John Hargreaves, Lynette Curran, Ray Meagher, John Meillon with a special guest appearance by David Gulpilil as Brian.

Showing at a cinema or drive-in near you. Certificate X.

Eighty

1991 - Glenn and Nicole

In My Father's House There's Many Mansions

"I can't stop smiling."

She was hunched on her knees peaking out through the curtains.

Nicole turned back to look at him over her shoulder. It was cold in the old combi-van, sat under the withered silver birch trees towards the back of the junkyard; he could see condensation on the windows.

"I'm a dragon. A taniwha." Nicole blew clouds of hot breath towards him.

"Aren't you cold?"

"Nah, I'm fine."

"Make us some tea, sexy bum."

"Make it yourself."

He stands up, putting one of her Blinky Bill socks over his cock, before hopping down off the rank fold up bed to tend to the stove.

"God, you're off."

"If he gets any smaller, he'll disappear, besides I don't want to get any boiled water dripped on him."

"I'll make him bigger again. Keep him warm. I'll put him on my tongue."

She wriggles to edge of the rough mattress, assumes a position on all-fours, opens her mouth and lets her tongue roll out, mock panting like a dog, grinning like a split sausage.

Eighty One

2018 - Glenn

Days Ignored

Glenn lives in the past. Nothing from the time he thinks about exists anymore. The glass wall he stands behind is too thick and he doesn't think the apparitions he observes as a constant can hear him. The same mistakes will be made. Always the same.

The past awaits: the streets are empty, the daylight barely penetrates into the buildings, the breeze is slight but not much else living stirs besides him. There is a slight ripple in the leaves on the trees lining the street. A strip of bark peels back in a narrow curl from a eucalyptus trunk and the sharp grass parts as an ancient cricket embarks on its next top-secret mission. Nobody remembers the quiet moments between the memories. Waiting to be replayed. Awaiting redeployment.

The insects are holding their breath. And the cicadas stop whatever they are doing to watch what has already happened. Will it be different this time?

Eighty Two

1994 - Vella, Glen and Mr Madonna

All Out Of Love

The locals called you Harry Palmer if you were the kind who got spotted at the Palm Club more than once, *"Arr yeah, he's a right Harry Palmer that one."*

It's the place where strippers went to die on stage. Don't go.

The gruff yet warm voice pipes in through a speaker, it's almost like Derren Hinch himself was back there behind a matted velvet curtain. *"And now, all the way from North Dewhurst, the Old Boilers! Hahaha, no not really. For one night only at the Palm Club, we have Candace Marie, so keep your 'Nuts In May' firmly bolted in your shorts fellas, cos you're in for a true North Queensland treat tonight."*

Karyn White's 'Superwoman' fades in and an older woman in a large duffle coat, woolly bobble hat and big Michael Caine glasses started to do her routine around the sad stage lined with floor to ceiling silver paper streamers. She attempted to lip synch some of the words but its clear to anybody paying close attention (nobody is) that she only knows the chorus. This bottle blonde wouldn't be stealing any hearts tonight. She was on first because she had an early shift at the foundry canteen tomorrow. Leigh, a.k.a. Candace Marie had thought she'd get bigger tips if the fellas up there recognised her, but out of the few that came, as in turned up, all she got was their judgment or the odd quip about keeping down their breakfast.

"I'm not the kind of girl that you can let down," is sung under her breath as she undid the last toggled button on her duffle coat. She notices Mr Madonna in the wings telling her to speed things up.

She tipped a wink at Glenn and Ed. Glenn was the new bartender, and Ed managed the motel bookings and chalet maids.

"Don't like yours much, Glenn."

"The amount of clothes she's got on we'll be here all night."

"Believe me, it's a disappointment. Men pay her to keep her coat on."

"Don't be cruel."

Laine is sat by herself at the end of the bar sucking a cocktail from a slim Jim through a curly straw. Then stirring the melted ice around with her straw. She's watching Leigh's routine as if she's taking mental notes.

"You think Laine's planning on taking a job here?"

"Who'd pay to see her tits?"

"Come on Ed, don't be coarse."

"What do you fucking care? She's a donkey toilet."

A brave sort is sat at the edge of the elevated dance floor and happy to be throwing his dollars away: turns out it's Vella in red sunglasses and a stupid Hawaiian shirt (again). Leigh is seductively tucking the tens and twenties into the elastic of her panties. Vella beckons for her to crouch down by him and he whispers in her ear, *"Do I get a married man's discount?"*

"I'm not a fucking hooker, I'm a dancer." She stands up and drops the routine, stops to gather her clothes and disappears into the guts of Motel 501.

"Sorry to end that one on a cliffhanger, gentleman. But this is not, and I repeat not the place where whaling has been legalised - no don't get Greenpeace on the phone just yet. Because you haven't met our next girl who's come all the way from North Dewhurst. For tonight and tonight only, it's Portuguese Paulaaaaaaaaa!"

Nobody's ever sussed out who the MC is. Even the girls don't know because if they did, they'd probably string him up by the bollocks.

Vella, who is fucked out of his trunks, starts to demand that a Maltese queen turn up to sweep him away. Not some Portuguese prostitute. When he's allowed himself sufficient time to come to a boil, he throws his glass on the floor and stumbles to the bar.

"Hey you. Glenn. Give me drink."

"Sorry Marcos."

"I want a VB in a cooler, do it"

"No mate."

"Ed, tell Glenn to give me a beer."

"No you're drunk. You're a cop. So no."

They all turn to see a door open as Mr Madonna marches
through in step; historically bad coincidence abound as 'I'm
All Out of Love' by Air Supply bursts out of the bass bins.

"Looks like my lucky night," rejoices Vella, folding his
sunglasses and placing them on the bar. They fall on to floor
and he shrugs, just as Mr Madonna arrives to face him. No
words are uttered. It's all over very quickly as Vella coal-hauls
Madonna in the goozegoggs and as the latter doubles up,
winding the gay man mountain with a left-handed uppercut.

*"(((((((**Boom**))))))!!!"* shouts Laine from the end of bar.
Madonna says, *"Farrrrrrrk!!"* And it's the end.

Nobody notices that Paula is completely naked sat on her arse,
with her legs spread in the air. Vella, a virtuoso with his fists,
would have gotten all the tips if fighting was the kind of thing
men paid to see in a strip club. The mighty Mr Madonna was
on his side, prostrate, mewling quietly like a fucked up cello.

"I'm all out of love, what am I without you?"

Eighty Three

1991 - Glenn

A Childhood Replaced By Fear

The band, Son of Dad, that played that night at Sapper's party behind the sugar chiefly revolved around two brothers, Liam and Jules Embrey. They were modelling themselves on the Red Hot Chilli Peppers and The Pixies. We were all squashed into the considerable lounge space shouting along to some chant about not listening to authority. The guitarist was wearing a blonde girl's wig - 'like really cooool, man'. I think they were serious about their music, we weren't - they were just a bunch of nerds that found a novel way of getting theirs cocks strangled by the moodier, arty girls - rock-n-rollllll. We all got fucked off our faces and pushed all the garden furniture into the swimming pool. Robbie Diaz uncharacteristically drowned a bunch of pot plants and threw Caitlin de Jesus in after them. The singer could be heard better in the garden parallel to the din inside the house. His name was Mike Rowan-Peters, had a real-stick up his ass. Boy could sing, but. Made me sick.

Mr Coffin Man was there too and he was stood with his elbow parked on a short girl's head, for some reason she found this behaviour hilarious and was bellowing at some other kid with a camera to take a picture of them but they were being ignored - so they just stood in the pose locked into the lamest joke ever. On the way up the driveway we switched the letters around on the signpost from The Pines to The Penis. We did it every time we went over to Sapper's. No pine trees grew within 10 kilometres of the place though, but there were a few straggly eucalyptus' that would end up draped in toilet paper by sunrise.

Whenever I think back to this party, I hear Mike's band play tunes that weren't even out back then. My chronology is all fucked up. I hear them play versions of AM 180 by Granddaddy, or 1979 by Smashing Pumpkins. I saw the video for the latter a few years back and it was like switching a light on in a cold, dusty room I'd left unlocked but never revisited. My own recollections meshed with those depicted in Billy Corgan's fictional version. The couple kissing in the shower; did that happen at Sapper's party as well? I know we left to go to the bottlo at the end of the night - me, Robbie and three younger girls. "Wanna come for a drive, we're going for drinks." We didn't wreck the shop though like in the rock video, we did have to drunk drive though and made the most of an empty parking lot to peel some rubber and make our captive girls scream. I really can't remember who they were. The blonde in the black Adidas tracksuit top sat up front with me as I leathered the Datsun around the lot. I badly wanted to leave flames behind in my wake, just like Michael J Fox's DeLorean in 'Back To The Future.' When I finally brought the car to a halt the girls all got out and walked home, unimpressed. Robbie and I shared a four pack of beer that we'd bought from our friend, Reedo, who happened to be on-shift at the drive-through, a bit of lucky timing. I'm sure the sunrise was all it was supposed to be, the dark shimmer comes to light, but we were talking too much shit to notice. Robbie set a dog off barking with a mega fart. We ran home hooting at our teenage despair too drunk to start the car. A new day had begun but it forgot to mark itself out as special; it all happened over twenty years ago now, another party.

Half-remembered, half-seen. Never talked about, because everybody has else moved on.

I ask myself have I really done it all harder, funnier and better? Did we honestly have 'badder' tunes back then, better clothes, more sex. I rarely feel the need to castigate myself because the young things I know generally hang themselves out to dry with their dumbo comments for me anyway. I work with a lot of twenty-somethings, most of them have gigantic mouths - nobody seems to know a thing about what's come and gone before, be it historical, or something to do with literature, films, TV, science and so on. I get looked at like I'm the stupid one, because of their own ignorance and lack of basic curiosity, I get to be a reluctant comedy foil. Yet I know my tastes aren't esoteric. They're just lazy and unadventurous, the lot of 'em. "What? You mean isotonic, right?

II

There's one person, or at least most of a person, in the office who half-likes the same things that I do or at least knows of them; a strange and gloomy creature of a sub-editor called Leni, but I feel like a desperate creep hanging around with young women twenty-odd years younger. She's intelligent, and has bit of interest in a world beyond the windows of her mobile phone. But she's trapped herself behind a mountain of insecurity laced with a lack of self-worth and monstrous self-hate. It would seem that she wants nothing more than to be accepted by her more ordinary colleagues. To be the centre of attention, to be the alpha-cat.

I think Leni is very attractive but unaware of the powers she could wield over men like me, yet she wears this damaged nature in plain sight for all to avoid, it's like a smell. She sits with hunched shoulders as if embarrassed by her breasts and rarely looks anybody in the eye, all this sounds at odds with her flashes of brilliance but I don't know her well enough to ask where all this hurt she's bottling up comes from, or why she's chosen to hang it off her (and then ignore it accordingly). Speaking very quietly, her words are well-chosen and deliberate but I feel that she's somehow missed out on all the real fun. Settling for safety and convention, rather than risking it all for a life of adventure.

I always listen out for her comments deep inside the racket - a silver thread in the banal bilge that passes for small talk amongst the prams and prols in the office. The other day our team was talking about love and romance, and Leni chipped in to talk about an old flame of hers. On an early date he had flown her for a weekend to Sydney and that he'd taken her to see 'Norma' at the Opera House.

"Who's Norma?" asked one of the idiots. How we laughed, but as the story unfolded, she told us how her paramour had gently taken her hand in his and how she had noticed that he was gently trembling. No other details were offered. Leni's story was quickly steamrollered by some drunken pantomime scooped out by one of the others. Was this shy boy her first? Was this a confession to me, because she knew I'd be the only one listening to her steady, quiet voice in amongst the puerile shit. It's the only time she has ever picked up and held my gaze for longer than two seconds. I held her eye as she talked about this nervous boy of hers, and I then understood the extent of her unhappiness.

Eighty Four

1994 - The Chorus

The Truth In Sunday Dress

"What about the night that Kerry got kicked out of town?"

"He wasn't so much kicked out of town, as that one day he was here, and the next he wasn't."

"They found his girl kneeling in the road by the gateway to the speedway."

"Fucking druggy."

"You don't know what you're talking about. She was that pregnant one remember."

"Nope."

"Then stop flapping your lips about stuff you know nothing about."

"Well, what happened then? Fuck's sake."

"He knocked some college kid up. She lived on the hill over in North Dewie. Good sort, nice family. Pops owns the sports shop."

"Mr It's Big!"

"That's right, the bloke on the telly who would stomp around town like King Kong yelling 'It's Big!' when his winter sales came on in his ads. His kid."

"Fallon. Yeah, she's a sort. What happened to her?"

"Went to Uni down south. Got rid of the kid and split town."

"Split town."

"Yeah she split."

"You mean she skipped town."

"No. She split town you dag."

"So this was Kerry's girlfriend."

"No. She must of loved him though or something. He got her up the duff. Shot through and that's it. No one saw or heard from him again."

"Well mate, that makes him lower than a snake's belly button in my eyes... Some fellas, ay!"

"Word is he stole a bunch of money from some out of towners. The cops, Johnny Pearce and Pommie Pete intervened caught him down in Sarina, brought the money back and that was that."

"Kerry's probably buried out in the bush somewhere."

"That's the thing about this place, one highway in and out.

First place to fill up with petrol is Sarina if you go south, Prosperpine or Shute Harbour in the north. No escape."

"Unless you fill a load of jerry cans."

"I don't think he was planning his escape for long, else he'd have thought of that."

"Bet he had a ton of them lying around the speedway too."

"Rusted out like everything else down there now."

"I reckon Johnny had his henchman Pete kill Kerry. Bury his greasy haired corpse in the bush. Or set a match to him, Kentucky Fried Kiwi Cunt."

"KFKC. No thanks."

"I don't know a soul that's heard a peep from him. Not a one."

"I think he got sent off because he was sniffing around Nicole too."

"I'd loved to have had a crack at her."

"Should've joined the queue. It was long, but relatively fast."

"But Glenn put up a roadblock so to speak."

"Yes, he beat that girl into next week. Gouged her face, her legs. Dislocated her jaw and fractured her arm. That's what I know anyway."

"Strong tranqs for life I reckon."

"How'd you know?"

"Remember Toe Bows? Was in a car wreck. Smashed up his cheekbones and all sorts. Goes around still, ten years or so later looking like The Mummy with balms and bandages all over his head. You get high just sniffing the air after he's walked through – all the potions on him."

"You're equating Nicole's beating to a car crash injury."

"Yep. She got pulverised."

"How the fuck she escape hospital then?"

"Well, that's how it was told to me. Just what I heard."

"You're a bright spark, aren't ya?"

"Eat my shorts."

"No thanks, now get back to work or I'll dock yer."

Eighty Five

1992 - Fallon

Build A Fort And Set It On Fire

Poor Fallon Biggins - the olive-skinned, beauty with strong legs, good glutes and those crisp white blouses that enhanced her easy looks. She had a winning smile, a deep laugh and as smart a collection of old novels as the city's sole book emporium would allow lining the walls of her bedroom. The tomes took up the space usually reserved for torn posters of dopey pop stars with skids in their undies. Nevertheless, she got her enhanced education and ideas in the pages of well-respected books not from teen gossip or style mags. Dead people like Anais Nin, Henry Miller, Percy Bysshe Shelley, Francoise Sagan taught her that boys and men were as fucked up as she thought all her girlfriends were. Their books told her how long to wait and how deep to wade out with a bad man. But even the best of us would exchange an educated mind for a bit of rough (if nothing was at stake / nobody knew).

A well-sketched story or sharp depiction of a dashing male hero or a sexual composite was ill-preparation for the unimaginative realities that awaited her. These types of men were a myth in Dewhurst. Nobody so exotic as a Serge Gainsbourg-type with a stripy hooped top and a droopy cigarette came within a 1000 kilometres of the place. *"Ou est Jules et Jim?"* A bottle of A$20 white-wine and a fumble at the drive-in was the best she could hope for.

Kerry the shark was smart enough to have read beyond

chapter ten in the 'how to score a root in Oz' book. His
baby blues, and a well-rehearsed expression of someone
who was really listening and ultimately showing a genuine
interest in his quarry would get him further than most of his
rivals that thought a dirty joke was all it took to send them
on their way to knee-trembler's heaven. A worldliness and
a bit of experience, he took his slice of greasy under flesh a
few times, smearing his face against Fallon's, smudging her
lipstick, mussing her straight dark brown hair, forcing her to
taste herself on his underwhelming dick. In the end he cut
in too close and pressed his life force against the walls of
her pristine uterus giving her a fucking horrible baby. 'Point
Break' junior. Hang ten, ferken loosserrrr.

That day, she caught Kerry just in time, leaving the speedway
with his clapped out yet confident sports car full of broken
shit…a surfboard he had for show, as it was part of the
uniform, stuck on the roof rack. He wound down the window
and asked her how she was. He smelt sweaty; did he use pig
pheromones? There must be some trick because again she
finds herself magnetically attracted.

"I'm pregnant."

"I thought you looked a bit different."

"Yes, I'm bigger."

"And I suppose you're here to tell me it's mine. Am I right?"
He sniffs to clear his nasal cavity.

"Of course. I haven't got with anyone else."

"Well, you timed your getting pregnant just right, see? I'm leaving Dewhurst."

"Now?"

"Right now. You need help naming it?"

"What?"

"The sprog. You need help naming it? The least I can do. Most I can offer."

"You want to name it?"

"Yes why wouldn't I?"

"You're fucked in the head. We need to talk about this. I need to tell my parents."

"Shh, shh. Come here. Don't get wound up. It's OK."

Fallon found that she does still need comfort from this dirty man, so she crouched down by his car window. There's no logical reason for her actions, she can't summon up the will to resist. Pheromones?

"Fallon." Kerry reaches up to stroke her face with his fat, mangy forefinger. *"You want to know how many college girls like you I've shagged up there in my hut?"*

Fallon steps back away from the car, she gets the feeling she's on the receiving end of a very bad joke.

"Fucking dozens." He spits.

He throws a balled up twenty on the dust, *"That's for child support."*

Then he drives off. She tries to keep up with his car as it goes along the potholed driveway to the road, but she's not fast enough. Soon Kerry the wanker has gone, she watches the car barrel away toward the inappropriately gorgeous horizon - there is even a cloud of smoke scraped across the tan scuffed sky. Out of breath, Fallon stops running.

The sky above the sugar is too golden to be anything but the fool's kind.

Eighty Six

1991 - The Chorus

The Southern Cross

"Did you know that the song 'Downbound Train' ends with Bruce working on a railroad gang building the very thing that sped his love away from him? The impossibility of salvation is palpable."

"I'm trying to sleep."

Eighty Seven

1991 - Glenn

No Man's Land

The front left tire on the stock car hits a rock making the vehicle bunny hop to the left, almost. He feels a pain in his right buttock. Red clouds of dirt fly up. The engine gives out and the bent-up auto chugs to a halt. Glenn looks over his shoulder to see if any other drivers are speeding up on his left hand side. An escape to the no-man's-land at centre of the circuit is essential so he doesn't get barged by the remaining race-cars. Glenn sees Skids Yahnundasis hop into the rescue truck used to retrieve stranded drivers and shunt dead cars out of the road. Now!

Glenn dives out of the car and hurls himself into no-man's-land as three cars bear down on him on the straight. A bit fucking dramatic but hey, he thinks. He pulls his helmet off and punches the air, the crowd goes wild. Friends, yet no family, clap and yell. Skids, skids his pick up onto the patch and tips him a wink.

"Should keep your helmet on until you've left the track area Glenn. You know that ya fucking nong. What are yer?"

"A fucking nong, Skids."

Eighty Eight

1991 - Pete and Nicole

Oysters, No Pearls

"Did you listen to my tape Pete?"

"Soldier boyyyy, oh my little soldier boy! I'll be true to youuuu…" He sings. His gravelly voice cracks and it embarrasses him. The dark cop finds that he's blushing. His eyes feel wet at the corner and as a smile races out the gate, he tries to hide a bead of saltwater that runs down his cheek. A tear by another name. So tender. Pete wants to put a distance in this run. She's engulfing him with her sweets. He grits his teeth and pictures a boot heel grinding some granulated sugar into the ground. The unholy visual metaphors of an unimaginative thug. Such involuntary and crass symbolism shames him even more. This wasn't the first time he'd have her, but he'd been altered. Time for a change. Time decays all good things.

"I love Motown…" Nicole rummages in the bag in the foot well of his white car. *"I made you another one today… at Fallon's house. She has more LPs to choose from. Don't worry, I made out the tape was for Glenn."*

"Let me get into this first tape and then you can give me the next one."

"Can we play it?"

"When we're on our way again, yes. It drains the batteries playing tapes when the engine's not running."

"I know. Dad told me."

"We'll play it soon, bub."

She smiles.

Fucking women. Girls. Like honeyed quicksand. They keep on drawing him back to places he's sworn he'd never go back to. Every sweet time is the last time.

He's no villain, he thinks to himself. This Pete's just an off-duty cop with a hard on. All of a sudden he gets an urge to send his 16-year old adolescent self a message. Once upon a time his young self was unnaturally anxious that he'd never ever get a girl to even speak to him. He strains to project back to his earlier self a positive sign that even in his early forties he'd have beautiful 18-year olds begging him for his sex. Then quite unexpectedly, he actually sees himself, wavy crap hair, stood 20 feet away on the green verge that ran between the road and the sugar. The boy about turns and disappears into the cane out of sight. Somehow Pete was able to track down his 16 year-old-self but it would seem his projection didn't want to be found for long. Younger Pete had been 'put-out' by his unsettling, erratic fervour. Perhaps this boy version had sent him a message back reminding him that this was not right. Even though he was a single man in his 40s, this girl could cause him nothing but trouble if he crosses this very enticing line again. Johnny would have the answers. Maybe he could persuade his buddy to help him remove this damned spot.

"No. I'm going to drive you back to your car. I can't be here."

"But you are. You're here."

And there he is.

Eighty Nine

1994 - Glenn and The Nurse

Oh How We'd Laugh Back Then, Like Tomorrow Wasn't There

"Fighting at a funeral. I've seen it all now."

"Was that the last thing left to see then Nurse?"

Glenn laughs and winces. Accidentally, he gets a nostril full of the sick / sterile pong of the hospital ward. The nurse is a homely sort, easy to smile and laugh, not jaded and constipated like the ward sister.

"I need to see to your hand next Mr Comedian. You didn't get duffed up for telling lousy jokes did you?"

"No. I got roughed up for spitting on my father's coffin and assorted other bits."

"So, you're the late Johnny Pearce's jailbird son."

"Well, that's one way to describe me."

"And now you've come to spend time in another institution, here with me."

"Yes."

"So you know Roo Stamper and all those pricks."

"Yes, I do, but they're no mates of mine."

"This is a nasty bite too. Dog bites and a fractured hand. What a guy!"

Ninety

1991 - Pete and Johnny

God Won't Bless The Person You Think You Are

"What's that tune you're always humming, mate?"

They were driving across town; some curtain-tugger had reported a violent domestic in Black's Beach. The sun wasn't due to show its face for at least an hour, so it had to be 'an end of evening / post-party' flare up. Johnny Pearce and Pete Wilson were on the night shift together and with the roads so clear the police 4x4 was going over 100 kilometres per hour through the cross streets to meet the highway north at the bridge by 'Slack Macs'.

"Not aware of a particular tune."

"Yep, there's one you keep going back to. And I keep on meaning to ask you what it is. Cos I think I heard it on the radio at home a day or two ago."

"What was it?"

"Can't remember."

"Lot of use you are."

"Want the rest of me Chiko Roll?"

"No, you're alright." He gave Johnny a sideways smile and

shook his head, as he watches him polish off the rest of the poor man of Australia's diet cornerstone.

"Revolting," smirks Johnny.

Ninety One

1970s, 1980s, 1991 - Pete

One Fisherman Spots Another From Afar

Pete is 10 years old and the floorboards in his new Australian home are warm. The floor-to-ceiling nets are blowing in and out of the veranda doorway. He hears his father singing an old Tony Bennett song to himself, reading his paper, whilst sat beyond the sultry drapes. Pete receives his first ever mosquito bite… and it's incredibly itchy, flaming 'eck. He sees the article on his forearm and he smashes it. The thing was full of blood, a sack of flying red plasma - dead now. It was the second living thing he'd obliterated that day. Pete had cornered a mouse in the sickly yellow spare bathroom next to the utilities room downstairs. The boy had bashed it with the new toilet seat that had been waiting to be fixed in place since they'd moved in. He threw the mouse's body in the bath and then ran the cold tap slowly, observing a narrow trail of blood seep from its mouth. Mice were so much smaller than he'd been led to believe. Wiping the new toilet seat clean of any discernible traces, he'd leave its carcass for his sister Lou to find (ha ha ha). Now he felt remorse but he figured it would fade. Pete was wrong though because even now that little mouse was able to weave its way back to the top of his pile of guilt - the slowly running water, the stringy blood, the ease with which the action of death dealing had come.

"Once upon a time, a girl with diamonds in her eyes, put her hand in mine."

It seemed this was the only part of the song Mr Wilson knew,
as he absent-mindedly thumbed his way through the local rag.
Pete's dad had brought the family over to Australia as part
of a recruitment drive for schoolteachers. It had taken them
nearly a month to get to the new house here in Queensland.
They came from England via Singapore and then had around
a week in Sydney whilst his father got allocated a school and
also a place to live for them all. His dad was given a spot at a
high school in Dewhurst, a long way north he was informed.
He was hoping for Sydney but they got sent all this way with
the promise that things would change once he'd 'proven'
himself. But his father took to Dewhurst life like a 'salty' to
water. The pictures in his head of cold beers and barbecues
on the weekend weren't a fantasy. He could really go to the
butchers and order a load of sausages and chops by the pig.
"Half a pig please, Doug."

Wilson senior could play his beloved cricket with a better
standard of player, he could afford a boat to go sailing in.
Most of all he wasn't in the north of England with his thick
family: angry, drunken brothers, depressed women, hard fists,
damp bedrooms, black rain and canned food. Eventually
Pete's mum, Claudine, took a managerial job at the newly
opened supermarket, Coles, and all was well. Within two
years, people thought his father was an Australian too, so
easy did he pick up the accent and the mannerisms. It was the
same way that surfers all speak the same, vicars, or effeminate
homosexuals; maybe his father had secretly taken a course on
how to be an Australian and had come top of the class.

*"G'day sport, how's it going cobber. Got a cold tinny mate?
Cor, she's a sort, right? Fair go. Onya mate."*

Pete moved south after leaving school to go to college to qualify for police training. He enrolled at the Police Academy in Yass, near Canberra on graduation, before winding his way back to his Australian home. Before he did that he lived with another cop called Jess; during this time, he was a beat cop in the Blue Mountains area of Penrith. Pete loved and stayed with Jess for ten years before she had an affair with a friend of his, Barry Fox - she got married to the prick within a year too. People really were like monkeys, they couldn't let go of the last vine until they'd gotten a firm grip on the next one - the fear of spending or ending their time alone. Jess made him sick with how basic she was. Last he heard when he ran into an old mate on the force, was that she'd got two kids, girls called Jodie and Eve. Ballerinas. Barry had gone on to run one of the regional TV stations. He never clapped eyes on the arsehole again, perhaps on purpose, so that he wouldn't have to do the whole, 'Is he better looking than me - kinder - a good dad - a better lover?' thing. Fuck that low-life cunt. Pete also gleaned that she'd dropped out of the force and was a security advisor-cum-consultant to small-businesses across Hay Plain to Mildura. The one thing this prick Barry didn't have though, were her young years. He didn't have their time together, couldn't steal it from him even if he tried. The memories, shared intimacies, secrets and dreams. Fox had come to her afterwards, after she'd become no use to him, frazzled by work, worn down by coarse, sexist colleagues, cynical, tired, boring, and alcohol dependent most probably. Why fight for her? She was gone, spent out, and plus she didn't want him anymore. Jess had wanted ballerina girls, and a large house in Wenty Falls, other suburban mums to compete with and that's what she got, plus the unwanted side-effect of a husband that would probably always be out on the hunt for more new and mundane love assignments.

After Jess confessed to being in love with someone else, Pete
had simply walked away, and because of that he never saw
her again either. She came and collected her stuff from their
shared house through careful co-ordination, delegated friends
and usefully deposited keys. It was like he had turned off a
light. There was no need for retrospection and the hole she
left in his life was filled back in with dirt, shit, live culture and
a heavy blackness. Pete toyed with the idea that he'd never
loved her. Perhaps this was untrue, but how much of love
is habitual, how much of it is fulfilling a need as simple as
eating or sleeping? There would be others but the ease with
which he pulled away from his life-partner, the 'love' of his
life, almost overnight and without much sadness troubled him
to the core.

Pete tried the club scene and found although he was no
beauty, women found him attractive. He farted about with a
few, never getting all-that close out of both tepid pride and
boredom. The fractious routines of the courtship bored him,
even the forward ones cooked up a frustration in him that
wouldn't dissipate. Inchoate love affairs - all the preening and
grinning like a simple minded fish through a procession of old
jokes and tales of old boyfriends.

Then one day he snapped and he slapped one of these girls in
the chops for getting on his tits about nothing. The girl was
from Norway. Her name was Gun. This Nordic beauty was
slightly overweight but her flab evened out because she was
six foot or so, so clothed she was dramatic and striking, naked
she was full of lumps, dips and oddly placed bulges, but God
she was affecting, his loins always stirred unfairly in response
to the memory. This archetypal Scandinavian princess worked
in a bookshop and was generally fairly closed mouthed about

most things. She quietly went about her life and only homed in on Pete when she needed some company to go to a party or to a movie. He'd slept with her on and off for about four months whilst seeing a second girl, about whom he can now only recall some small details. Gun had discovered early on that their companionship was little more than a sham but one day quite late in the cycle, she had asked him to account for himself. With nothing to say, he just hit her across the face. A backward swipe with all the weight of his arm transferred to his hand - just like you'd see Nazi villains in the movies do.

Gun, flew to hit the floor and he felt an unfamiliar tingle of excitement - a building charge. These women were so mouthy, so dominating yet physically lightweight - yet now he had discovered the way into gaining the upper hand, a way to outstep the smart answer. What a fantastic revelation. She tried to get to her feet and he pushed her down again this time with an extended foot, not hard, just enough to stop this bitch reclaiming her balance. By now she was foaming at the mouth, popping off at him something blue, calling him every name under the midnight sun - from her perspective she was rightfully outraged. But every time she tried to get to her feet he kicked her down gently like a cat playing with a mouse. Each time he did it, it tickled him. Pete was strong / Gun was pathetic. After a minute of her shouting and crying he balled up his fist and hit her in the face again. And with this action, he felt free. He felt good. The feeling was electric. Pete got a real boost out of seeing her scared, tearful face - the inconsolable Gun curled up in a ball as additional blows were lowered down. New feelings in an old room. A line had been set down, society had drawn it, and he'd crossed it without blinking.

It seemed like time had no thought for any of them, it all just moved ahead on its relentless course. A fault line had opened up and all these women, like Gun, had fallen down it. He'd discovered a talent that day with Gun and he had since trained himself to bleed the feeling slowly for pleasure and effect - the occasional unsolicited physical punishment of any woman who sought intimacy with him.

Eventually, a post came up in Dewhurst and he returned home to where he'd grown up. Johnny Pearce took him under his wing, his welcome gifts were a night sat on surveillance in one of the police rovers, one of his Chiko Rolls and a can of Coke.

This man in Blacks Beach, to whom he and Johnny were attending to that morning was really a fellow collector of the same colour discourse too - a brother in arms in this war against fucking idiot women. But the good and decent weren't on their side, the hypocritical nice people that buried their vices in closed-off shaded rooms. He was a cop. A custodian of the law, he could even be untouchable.

Ninety Two

1987-1988 - Glenn

History Is Written By The Victors

*Mr Ball, would always whip through his lessons like a fucking
whirlwind. Looking back, we were lucky to have a teacher
who was interested in engaging us. I always remember one
about Queen Elizabeth I and her really being a man, replaced
by a changeling (if that's the right word). There were others,
but fucked if I can remember them.*

*His class was the first place I remember taking any real notice
of Nicole. Before that, she was just Nicole who walked down
our street with the other girls, the fair one. That's if I even
knew her name before then. I think I probably did, but Mr
Ball's history class is where my earliest solid recollections of
her came from. I suspect Mr Ball gave us those conspiracy
theories to challenge our perception of history. As far as the
documented past, world events are concerned, we only get
the broad strokes, no sense of the minutiae of each event. He
asked us to look closer and then question the validity of what
we were being told. With his conspiracies, as outlandish as
they were, he wasn't asking us to buy into them, but he was
probably asking us to compare them to the material that
was served up to us as bona fide fact on a daily basis via the
TV and newspapers. Just because it's taught to children in
schools on a massive scale, doesn't mean it's the truth, right?
We just needed to know it all to pass some bullshit exam that
doesn't count for shit to us in adult life."*

*

"Right, that all took a lot less time I planned, which means?"

"We can go home early, Mr Ball."

"No, shut up."

"We get to listen to one of your boring conspiracy theories?"

"They're not mine. They're everybody's. And some of them could well be true. You decide."

"We'd sooner go home."

"Shut your mouth Dobson."

"It's Robson, sir."

"Well, who's Dobson?"

"There isn't one."

"Yes there is, Michelle Dobson in 8G..."

"He's hardly gonna mix me up with her is he?"

Mr Ball, who had been holding a large book under his arm for sometime dropped it on to his desk with a bang.

"Who believes in aliens?"

"You mean like fobs n' wogs?"

"You've just bought yourself a week's worth of detention moron."

"Fuck."

"And another week."

"But."

"But nothing."

"It's half-term break next week."

"You wait behind after class. NOW I repeat, who believes in aliens from outer space? Don't answer that. How many of you have considered that aliens might have been here all along, observing us from outer space. Have you entertained the thought that we could be the aliens? Who's heard of the Black Knight?"

"Can we just get up when the bell goes? This isn't curriculum."

"In 1960, the U.S. Navy's Dark Fence radar system made an important discovery. They had detected a large object in polar orbit around the Earth, estimated to weigh as much as 15 tons. What was particularly odd about this was neither the US nor the Soviets had the ability to put objects into orbit back then, and the purported weight was far beyond what either country were capable of getting into space."

The bell rings. The class charges out the door, all except for Glenn and Nicole.

"Go! Get lost." bellows Ballbags, flicking hair out of his eyes.

Mr Ball begins to pack his bag.

Nicole who was sat nearer the front of the class looks over her shoulder at Glenn. *"You walking back the same way?"*

Ninety Three

The past - The male of the species

The Coolidge Effect

What happens when you drop a male rat into a cage with a
receptive female rat? First, you see a frenzy of copulation,
followed by a progressive reduction in activity. The male is
seen to tire of that *particular* female. Even if she wants more,
he has had enough. However, replace the original female with
a new one, and the male immediately revives and gallantly
struggles to fertilise her. You could repeat this process with
fresh females until he is completely wiped out.

This is called the Coolidge Effect - the automatic response
to novel mates. Don't tell your husband about it, he'll use it
as an excuse next time you catch him with his undies down.
Now let me try and find a female equivalent study that proves
it's the same for girls, only better.

Ninety Four

1991 - Glenn, Robbie and Crusty

You Got Friends, I Got Friends Too

Robbie -   *"Oh here he comes... Where you been bludger?"*

Crusty saunters round the corner and plonks his arse on the grass next to Glenn and Robbie.

Crusty -   *"Was over Bradley's playing pool."*

Robbie -   *"We been here ages, fanning our balls waiting for you."*

Crusty -   *"Should've had a cuddle instead."*

Robbie -   *"Fucking dickhead."*

Crusty -   *"Anyway, here's why I was late, crazy shit. You know what a stinge Brad is, right? We're playing for hours and I'm getting seriously fucking hungry but he's not offering any food out, not as much as dry roasted peanut mate."*

Glenn -   *"You're always bloody eating."*

Crusty -   *"Yeah, pussy and eggs for breakfast."*

Robbie -   *"Will you just shut up."*

Crusty -   *"Look, I just needed some tucker mate, what's
              wrong with that? Anyway, I've asked him like
              three times to rustle something up, but he says
              he doesn't want to get in trouble with his mum.
              Fucking poof. So I say to myself, "Fuck it, I'm
              gonna do a fridge raid..." So I tell him I need
              the dunny. On the way upstairs to the kitchen,
              I walk past his parents room and I spy a tube
              of Pringles on the floor next to the bed right?"*

Glenn -   *"Is this actually going anywhere?"*

*"Fair go, anyway, I sneak in and pick up the tube of chips
right, I take the lid off only there's no chips inside. It's a
fucking dildo!"*

"Argh, yuck..."

"Yargh, mate."

*"Yeah, imagine if I hadn't have looked in the tube first, I'd
have had Bradley's mum's dildo in my mouth..."*

"What flavour...?"

"I told you I didn't taste it to find out..."

"No the Pringles, dickhead."

"Oh. Sour Cream and Onion..."

"Ah that's disgusting."

"I know right. I just threw it on the bed and went back downstairs to play pool. Cured me of my appetite...."

"And he never ate Sour Cream and Onion flavour again."

"Hahaha, shut up."

"Come on, we're gonna be late. Time to watch some touch footie up at the school. Girls' squad are playing."

"Mumble pants."

"Ey Crusty, tell Glenn why you call 'em mumble pants."

"You can see the lips moving, but you can't hear the words."

Crusty followed the quip with a titter and a thick grin.

"Fucking no hopers."

"You coming then?" asked Robbie.

"Nah".

"He's seeing the Boobers for his tea, aren't yer Glenn."

Crusty half-heartedly begins to climb the saggy chainmail fence of the sunken tennis court at the corner of Bates and Manuel Street. A sinkhole had opened up five years earlier about four to five metres in diameter. Sharp blades of tropical grass and weeds came up through cracks in the court's asphalt surface. The gates were padlocked shut but the fence bowed enough at the western edge so that you could get in if you really had to. It was still a hangout but no one really went inside the fence perimeter these days, and instead they just sat on the ascending grass verge between the edge of the court and the pavement.

"Not decided."

"You finished with Nicole?"

"Fucked if I know, not seen her for days."

"So The Boobers jumped in the hot seat?"

"Shut up, we're just gonna hang out."

"Where you taking her?"

"Might go to the drive in, stop at Red Rooster".

"Class act aren't you?"

"Romantic," sniggered Crusty. *"I hear she's finger licking good,"* dropping down off the fence.

"That's KFC dickhead."

"I was talking about Jocasta, poofter."

"He did say 'she'." Robbie pointed out.

"Leave it out eh?"

"Stop being so fucking serious. We're off anyway. Fucking

missing some prime time perving whilst you mope about. Got vagina all day like a toilet and he's still depressed. Let's go."

Robbie stands up from the grass verge and stalks off in the direction of the floodlights at the school sports ground smearing the town's dark sky with a white haze.

"Don't be fucking late tomorrow morning. 5.30 at the Marina," Glenn shouts to Robbie.

"Yeah," adds Crusty as he walks off following Robbie.

"Catch you later, dickhead."

"Eat it, Crusty."

The two mates walk to the junction of the cross paths a few yards down the slope. Crusty stops at the corner, turns back to Glenn, grabs his own nuts and gives him the finger before rolling out of view behind some garden foliage. Moths to flames. Zombies to a bare arse.

Ninety Five

1991 - Jocasta

Tell Me

*Siri Nguyen had been saying for months how hot Glenn
Pearce was getting these days. Elbowing me in the hip every
time he walked by - some days we may get a "how's it?" out
of him but little else. I had an eye on him, but then I think I'd
fantasised about most of the boys in our class idly at some
point. Each of them weighed up, some days I could really
fancy someone, then the next day pay them no mind at all.*

*Girls were getting caught up with boys all over the place now,
falling like nine-pins. Loss of virginity processed while-U-
wait. Word got out that I was a bit keen on Glenn, although
I'd never said as much - I didn't do much to stop the jungle
drummers drumming.*

*Then one day, that nobody with the crooked teeth and poor
skin, Nicole, marched right in and suckered him. Snapped up
by a dag with no character: shit clothes, terrible music taste,
cheap perfume, and that annoying whiny voice. Why do guys
go for such insipid little girls? Flower print-clad homunculi
with flat chests and no style. I can't stand her, or her ancient
dad, cluttering up the neighbourhood with his smashed up
cars. Last of the bogans; this ain't Mad Max.*

*Then there he was, A$4 bucks short for his petrol at the servo
asking favours off the first person he knew. Me.*

II

Jocasta & Glenn

"What's showing?"

"Rocky V and Backdraft double-bill."

"Seen 'em."

"We don't have to go to the drive-in. What's on at the main one?"

"Either Silence of the Lambs or Robin Hood – Prince of Thieves."

"You bothered by either of 'em?"

"I don't mind... I'd sooner go somewhere for some food and drive around."

She said it nonchalantly but at the same time she takes a small step backwards towards her car.

"Why'd you have me pick you up here?" she adds nodding towards Dean's clammy Queenslander. The bull's horns gripped. There's no scope for avoiding Jocasta's gaze.

"I was working with Dean on something. He needed an extra pair of hands to help install a new head gasket into Flick's mum's car."

"Whatever that is." She walks around to her side of the car

and opens the door. *"So it's not because Nicole's around here someplace and you're trying to give her the shits."*

"No."

"I know you're using me Glenn."

"I'm not."

"You are. But here I am. I guess I must really be OK with that, ay."

"Come on Jocasta. Go easy."

"Don't you clowns call me 'The Boobers' or something?"

"I don't call you that."

"Your mates do."

"Quit being so weird."

"Do you want me to go home?"

"I just want you to stop it with the interrogation. I got your message. I agreed to go out, here I am, I'm not here under protest. Let's just go see Backdraft, or get a burger as mates. It's not like we're getting married is it?"

"You're cuter when you get heated and self-righteous."

"Stop fucking about Jocasta."

"Shall we start again?"

"What? Yes. Happy to. Go for it. Whatever."

"I'm going to drive around the block and come back in three minutes."

"You're really gonna do that?"

"Yes."

Casually swinging the keys on her forefinger, she gets into her car, without looking back at him. Glenn catches a glimpse of her thigh before she pushes her light blue dress down flat along her legs and leans out to close the door behind her.

Slowly driving to the corner, Jocasta performs a perfect U-turn at the entrance to Timor-Leste Street and stops at the T-junction. And there she sits, looking at him over the steering wheel. Is she blinding him deliberately with her full beam? He shields his eyes from the glare. The car hovers at the bite point and the engine of her sad hatchback growls.

As the remains of the day seep away and the light dies behind the pine trees at the head of the rise, Jocasta releases the clutch. She turns back on to his street and drives past him without stopping. He waits by the kerb in the warm breeze as the nearest streetlight flickers.

A cane toad clambers out of the gutter in baggy fashion. Three minutes pass. Then another three.

About an hour later Glenn drives across the few blocks

between Dean's place and the Queenslander he 'kind of' shares with his dad. It's a short drive, and a good walking distance via a couple of small neighbourhood shops. Stopping in at the clapboard convenience store, Mully's, he buys a pack of Samboy chips and plays a game of Pacman on the console at the back of the shop. The obese Pommie Bill, the till-jockey stands at his shoulder watching with him, all fat belly, stretched t-shirt, ratty goatee and a black Raiders' baseball cap - NWA and The DOC-style. He was on an extended holiday, earning his money for a flight back to the UK off his Aunty Marilyn, who owned the place.

During the course of their intergalactic maze chase, a small crowd of locals had gathered at the till waiting to buy this and that. A clapped-out, puny dude aged about 50, dressed tip-to-toe in denim with a pencil moustache, tells Bill, *"You're bang out of order..."* for making him wait.

"You got somewhere important to go have you, mate?"

"It's not the fucking point. Now give me a box of Durex."

"You're kidding right?" snorted Bill.

The gaggle of BMX kids in the line behind him set off in peals of laughter.

"I thought I told you little shits to leave your fucking bikes outside."

"Aw come on Bill."

"Durex, wasn't it?"

"Is that why you're in a rush?" says one of the punks.

"Don't be fucking cheeky."

And so the exchange went on, culminating with all the kids all bickering and marvelling at how such a weirdo could find someone to go 'down the road' with him. Bill clears the idiots out - they buy a Viennetta roll to share on the humpy across the road.

"I bet you can't eat a Cheeto and some Viennetta at the same time." He allows another one of them rent the video of Cyborg, rated M+. *"Village Roadshow Pictures gives you a dare."* The kids pronounce Jean like the trousers, 'Gene Clawed Vern-Demmes'.

Once the squirts had cleared off, Bill presses play on the grimed up mini-ghetto blaster behind the till. *"Got posted a few tapes of Tim Westwood from my mate back home. Be ages before it comes out here. New Ultra Magnetic MCs, Lord Finesse, Craig G."*

But the tape is skidding and moving slowly in the shitty deck. *"Back to 4DW I guess."* He shrugs stopping the tape.

"The place with the hits. See ya Bill."

Ninety Six

1991 - Glenn

And So It Is

It's dark by the time Glenn pulls up outside his house, he notices Jocasta's car sat on the driveway. There are no lights on at the house. There's a chink of apricot coloured sky, an economic display of the dwindling light, the sun like the smudged cherry of a dying cigarette.

He wanders across to her Ford, discovers it empty, the bonnet is cool to touch and he absentmindedly runs his hand along its edge, skirting the windscreen, the roof.

Then he sees her. Rooting himself to the spot, Glenn gets butterflies and his throat dries out.

She's sat, waiting for him halfway up the staircase to his front door. Without saying a word she slowly parts her legs.

Jocasta exhales a long stream of smoke and stubs her cigarette out on the concrete step. Rising to her feet, she turns to walk up the untravelled steps ahead of her. The air sinks, indeterminable and he follows.

Ninety Seven

1994 - Vella

Mislaid Ice Cream Days

Vella had driven back to Motel 501. The front of the police rover is pointed towards the neon palm tree so he can get an unspoilt view of it. Beyond the intermittent traffic sounds all was quiet on the lot. He loved this artificial tribute to the tropics. The tree's lush green leaves gamely represented by four green strip lights. Vella thinks his love of coloured lights, neon, and his career in law enforcement could be related. He deploys his blue police lights. Yes. It's true. The electric blue jets of light ricochet across the facades of the horseshoe of motel buildings prompting a few of the occupants to peak out from behind their curtains. What would they think if they knew that he'd just driven all the way across the city to watch a neon palm tree blink from red to green and back again?

In Malta, it's customary for all ex-pats who return to the island to retire to commission a statue to be placed outside the front of their house. The edifice is intended to represent the career or how the owner has made his money during his life up to that point - a bold status symbol that in many cases defies taste, style and humility. Vella has an idea on one such evening sat, half-drunk in the sandy motel parking lot - perhaps he could buy a palm tree like the one at Motel 501. The only thing in this whole city he had fondness for.

Ninety Eight

2019 - Glenn

Among The Living

Had no one to tell this tragic tale to when I got home to my apartment, so I'm telling it to you. We got these air wells at work just so that the offices on the inside of the building get some sunlight, but no view. They've all been covered over with netting to stop the pigeons and other wild birds getting in, laying eggs, nesting and shitting all over the shop. Well, that's the idea, but every once in a while, one will wriggle its way in and then lose its way back out, so that's it really.

Until today, we'd grown quite attached to this young pigeon, with a beautiful white breast. Poor fella had gotten in and was living the dream getting by off our chips and crumbs - some dumb arses would throw in a strawberry or a slice of cucumber thinking that wild birds could eat any old stuff. Anyway, he was enduring somehow, but he was getting no smarter. We even gave the chipper little sod a name, Eric. Some of the seniors wanted to see the back of Eric and this morning they suggested that we leave the window open to see if he'd walk in of his own accord, and we could then help him on his way out through one of the street-side windows. Office he-man, Dave Riekken was the one to 'man-up' and catch Eric the minute he stepped over the windowsill in search of more Samboy chips.

Unfortunately, come the moment, Eric flew up and got sandwiched between the window, the blinds and the pink fluffy towel Dave was trying to wrap him in (what was he doing with a pink fluffy towel?). After a squabble, Eric relented and allowed himself to be gathered up. As the bird was being ferried to an open window on the other side of the room it seemed to be gasping for air or screaming silently, its head jerking forward and backwards, 1 - 2 - 3!

Next thing we know, Dave has launched Eric out of the towel skywards, up through the window, only for the poor sod to plummet like a brick to its doom on the busy pavement one-storey below. We hear a woman call up, "You just throw a dead bird at me?"

"Oh no, is he dead?"

"He's a goner, doll."

Dave rushes out of the office with the towel. Everyone in the office begins to laugh hysterically, tears coming down with their mouths gasping for air, not all that unlike Eric's as he had experienced, what I realised shortly afterwards, to be a heart attack from sheer fright.

I looked out through Eric's exit window a few minutes later and I saw Dave crouched down next to the bird's corpse, gently wrapping it in the towel. The bird's wings weren't outstretched. Perhaps they had been broken when he'd gotten himself captured. Dave was quietly explaining to some ladies who had gathered around that the bird was still alive when he threw it to freedom, but somehow, this makes the whole situation sound worse.

Dave was silent at his desk all afternoon - somebody makes a 'missing pigeon' poster adorning a photo of a fine specimen enquiring: "Have you seen my brother?"

He doesn't react - clearly moved and upset by his high-profile mistake. Fella only wanted to be seen as the caring, in control one, and now he was a comedy pigeon killer.

"Funny fuckers aren't we?"

Anyway, when things had gotten less hysterical in the office and boredom resumed, I began to think about poor old Eric as he died from a dose of undiluted terror. Hopefully our feathered mate was dead before he knew what was happening, before he hit the ground.

Dead Eric is in the bin wrapped in his pink towel at the corner of the street, still. A shower passes over now and I can hear the raindrops rebounding off the sloped kitchen window.

All the little animals, gather round.

Ninety Nine

1971 - Aggie

When I Think Of You

Aggie lived in three different areas of Sydney during the years of 1970 and 1971: Randwick, by the racecourse; Glebe with its beautiful narrow streets; and Woolloomoolo with it gigantic flights of stairs filing their way down to the busy water's edge. She spent her spare time between the city's art galleries because she wanted to learn a bit more about her new country and the parks. But she became lonely so she made an effort to attract some friends and people here and there to explore the nights with, firstly by taking a part-time job in a low-key live music lounge. A well-earned yet busy whirl of a social life meant that she came into contact with a number of square-jawed professionals that loved to play rugby - or footie as they called it down here. The odd new acquaintance would be from England and it would be nice to compare notes on how they were adapting to Australia too. Aggie also met a few Maltese, Greeks and Italians. She soon found out that black Australians were either hated or ignored by the whites in most cases. Those that did care about them misunderstood them. Aggie observed how peculiar it was, that in this land of opportunity, there didn't seem to be any room for them. The original natives. A bullshit artist called Clarrie Cotton explained their treatment away with a sentence that sound well-rehearsed as he recited it with relish, *"There was a war of occupation, and we bloody well won. Fair and square. Those black bastards had this place for thousands of years before us and what have they got to offer the rest of the world? A giant fucking flute, religious mumbo jumbo, shit art, and a bent stick."*

Clarrie the clown had also made the mistake of trying to woo her. But after he'd shown his colours as a card-carrying 'Australia for Whites' advocate, he'd had no chance. On arrival in Australia, she had been led to believe that it was a progressive place. As it was one of the first countries to give women the vote, but on close scrutiny that was just the one state, South Australia. By the time she died, it was still illegal to have same-sex relations in Tasmania. So for her it was a mixed bag.

Being young and single in Sydney in the 1970s was an amazing time. A blitz of parties and at least six new friends recruited every week; it was possible to move in different circles if one clique was getting on your nerves too. Each neighbourhood had its own collection of milk bars and pubs, so it was possible to avoid the heart of the city for weeks. Randwick was reasonably close to the coast with Bondi up the road for sunbathing and watching the lifeguard's profile. The sand was full of cigarette butts back then which was kind of off-putting and in the end she found a better place to sun worship.

Aggie rented a room at the back of a family house. The couple she rented it from had two sons. One was a teenager and the other was younger. The eldest son was called Cecil and he would always blush when he had to talk to her or when he was sent down to ask if she needed anything from the store (on his parents' bequest). Aggie was so unused to being the subject of a teenage crush, the object of this boy, who had to be 4 or 5 years younger than her. She also became aware

that her collection of underwear was dwindling. Unwilling
to embarrass her landlords, she didn't bring it up, but she
did move house to a shared apartment with a young married
couple who were trying to make the mortgage in Coogee.

The place in Coogee was covered partially in ivy and had
an unusual pointed apex tower like that of a rural American
church. The couple Troy and Clara, didn't know the building's
history, so Aggie said she'd see what she could find out
seeing as she now worked in planning at the City Council.
Troy and Clara could be heard having loud arguments about
money and sometimes another girl's name came into it. Turns
out that Troy's sister Mary, was a drug addict and had asked
to stay. To this request Clara had said no, because druggies
stole and were generally of low character but Troy must have
talked her around. A week later the junky sister was moved
in, so she moved out to a small one bedroom street house on
Yurong Lane in Woolloomoolo. No house shares, no troubled
relatives, no stolen knickers or bras. Aggie then made herself
a simple rule that no one but no one would make it over the
threshold of her new home until she suspected there was a
good chance of love. This new rule wouldn't stop her staying
over at the odd cute boy's house though. Not once did she
encounter anyone from work after dark, so what she did at
night never came back to haunt her in the daytime.

Then one day she craved vanilla: she wanted to slow down.
Out of the all the flavours and toppings, she just wanted
one thing. One person. One mind. One cock. With nobody
knowing where she lived, her three months of what your
average person would call mildly debauched behaviour
came to a halt. It was time to talk to the wiry looking young
chap who was found staring at a painting of runaway sheep

whenever she went in to the AGNSW on her lunch break. With his hat pressed flat against his heart, this stranger looked as if he was worshipping this work of art. She would find something interesting to say - an appropriate opening gambit.

One Hundred

1991 - Dean

The Winds Of Change

Nicole, her friend Fallon and her sort of friend, Ursula danced around her bedroom singing along loudly to *The Horses* by Daryl Braithwaite. *"That's the way it's gonna be, little darling."*

Dean is working below and Bets patiently watches on, sat close by. It's almost her feeding time. He looks up at Nicole's window but beyond seeing the odd flick of Fallon's long black dancing hair he can't see the girls from down here in the garden of cars. He can just hear the blaring pop music and the girls' excited voices.

"We'll be riding on The Horses!!!"

Dean lets out a fart that sounds a bit like the buzzer on a quiz show, he thinks, sorry Bets, that's not the right answer. The dog gets up slowly from its comfortable spot and strolls off.

"Don't worry, Betsy. It'll all blow over one day, ay girl." he says wafting the smell away, laughing to himself. Dean lights a cigarette; the flame is bluer than normal.

Where does the time go? One minute she's a child... Nicole. She danced better than the girls on the TV.

One Hundred and One

1991 - Skids

Round And Round We All Go

Faroukh 'Skids' Yahnundasis was a successful thief. He
never had to answer to the law at any point. His motto was
never to get cocky, don't ever, ever confide in anybody unless
they have as much to lose as you do (and even then be very
fucking selective), don't boast about your spoils, never show
off what you stole, and most of all, really don't underestimate
the people you're stealing from. Skids stayed in the shadows
and would only take the things he needed, but it was mainly
cash money that he took. He never got too techy or ventured
into areas where a paper trail could emanate from the
skulduggery. If his underhandedness was ever work-
related, he would only steal 'big' once in a blue moon when
he knew that he would be one of a few under scrutiny.
Nobody bothered him anymore and you might say that he
had become rehabilitated all by himself - as he had gotten
older he was less inclined to take any risks and after a time
he stopped stealing altogether.

In his expansive garden shed was the best slot car set-up in
North Queensland, bought with a combination of wages,
and stolen cash along with Christmas and birthday presents.
His set-up was 9 x 5 metres, and the level of detail was
astonishing. There were figurines in the stands cheering on
the drivers, support vehicles in the pit stops, ordinary cars
that were the same scale as the slot cars parked along sections
of the track, logo'd up railings alongside flags and banners.

There was even a town, with shops, houses and a tower block and an authentic scaled down replica of Istanbul's Grand Station. The slot cars had the right livery to match the existing teams of the day too. The love and hard work that Skids put in was astonishing, he'd ordered parts from all over the world and spent an absolute fortune on the cars, the landscape, the fake flora and fauna, and the buildings (there was even a fully operational, to scale, railway circuit). Aside from being a good thief, the shed also doubled as a social spot for the local dodgy bastards to occasionally leave their stolen goods since the speedway had gone out of business when Kerry shot through, although hardly anyone of them knew that he was cut from the same cloth.

But the slot car track and the set up was too much hard work to simply be a brightly decorated backdrop for the dishonest and the ugly, at least it was until Pete Wilson, shortly followed by Johnny Pearce, walked in one night asking to join the club. It was all quite innocent as they'd both decided that they needed a 'nice' hobby where they could bond with the community on a 'buddy' level. The subsequent redistribution of contraband by Skids and the boys turned out to be a real team effort. Everything had been vanished expediently by the second week, anything they couldn't shift was burnt out on a vacant lot at the south end of the city.

Skids and his chums were left scratching their heads a month later when no bust was forthcoming and the new outsiders actually started to get good at the circuits having gone as far as purchasing their own slot cars to race.

One Hundred and Two

1994 - Gully

A Century Of Storms

*I saved up all my piss for hours the morning of Johnny
Pearce's funeral. All through the eulogies and there were
loads of the bastards, and I was busting - there were a few
points where I was holding it in so hard I thought I'd have a
puncture. I would've rolled into help Glenn but I'd have peed
me pants. Yet I held myself all through the scrap as well, all
through the police rolling in to take Roo and the rest of those
lads away. I had to wait until everyone had disappeared.*

*When I was finally able to piss all over Johnny's coffin I heard
some kids laughing. The little buggers had been hiding out
during the funeral, I'd seen 'em earlier. But I couldn't stop
mid flow so I carried on, and the piss just flowed and flowed
- droplets bouncing off that rat bag's coffin lid. When I'd
finished, these young lads came to edge of the grave, looked
up at me lent on the handle of my shovel, and still sniggering
took a piss over the edge themselves - all three of the little
shits. I left them to it. I thought that I could always come back
to fill his hole in later, perhaps more of the townsfolk would
want to pay their respects in the same way.*

*

The idea of urinating down onto Johnny's coffin had come
to him in a dream. He wasn't accustomed to such displays of
depravity but this man had irrevocably ruined his life for the
worst and nothing could unravel the pain and anger he had left

brewing all this time. He waited forever, and he'd retained his position as city sexton this long especially for this moment. But was that even true? Did he feel released?

In the distance he observed the lads, no more than eleven or twelve years old head off towards the cemetery gates. Long walk back to town for them he thought. He noticed that the boys had brought a picnic along with them and left their lolly and chip wrappers behind a neighbouring gravestone, or heaven's stones as he still called them. He kicked the papers over the edge of Johnny's hole and watched as they fluttered down on to the wet coffin. There was all kinds of stuff he was going to throw in, he even had a septic tank to empty out from the spare caravan where he'd hidden Johnny's runaway wife, Glenn's Mum, Aggie, a decade earlier.

"Yes Johnny boy. We hid out right over there. She came to me, you sent your attack dog Wilson after me but yous never found her, sport. And now you never will, ay."

Gully walked with intent back to his studio shed. It was a fair trot to the end of the graveyard but he had things he still needed to give Johnny boy.

Moments after, Gully returned to the graveside where he'd hauled a painting of a woman with a black eye, bruised lips and breasts. She is draped in a red robe.

"Now you can take this reminder of what you did with you to hell and eternity."

He drops the painting down the hole. It lands facing upwards.

"Aggie." Her name escapes Gully's lips as he sees, really sees, the painting for what it is for the first time in years.

The shovel is within arms reach. No septic tank necessary, his revenge was complete. He heard a magpie burble in the trees close by. He decided that he'd walk out to Slack Macs to pick up a simple burger of some description after the hole with his sworn enemy in was full and forgotten. A$4 and change was all this deliverance was worth to him.

But I'm still here he thought, casting an eye over the now quiet graveyard. No bird song now: a disquieting sea change, a drop in air pressure.

"I'm still here. I'm still here. I'm still here." Gully barely more than muttered under his breath with each shovel of dirt delivered. A steady rhythm established itself.

One Hundred and Three

1986 - Aggie

Nothing Further Then, She Uttered

Johnny Pearce was already present in the threadbare, bald-floored Room 6 at the Motel 501, sat at his wife's side when Gully walked in. Pete Wilson was also present, stood by the door he planted his hand right in the man's chest on arrival.

"Fuck off Wilson," Gull shrugged him off and strode into the room.

The vomit in the double bed had been partially concealed but was soaking through the thin cover sheet, however Aggie had been cleaned up and was looking dazed; her eyes fixed on the fly screen covered window to her right. Her eyes moved to Gull's own as he walked towards the bed and then back to where they began. He could see a jar of tablets on the bedside table. The scene had been painted in bold strokes - even an idiot like him couldn't have missed the signs. Johnny stood upright, the chair he was sat on skidded backwards a short distance.

"I'm gonna make you pay dearly for this. Mark my fucking words." The voice firm, determined and certain, perfectly controlled. He then calmly retrieved his chair and lowered himself back down onto it. On picking Aggie's hand up, she weakly freed herself from Johnny's hold, all the while still looking at nothing but light coming into the room.

One Hundred and Four

1986 - Gully

Don't Be Afraid That Nobody Loves You

What an unholy fucking mess. The ultimatum delivered, Aggie had attempted a third and unthinkable way out. Gully's ham-fisted demand had basically boiled down to, *"Leave Johnny, and come and live with me at the necropolis, or let's stop seeing each other altogether."*

They'd been meeting for coffee initially, just a catch up, but then he'd invited her back to his studio to show her his paintings. After years of no contact, they were back where they started. Aggie had made the first move by kissing him forcefully. Pushing him up against a wall flat palmed, the same place and degree of force that Pete Wilson would use to prevent him from entering the room at Motel 501 just now.

"If this kiss is a tiny yet sweet slither of cake in a lifetime of meals, then it's just happened. How I wonder."

It was only as Gully began to walk across the motel lot in an furious haze that he finally saw it, usually known for being astute, for once and when he needed to be quick he was slow. Aggie hadn't needed a clean break from Johnny, she'd just wanted someone to hide out with from time to time - a respite. He was the respite. Just like playing an old record, or looking at an old photograph, Gully, to her was like a faded keepsake she could take out then put back in an old biscuit tin before she returned to reality. Aggie already had one shitty husband, what made Gully think he could be a better alternative, offer her more, sat in his tarnished, green mould-coated caravan, painting portraits of the mediocre and the local 'beautifuls'. Failed, ersatz art-historian/artist-cum-grave digger versus a corrupt king shit. They'd already taken one good swing at it. Life didn't give you second chances, at least not ones with a clean slate.

Whatever happened to that young boy he once was; sensitive, golden haired Gully from Bateman's Bay, the boy who loved to draw and paint, who even loved to write about the paintings he saw? All those thoughts and loves were lost on him. He recollects the day he met Aggie, stood in the AGNSW in Sydney Harbour gawping at a painting called *The Breakaway*. How had they ever gotten bored of Sydney - their dearest and best?

Gully winces as he pinpoints, for the billionth time, the day their fortunes together changed for the worse. It was the minute their first house together in Dewhurst got burgled. It was in that single moment that Johnny Pearce, then still a mere police constable, attended the call-out and sized her up for later. What spells had he borrowed to spirit her away from him? Pah, spells, he was no sorcerer - the man had barely read three books in his life. It was this heat that fucked it all up for them all. Got people all hot and bothered, a city full of naked shit bags spread eagled on their backs - post coital under cartwheeling ceiling fans. Genitals cooling off for the next go around. Human decency locked into a stagnant holding pattern, perishing in hope for a word with the slightest accent of comfort.

II

Gully wasn't afraid of Johnny, or his dog Pete Wilson, he'd
kill the pair of them and bury them somewhere they'd never
be found. He didn't care. As the night was going to be an
extra hot one, he planned to hide out behind a heaven's stone
with his undeclared revolver and the licensed shotgun he was
supposed to use for killing vermin and poisonous tree snakes.
Let them come. And try they might but he'd be ready.

One Hundred and Five

2019 - Glenn

All The King's Horses

I don't remember the details of many conversations we - me and Nicole - had. It was a relationship built on short sentences or single words. Yet I felt the strongest pull towards someone else that I'll ever know. Every time I had day release from jail we'd get driven to Rockhampton. I'd scan crowds for her face, in the street cafes, the supermarket queues, passing cars, darkened cinemas. What would she even be doing in Rocky? But I still looked for her. Every girl had her face, I heard her voice and laughter in the street noise.

When I was locked up, I'd wonder who was talking with her, touching her, every man wanted to be with her, each a possibility and I'd feel sick. A mild quaking in my hands. Songs on the radio. Girls on the telly.

II

Pete Wilson had run away to England by the time I had turned up for Dad's funeral.

Him and Dad had made a formidable team but then he had stood alone and it wouldn't have been long before people sought to level the playing field, get a bit of payback for what he'd done to Nicole. I heard the stories in jail.

None of it made sense and each of the possible truths didn't ring in tune either. It's not like a fucking story book where people are predictable, people conform to type, I wish I could boil all this down into a one simple storyline but there's too many fucked up variables. I line up the facts yet there'll be one element to contradict everything else, then I'll go back to beginning and try to work it out from another angle, yet again I'll come across another misalignment in the telling. I'm missing something but there's no outcome to this and there's nobody's left to account for themselves anymore.

The lie makes more sense, a tale of convenience for the stupid people to follow - the popular version. Fuckwits like Roo Stamper follow this fabricated version that I took and smashed the one thing I've ever loved, my Nicole, but my truth is this: Dad just watched, eating a fucking Chiko Roll and guzzling a can of coke as Pete Wilson destroyed our lives in less than 2 minutes. Less than animals, with no motive, or reason but to wreak havoc for kicks: they changed everything forever. They had me locked up in a soundproof police rover as I watched on, too scared to look, too angry to look away... I can't get around it, or through it. It's not an ending.

One Hundred and Six

1991 - The Chorus

He Or She Who Laughs Last Is Slow

"You're not a real Australian until you've been to Mt Isa."

"You ever been?"

"Nope".

"Where were you born?"

"Townsville General Hospital."

"Where was your Dad's dad born?"

"Dunno. New South Wales."

"Then it's bullshit."

"What is?"

"That slogan about Mt Isa".

"I know."

One Hundred and Seven

1991 - Glenn and Nicole

I've Been To Those Other Places

"We're ranked about fourth in Dewhurst at the moment."

She sits down heavily next to him unfastening her shin pads. Nicole props her plastic cricket bat against the neighbouring chair. *"Can I have a chip?"*

Glenn offers the bag to her, *"Think you'll win the league this year?"*

"Early days… Wasn't expecting to see you. Everything OK?" She kisses him affectionately on the cheek, then she pops a CC'S corn chip in her mouth, crunching it loudly.

"Yeah, just thought I'd hang out. Been ages since I came to watch. Where have you been? Not seen you in about a week or something."

"I came to look for you yesterday, but Crusty said you went out on the Sea Cow with Robbie."

"We went for an early morning fish but were back by 11."

"Oh. Catch much?"

Glenn could detect something in her voice. They'd never had a fight or even a serious disagreement. What was she hiding?

She sounded almost afraid, but maybe she'd heard about Jocasta's visit.

Everything goes away if you choose to leave the doors open.

"An ocean's worth. It's in the freezer. Fry you up something later."

"Sounds good."

There was a game still in progress in the next court. He sees Pete Wilson fielding for the defending team. *"I didn't know the police had an indoor cricket team."*

"Not sure they do. You wanna go, you made me hungry."

As they leave, Pete watches them but misses a chance to catch out the batsman, a real dolly drop.

"Come on Pete, wake up. Stunned mullet!" shouted Brett Coulson.

Nicole throws Pete an apologetic smile as she slips out of the hall, but he doesn't see it, instead the intention bounces off the breezeblocks and assorted crash mats.

"I've missed you," she says to Glenn, as she pictures Pete in her head.

One Hundred and Eight

1991 - Pete

What Good Am I?

Fitting in. Catching a 'coldy' after work with Brett to make
him feel a part of the team. Pete thought the young copper
was a try hard. He should speak plainly and tell him he didn't
really want a mate. Him and Johnny had this thing and he
didn't want to share it, not that this do-good lick-arse would
want a piece. There's a spot on the cricket team - the guys are
screaming for new blood, Pete had told Brett as deflection.
Brett had snapped up the chance to get involved with the local
team, why Pete did it was a mystery. Johnny had told him, be
seen. Join the men's groups, if they know they've got a cop
hanging around it gives the prols the illusion of friendship and
free will - in return what you gain is a lower local crime rate.
What bullshit, he thought.

Pete was alright at cricket, his old man had been friends with
the fathers of half the men on the team. So that was another
reason, he was easily accepted into these diversionary clubs.
Johnny had also told him about a slot car club over in Sandergrove that he might join too.

On the other hand, Johnny had enrolled him into a very
exclusive club, a cabal that a certain type of man would kill
to join. You only got to know about it if you were on the
receiving end - no bystanders knew what the two men were
up to, so they couldn't even ask if they could join up, because
the option was under a cloak. The club barely existed; anyhow

it was more of an accord between two men. Pete was utterly addicted and was enthralled by the fact that he'd found someone like Johnny who shared his enthusiasm. Johnny had once joked that one fisherman spots another fisherman from afar. At first he didn't understand what he was getting at. Then he did.

About 3 years ago they went to break up a drunken fight between two women one hot afternoon - they were squabbling over a man - some tattooed dole-bludger. The women were in the street near a public phone box at the car park end of Hunters Beach, near by the toilet block. One of the women had called it in and said she had been chased up the road by the other woman and had barricaded herself in the call box. The woman doing all the shouting was a Laine Barclay - a short-arse blonde who already had a reputation for trouble. She was yelling and banging her fists on the plexi-glass saying that no one was 'gonna' tell her who she should or shouldn't fuck whether they were married or not. A real classy bit.

*

As we got out of the car, Johnny got his revolver out holding it by the barrel. Before Laine could react, Johnny hit her in the back of the head with the gun grip. As she fell down, he then yanked the door of the phone box open and pulled the second woman out by the hair, screaming and threw her down on to her knees. All this happened in under 20 seconds, no fucking about. Laine was still yelling, clutching her head, blood running through her blonde hair over her face. I watched as Johnny booted her in the side where she lay on the road. The first things he said was, "On your knees the both of you, and by Christ if either of you say another word..."

*The two women complied, the second woman was sobbing
quietly, mascara running down her face. She was older than
Laine; bit of nice mutton dressed as lamb.*

*

Pete recognised her as an old colleague of his late-mother's
from Coles. She was a weekend girl back then, but her name
escaped him, Joan, Jayne or Jen. She was a year ahead of him
at school as well. Whatever her name was, she recognised
Pete. He had asked her out when they were young and she'd
just gently laughed him off because she hung out with the
bikers and he was just a wavey haired boy with bum fluff and
a soft voice. Whatshername had been kind about it though and
was flattered that a younger boy like him had had the guts to
come across. He'd heard no more about it, so she hadn't told
anybody or made a donkey's arse out him in front of the other
girls or his mates.

"Johnny let her go. She's the one who called it in."

Without missing a beat, Johhny crouches down in front of my
old school crush.

"What's your name, my love?"

"Sophie."

"Sophie what, darling?"

"Sophie Moore."

*"Well Sophie Moore, do you want to see what happens to
women that waste police time over low-level shit like this?*

*We're not interested in the scuffles of pissant cunts like
you and your petty bullshit. It's fucking squid-piss, all this.
Fucking mongrels. We're sick and tired of it."*

Laine sobs, *"I've got blood in my eyes, I can't see."*

*"Shut the fuck up and wait your turn. Now, Sophie you know
Pete. We all know Pete. Pete, show her what you do best,
mate."*

*

*"That's when all logic went out the window. One minute I was
going to defend her honour, then she looked up at me, then
spat on my shoes. There was no reason for doing what came
next other than for the thrill of embroiling myself in something
so despicable and illicit, it wasn't as small as simple retalia-
tion. It was like Johnny read my mind as he dragged Sophie to
her feet, I walked over and punched her in the gut as hard as
I could. That's when the screaming started, the high-pitched
non-stop, one-note shriek - fear. On she went, every blow
caused her to screech even more at the top of her lungs. Laine
tried to scramble away on all fours but Johnny put a boot in
her back and she went sprawling. Johnny got a hammer from
the trunk of the car and demanded that Sophie stop it with
her infernal racket. But she was hysterical, swinging her fists
around, bloodied face and arms. Johnny dropped the hammer
on the dirt road and knocked her out cold with his fist. Down
like a slaughtered bull.*

*The next day, I left a bag of money on the doorstep of the
local biker chapter under Johnny's instructions, so there'd be
no reprisals after what we did to Sophie. Johnny explained
that we would be doing the town a favour if the prols on the*

poor side of town, with their own stuff to hide, stopped calling the cops every 5 minutes. It would go on to become fairly uncommon as rumours spread, but any domestics that did get reported were ours to put down. We'd finish the job the husband or boyfriend didn't.

For future 'incidents' or club meetings as he called them, Johnny advised me that there was to be a maximum of three body blows each, and you had to make them good ones. We never did anything these women couldn't walk away from. Strange thing is, is that when it was Nicole's turn Johnny told me to break her legs and only to stop when I saw the bones.

For years, you quietly think you're a freak, then one day you meet someone just like you and find that you're not alone.

You can go from day to day then something comes along that changes everything. What a funny thing to happen over half way through your life."

One Hundred and Nine

1994 - Uli

Can't Look At It, Can't Throw It Out

"The bastard better fucking settle up soon," thought Uli,
sucking on the remainder of a Winny Blue.

Some favour. 300 bucks he'd been fined for not collecting
the wreck in timely fashion. The one he'd dropped off
at Dewhurst Jail (PMRF) for Glenn Pearce. He'd never
begrudge Dean anything, but that fuck up had bounced off
the road and imbedded his tonner in a fucking muddy pile of
shit off the highway. *"Well I'm not fucking paying it,"* he said
screwing up his face. Nobody was around. Fucking smoke
had gone out. He felt in his pocket, nothing but a Durex.
Where the fuck was his lighter. *"No way. Fucking dog killer
can pay it."*

Uli stalks up the driveway to Dean's Queenslander and spikes
the court's summons for unpaid fees on a finial in the paint
chipped filigree gate at the foot of the front stairs. House
looked abandoned. He gets a strong whiff of girl's perfume
through the half-open garage door. Even at 9pm the air is
close and noisy with insects. But there it is again, the cloying
fruity aroma of some kind of all-body deodorant favoured by
young women of a certain age.

"Hello?"

Uli ventures forth and lifts the garage door. On the ground

floor there is a tiny apartment and a dunny off the garage area.
In the gloom, Uli could make out a trailer and the left over
parts of a motorbike of some description. Moonlight came in
through a back window aiding his progress and his limited
vision. The residue of light from the street silhouettes the
door left ajar to his right. As Uli pushes it open, he reaches
for a switch - a low-watt bulb comes on in the room to his
left, casting more shadow than illumination. The two rooms
in the tiny ground-floor apartment hadn't changed much at
all since he'd stayed there for a few weeks many years ago.
The wallpaper was the same and the bed hadn't moved. The
sideboard was sun kissed and worn out. These days the rooms
were full of Nicole's old things. Spread out on the grubby
double bed was a blouse and a pair of women's trousers.
Further attention to his surroundings gave up more anomalies
– in amongst the dusty tat were: kids toys, dolls prams, an
ironing board, car radios, piles of cassettes, CDs and a few
vinyl records. There was a smelly old microwave, its door
hanging open with the dark, dried out remains of a ready meal
plastered across its inside: why the fuck would you want to
keep that? Washing baskets full of Nicole's clothes vied with
the piles of comic annuals that filled the rickety shelves and
much of the floor space. Enid Blyton, 'The Secret Seven',
'Swallows and Amazons'. A poster from the film the 'Man
from Snowy River' was stuck up on the wall above the bed. A
sizeable, wooden toy fort lay in the shadows, plastic knights
on die-cast steeds, stood silently within its walls, swords
drawn but unprotected from the unstoppable layering of dust
that covered everything. The drawbridge raised - the fight on
hold. A buried clocked ticks.

All the girl's gear had been moved down here from her
bedroom upstairs, piled haphazardly, here in these gloomy

ante-rooms - a permanent half-light, the curtains drawn to expel most of the sun's glare during the day time; the yellow street lamps providing their colic rays at night. This space and its contents were too neglected to be a shrine, but dead or alive Nicole had achieved an unusual status - these rooms were haunted.

Dean was probably asleep in his hammock out back but he couldn't hear his mate snoring. Uli didn't particularly want to be caught snooping around Nicole's stuff, so he crept out the way he came in, undetected - like a fox.

One Hundred and Ten

1994 - Glenn and Dani

A Soft Spot For Repetition

Nurse Dani crept towards him, *"I thought that was you from a distance. Could you see me waving?"*

Glenn was perched on a bench near to the seldom-used city jetty. He was quietly observing a docked freighter, called Warratah. It was being used to dispense gravel via a mobile crane into one of a chain of five or six lorries. The tide was at its lowest with the boat rising slowly over time as its hold got emptied. He cast his mind back to a book he read and racked his memory to recall the words Plimsol Line but it stayed on his mind all day until he'd long left the waterside. Everything, he knew was precisely calculated in advance based on weights, tide times and the number of lorries needed to get the graded gravel into the stockades within a certain time window. The keels of the larger vessels, like this one, were literally centimetres off the riverbed in some places even at high tide. He'd read in the local paper that today's guest freighter had just come back from Singapore and was due to leave at 4am on the next big tide. The sound of the lorries' engines weren't that loud over here and he'd taken a few photos of the activity, he didn't know why. It was almost as if the hardworking lorries were re-enacting countless games he'd played alone with his toy trucks as a child. The reality looked every bit as fun, every bit as solitary, each driver alone in his cabin, grinding down the gears, right turn, reverse under the crane, forwards, left turn off the jetty, unload 300 yards away in the stockade, and repeat - a Sisyphyian order of bliss.

On quieter days, pied oystercatchers, curlews and other waders would look for food beneath the concrete jetty. Their calls echoing off the surface of the waters and the low bottom of the boardwalk conjuring up a fantastic effect, giving up an odd audio illusion that the birds were trapped inside a stone chapel.

"Hey, what you doing out here?"

"I read in the paper that a ship was in. I like to watch them load and unload."

"Never seen the jetty used myself."

"It's a rare sight. It's what stands for entertainment around here."

The crane drops a shower of gravel into one of the trucks.

"You know, I still don't know your name?"

Glenn turns to look at her but she's stood in direct sunlight. He tries to outflank the glare with his hand as she sits down next to him; still a shadow.

The red nurse is with her black and white mongrel that has charged off on towards some mud flats. *"Well the dog's called Geoff. And my name's Danielle. But friends at the hospital call me Nurse Dani."*

"Dani."

"Yes. So now you know. Just don't ever refer to me as that to anyone else in the context of you know what."

"Right."

"I haven't seen you for a few weeks. You met somebody. That's usually the reason for a gap in bookings."

"No. Just been, you know."

The dog stops running to sniff at something in the rocks that sit on the mud and sand flats.

"How's your hand?"

"Healing well." He wiggles his fingers.

"Think you'll be back?"

"To hospital or -"

"The second one."

The dog has since made it down to the water and is now running at full pelt along the shore. Dani leans in towards Glenn.

"I've got something for you, a souvenir."

Dani leans in and kisses him on the cheek.

Then she turns to watch the trucks for a minute. Nothing more is said as she stands and begins her walk back along the

path towards the jetty - whistling to attract Geoff's attention.
Glenn watches her until she's too small to make out anymore.
Always walking away. He inspects his bruised and bitten
hand. The sun burns his neck.

With the kiss Dani had confined herself to history. No one
ever knew about her and so far he'd never spoken of his
other worldly encounters with Dani, The Red Nurse, to
another living soul.

One Hundred and Eleven

1994 - The Chorus

Just A Face In The Wave

"I'm telling you, Dewhurst is not a good place to surf. It's shit mate."

"What are you on about? You got the north harbour wall where it breaks off the old jetty. Hunters too."

"That's two spots you've named, and if you think they're good you need to travel a bit more."

"It's fucking great. You can catch 10 footers on the regular."

"Once a decade if there's been a big storm out to sea, but mate if you're happy to surf in a nursery with groms and kooks that's your lookout"

"Yeah, fucking King Neptune over there, so what makes you so fucking good?"

"I've been surfing all over Australia, Bali, Hawaii, Seychelles and, mate, Dewhurst has nothing that compares to even an average beach down on the Sunshine Coast. There's enough to fart about on, but like I said you can't go shouting your mouth off about how you're king of the mountain in a piss pot surf spot like this."

"A piss pot surf spot, haha. All the boogs love it up at Hunters."

"Doesn't that tell you anything? If it's a boog's break then it's not a good surf spot."

"Bullshit. You seen those guys out there."

"A bunch of poofters too scared to stand up and face the sea, that's all I've seen."

"The boogies rip up Hunters at high tide, the shories kick ass, bud. You should fuck off to Gold Coast, leave us all to it, you're just bored and old."

"It doesn't really matter what you ride, ay. But Dewhurst is not a surf town. Never has been."

"Ok your point is made."

"If the city put investment into building an artificial reef out there past the marina, that might just change this place for the better, put it on the tourist map. Sea swimmers, groms, boogs and you. It's lame."

"Well thanks for that arsehole."

One Hundred and Twelve

1985 - Glenn

Arise A Knight

Glenn reckons wet suits are for bloody wimps. That's what his dad always says yet he still wears one for surfing too.

The strong easterly nags at the peaks, slicing their tops off - sunset coloured beads of saltwater fly skywards. The water's about three metres deep or more here and he begins to sing in a low voice to chase away the fear inside. Now and again he'll feel fish butt into his legs and feet, as long as it's not shark or a box jellyfish he's OK.

"Apparently if a box jelly fish gets on to you, you still scream out from your coma," he tells himself.

For several minutes, there's a lull and suddenly the sea's become low on its stock-in-trade: its waves - the sky is hard. There he sits on the shoulders of the ocean as it undulates, worshipping its simple yet colossal movements. Heavy and alive, he imagines that he's so vital to his environment that he can feel the sea salt pulsate over his narrow body. Glenn punches his right fist into the air, *"Wahooooooo!!!"*

As if to answer his call, the wind picks up, snatching the sound away. He spots a sea change as the ghost of a once mighty storm picks up and the swell begins to gather a pace. The doldrums no more. Glenn points his board back to shore, how far away the land is, the fringe of saltwater and foam, and he begins to paddle, his power pack renewed, the crest of a waveform closes the gap.

Arise a knight, arise a knight.

One Hundred and Thirteen

1971 - Gully

'A Break Away!' By Tom Roberts

The tumbling sound of a rampant sheep flock hurtling down a dry earth worn slope, the red dust, and the one that got away. The renegade adolescent causes the other sheep behind to dart left and right around the half-rotten beast of a tree, now an island in the living flow of animals. The beleaguered wooden fence, destroyed without knowing it. Sun bleached grass. The boundary riders on their tamed brumbies are tilted in stasis to the right as the stampede congeals before his eyes. Gully loved this painting. He came by the gallery every day to look at it. Straining his eyes and ears for a sound, some movement.

Gully had read that the painter of this scene, Tom Roberts, though not Australian by birth, was considered, along with Streeton, to be the true founding father of modern Australian art. He understood that he too saw and knew Australia from within, and to record what he saw, he borrowed from the Impressionists - their robust, vivid, colourful and resourceful style. Most Australians at the time that *'A Break Away!'* was painted (circa 1891) were remarkably unaware of the nature within their vast land and through his works, Roberts offered an exploration for them.

"Nature's scheme of colour in Australia is gold, then blue in an uneven rotation," said the young woman standing to Gull's left.

Of course, she's right. The light reflecting off the floor of the exhibition space is golden.

One Hundred and Fourteen

1991 - Dean

Pour Down Like Silver

Dean knocks a neglected cup of cold coffee over the paper work he was looking at. *"Oooh shit."*

He slowly gets to his feet out of his dilapidated chair in the even more dilapidated office-cum-shed. Betsy gets to her feet too. *"How much can you eat, huh? Always hungry Betsy."*

The dog walks out the door, a slow wag of the tail in recognition of her name, an instinctive response. Dean looks at the puddle of coffee. Picks up the paperwork - sopping. Shaking the liquid off the top sheet he decides the damage isn't too bad and the subsequent pages of the balance sheet he'd been working on are virtually unscathed. Dean scrubs the coffee into the filthy red carpet with his foot. It was just another oil stain, mud stain, who knows. All he knew was that if he dropped any food down there it was Betsy's and no longer his. It was disgusting, but who went in there besides him and the dog?

Dean gathers up the paperwork and leaves the hut. The evening is warm and noisy with the sound of cars on the bypass, voices carried down from the school where Nicole, Fallon and others would be playing netball about now, birds on the wing and the incessant squeal of the crickets and tropical bugs. Dean files the paperwork under the windscreen wiper of a Toyota Corolla with three wheels and a cracked windscreen - salvageable, maybe. The car was once his own, and he hadn't driven it since Nicole was tiny and his ex-wife, Jeanne was still on the scene. They'd often drive up to her parents' farm out in a tiny place about 30 kilometres north of Dewhurst called Yalbaroo - the name of which he searched for in his mind for at least 10 minutes. As far as he knew the father was still alive, but the farm was rented out to some young fellas now. Nicole used to play out on the huge sloped field at the front of the property.

"Stomp your feet, make them snakes run away!" Dean would shout to her as the adults all sat on the porch supping cold beer in the shade.

"Snakes can't run. They have no legs!" Nicole would laugh.

Jeanne's father, Val, had bought the farm from selling his share in a quarrying business inland - it was right before a class action suit was brought against the mine for the mining and milling of blue asbestos. He'd gotten out just in time.

Decades earlier, a whole town, Volker, got wiped off the map quite literally by the Australian Government, totally de-gazetted. It was walled off, roads torn up, buildings dynamited, access signs and mile posts uprooted or painted over. All of its residents were relocated, the mines closed down and the town was gradually left behind by the outside world, all but forgotten. If you ever stumbled across it by some unholy miracle, the very air you'd take down into your lungs would happily shave weeks off your lifespan, a great reason to visit. Prolonged exposure to crocidolite exponentially increased the likelihood of contracting pleural and peritoneal mesothelioma - a terrible way to go.

So when miners and townsfolk began to die, the mine bosses
were made accountable, yet the government was too slow
to act and it took decades to bring a class action case of any
kind. Most of the bosses were without conscience and bought
their way out of trouble - payoffs were made to victims,
officials, government lobbyists - it was a real cluster fuck and
a scandal best left strangled in the desert.

Val was permanently paranoid that he'd be singled out to
account for all the pay outs to people when the whistle got
blown, so he accumulated every stitch of paperwork from the
mine offices to put him in the clear, but nothing ever came
out - the bribes kept everyone happy, somehow and he'd
never know how. Yet on the quiet he was a man possessed and
he thought about the consequences of his former company's
actions every day. He acquired copies of every stitch of legal
paperwork pertaining to international and Australian industrial
class actions he could lay his hands on. He wanted everything
in case they came a calling: the victims, the law.

Dean had been asked to assist with the delivery of all the
crates and boxes that turned up at the farm but had declined
to help. This was at the time he was having a bad time with
Jeanne and wasn't inclined to do any of her lot any favours at
all. The boxes got took up to the cowsheds, but when the farm
was rented out years later the boxes were transferred to the
house. To Dean's knowledge nobody ever showed up from the
mines, and even to this day he's sure nothing will ever come
of it.

II

The spilt coffee cup set in motion a muted chain of events that resulted in Dean taking a drive out to his former in-laws' farm. On arrival at Yalbaroo, he pulled off the Bruce Highway and parked under a row of eucalyptus trees about 200 yards down the hill from his in-laws' house. He saw his ex-mother-in-law sat on the porch staring ahead blankly, lost in her thoughts. She was smoking a cigarette. Dean entertained himself by absent-mindedly timing his own inhalations from his own smoke with hers. Jeanne was long gone now and he hadn't concerned himself with any serious thoughts about her in a very long time. His ex-wife had dropped him like a shitty stone. She'd fell in love with another man. What could he do about that? You can't force someone to stay in love with you. And you can't become more loveable to make them stay either. In marriage sometimes, love isn't enough is it?

What was his reason for going up to the farm that day? If he'd just shown up on his in-laws' veranda it would only arouse suspicion - he searched his mind for logic.

Looking up at the rural Queenslander, Dean liked that nothing had changed in the 12 or so years since he'd last been there. It was nice, at first, to get some fresh forgotten memories of Nicole as a girl back. Thoughtful, playful but inconsolable if you burst her bubble with adult cruelty.

He thought about a day when he was unloading a car from Uli's flatbed truck and Nicole had been fooling around with their first dog, Milt, in the close vicinity. She was *'The Man from Snowy River'* and Milt was her brumby and he'd already told her to go and play at the front of the house. The devil had flown first into his mouth then his body as he bundled himself out of the car, and jumped down off the flatbed. The drop was further than he thought and he landed unevenly in a pothole, hurting his foot. Nicole tried to move out of his way but as he went to grab her under the arm pit to haul her out of his yard, she veered to the left and he caught her at full-tilt, slamming her in the nose with his upturned palm. The dog started to bark uncontrollably as Nicole hit the ground. Uli had intervened at this point, not seeing the contact as an accident from his angle up in the cab of the truck. *"Dean, she's only kid. Fuck! What the fuck are you doing?"*

Milt continued to bark alerts, misunderstanding Uli's intentions to help Nicole to her feet.

"Go get yourself cleaned up, here." Uli gave her ten bucks in an attempt to stop her crying. *"She's just a fucking kid Dean. What's your game, we don't hit children, s'a fucking mug's game?"*

Dean grips the steering wheel with both hands and exhales his last mouthful of ciggie smoke as the memory draws old heat. He hadn't noticed or heard the ute draw up alongside his truck. He stubs out his cigarette. Inside the other vehicle is a young man, with blonde hair and a kind, baby face that carried a crap attempt at a goatee and moustache on it.

"Can I help?"

"Ah, no thanks mate. I just pulled off the highway for a short rest."

"Well this is a private driveway, just so you know."

"I never realised, I'm sorry."

"Sign fell down - on my to-do list. A long way down. No one ever really stops here anyway. Where you headed?"

"Not sure."

The young man nods, inhales a long breath, and looks ahead up the rising road. Without looking back at Dean, he begins to speak again. Even more friendlier than before.

"Well, it's no biggie mate. Stay here as long as you need, there's nothing big coming or going today and, er, safe journey."

"Thanks, I appreciate it."

"I do sort of recognise you though. Have we met?"

"I'm not sure. I live in Dewhurst. I fix cars."

"I'd assumed you'd come from Bowen direction, you know, on account of you having a rest an' all."

"No. I set off and suddenly felt tired."

Dean's mother-in-law stood up on the balcony at the house in the distance and waves. The young driver in the ute waves back to her.

"Well, I'll be leaving you. Enjoy Yalbaroo. This is all there is to it."

Dean smiles and nods: this, he already knew.

One Hundred and Fifteen

1991 - Pete and Johnny

No Other Evil - Get A Little Dirt On Your Hands

Pete and Johnny rolled up in the rover outside the soiled
bungalow. A very late night call - pushed so far into the small
hours there was a lick of tomorrow's light at the base of the
sky canvas. Even people with nothing conformed to a sad
file of rules and regs, a lack of imagination shared across the
species, poor or rich, all conforming to their furrow, *"Get
in where you fit in, yer fucking cartoons."* All these houses,
looked the same, a similar lack of care by the residents to
look after their cheap housing made them fall in line with
another - tricked into being cookie cutter cunts like everyone
else. All the tatty single-level Queenslanders had snazzy
custom-built or enhanced cars parked in front of them regardless of whether there was a hard standing or a torn up section
of mud and grass. The once white painted bungalow looked
like a perverted jack-o-lantern in the gloom, untrustworthy,
blinkered windows as eyes, the door depping for a fucked up
boxer's nose and mouth. A defunct fridge towered over the
front path. The door gaped open: an acidic fish smell mixed
with refuge on a hot day masked the cops' sweet cologne.
They'd bought each other identical Christmas presents,
an awkward embarrassment that both men are constantly
reminded of but never comment on. Tough cops, close like
lovers.

Dawn Carmichael, mixed race, half-Aborigine, half-bogan,
more bone than flesh. She was sat smoking cigarette and

nursing a bottle of VB on the front step. The men couldn't
see but her gums were bloody, and her knuckles ripped open,
bruises formed quickly around her narrow rib cage and
woebegone boobs.

Pete -   *"I gotta say Dawn, I'm pretty fucking sick of
                coming out here every time he raises his hand to
                you."*

Dawn -   *"It's called a fucking domestic Pete. He was
                gonna kill me."*

Pete -   *"Miles. Come on mate were you really gonna kill
                her? Or did you just give her a nice love tap to
                establish the order around here?"*

Dawn -   *"You what?"*

Pete -   *"I'm talking to Miles. Miles?"*

'The poster pin-up-no-more' Miles, curly hair sprouting out of
his shoulders and forest-like out of the giant hoop head hole
of his bloodied yellow and red singlet, shambled into view in
the doorway above where his partner in-brawl was sat. Dawn
had obviously got a few punches in as the fat lump had a
blood bogey temporarily sealing off one of his nostrils. The
once promising Miles had succumbed to boredom and class A
drugs at a young age, swapping potential for cheap thrills and
getting addicted to that mysterious ticklish feeling in his balls
that stopped him focusing on anything long enough to solve
whatever was happening to him.

Miles -   *"I'm not gonna kill her, course not. It was just a
               fight."*

Dawn -   *"Fucking liar."*

Dawn stood up and pushed past Miles and disappeared into
the house. They all followed suit. The house smelled like
'Lily of the Valley' and that oaty smell of bad drugs and
unwashed bodies. The room centred around a nice top-of-
the-range television, and predictably rotten couches, and
half-eaten take-away food. Nothing was out of place or
surprising in this scene to either of the policemen.

Miles -   *"Calm down, Dawn, come on."*

Pete -   *"Now you called us screaming blue murder,
               we've come over, yet you're still standing,
               shouting the odds. You look alright to me. Now
               I want to understand exactly what we missed. I
               mean, Miles, if you just gave her a stroke I don't
               want to have to come out here to find out how she
               felt about it. But if you're beating her the fuck up
               and got her close to death's door, we might, and I
               mean just might want to hear from you. We want
               a ringside seat. A bucket of barbecued chook
               wings, ay!"*

Johnny -   *"A cold Tooheys."*

Pete -   *"Or two."*

Dawn -   *"What the fuck are you saying?"*

Pete -   *"Shut the fuck up. I don't think we'll be taking
                Miles in this time. Waste of time. What do you
                think Sarge?"*

Johnny -   *"Well you see Dawn, we need to see exactly how
                events unfolded to assess if Miles needs to be
                booked or not. Now Miles. Go over to Dawn and
                smack her -"*

Dawn made a break for the front door but Pete was quicker
and slammed her in the face with his fist - a love tap. Then he
reached down to pick Dawn up with a handful of tangled hair,
who by then had a broken nose. He pushed her towards the
utterly bewildered and fugly Miles.

Pete -   *"Show us."*

Dawn -   *"No, get fucked."*

Miles -   *"Seriously?"*

Pete -   *"Yeah, fucking show us."*

Miles didn't need asking twice, he pulled his wife/girlfriend
towards him by the shoulders and backslapped her in the face,
hard. The small woman hit the deck with a clatter of clothed
skin and bone.

Johnny -   *"Any more?"*

Pete -   *"Kick the bitch."*

Miles -   *"No. No. Pete, Pete, I only slapped her. That's
                all."*

Dawn was on all fours trying to crawl away. Johnny grabbed her and pulls her to her feet.

Johnny -   *"If you don't mate. I will."*

Miles -   *"I've heard about you guys. The rumours. I never believed it."*

Pete -   *"Shut the fuck up and finish this."*

The lamp in the corner of the room flickered. All four of the room's occupants looked at each other in silence. Then the light went out. With only the TV to illuminate the room, the unlikely quartet watched as Mel Gibson jumped off a building, followed by his 80's mullet. The spell was broken. Dawn began to sob.

Johnny relinquished his hold on Dawn. The scared women then crouched down flat on her belly on the filthy red pattern carpet. She paws at it as if she's looking for a way out or way to escape into the system of interlocking green and yellow hoops and octagons.

Pete -   *"Let's go. The thrill is gone."*

Johnny -   *"Okay,"* then he spat on the floor

Pete -   *"Don't you ever fucking call us again. And Miles, you keep your mouth shut or I'm coming back here for both of yous. Fucking scum."*

Johnny -   *"Saved by a screwy lightbulb."*

Then Pete spat on the carpet too. Twins. He then stalked out of the house in-step behind his mate.

Johnny -   *"You left the blues on, Pete."*

The whole street was awash with the blue light as it silently revolved at a slow pace atop the police rover.

Johnny -   *"How's your fist?"*

Pete -   *"Bit sore."*

Johnny -   *"I got an esky in the trunk, some ice in there."*

Pete -   *"Fucking pussies."*

Johnny -   *"Nice tonner though."*

Nodding to the truck splayed on the driveway as they left.

They heard a door slam behind them and the two men pretty much ignored Dawn's shrill voice as it screamed at Miles from inside the house behind them.

The sun was rising. A new day. Doused hope. Black trees. An unfolding flower in a corporate bouquet sent without sincerity.

One Hundred and Sixteen

1994 - Glenn

Couldn't Wait To Get Going, Wasn't Ready To Leave

Glenn was wide-awake when he swerved to miss the dog with the name Sarah. The jail was only two and a bit hours' drive south of the neon baked city limits of Dewhurst but he'd booked a room at a highway motel and would sleep his first sleep in a comfy double bed in three years - the cool air-conditioning, the cold cotton sheets. It was a cut-price effort and it was all Glenn needed. He'd slept all day well into the quiet hours of the night.

His tonner, borrowed from Dean's mate Uli, cut through the black velvet night like an armoured Viking berzerker.

The dog rolled under the wheels, playing the bongos on the sump as it went. The tonner itself fishtailed and hit the raised earth bank - as the vehicle headed off the road and into a 360 spin, decreasing in speed, it sent red dirt skywards. Glenn's arms flew off the steering wheel and his head slammed against the door column.

The air was wet, so was his shirt, his shorts, his thongs, his drink had spilled, it wasn't piss, or maybe it was (details). Glenn did a slow inventory of his faculties - his feet were still atop of the pedals and he could wiggle his toes OK, yet one of his fingers felt very painful.

The car door voluntarily creaked open by itself like the tonner was haunted. The moment of truth eventually arrived as Glenn stood up straight - he was OK, yet somehow, the dog was still alive on the road.

The insects saw everything from their vantage point below the streetlight. There were so many of them in attendance, they all saw what happened, there was no point in passing on their version of events to their neighbour.

One Hundred and Seventeen

1995 - Vella

Is That A Dagger Or A Crucifix I See?

So within five months of her arrival in Dewhurst, Ari and
Vella and the children had then relocated again to Leura in the
Blue Mountains, two hours west of Sydney.

Nothing happens overnight, you can't change a man, but after
relocating, Vella swore off the booze and joined Alcoholics
Anonymous (just to laugh at the other losers locked in the
aquarium with him he said). With a renewed vigour and
a considerable promotion at work on the horizon, if he
continued to bring in good results, the Vella family were in
danger of salvaging all that was lost when he was pushed
out to Dewhurst. Ari wonders how they fell so far apart so
quickly, and why such fractures take so long to fix up again
- like a mining accident, some seams burn and smoulder for
decades beneath the surface, the fire of the matter only visible
through cracks and fissures.

Within a month of moving to the Blue Mountains, Vella
became good friends with his next-door neighbour, a Maori
called Tama, a self-styled guitar mechanic. With Tama's
help, Vella took up an old hobby of playing the electric guitar
and the two often sat in the former's garage talking shit and
jamming on their days off. There was even talk of starting up
a band.

Tama was a reformed holy drinker too and he told Vella how

he had wrecked his marriage three years before and was permanently estranged from his wife and kids who lived in New Plymouth, New Zealand.

"One fisherman spots another from afar."

Vella needed a friend and this fuck-up was a good fit.

II

Within another six months, Vella was dead: the result of a freak accident that occurred during a rescue attempt on some climbers, a day's trek south west of Katoomba into the bush.

When briefing his team on location, he'd stepped backwards off a cliff, mid-sentence, into a ravine. His last words were, *"Let's kick this pig."*

Vella's remains, which amounted to very little in the end, won't be recovered until everybody in this story is very old, long buried and forgotten about.

His lost body buckled as it hit rock after rock, pulverising him as he plummeted into the patiently receptive tree canopy way below. It is there that his rag dolled corpse remained, slumped over a strong forked branch some 25 feet above the valley floor for almost forever.

Within hours of his death, Vella's unembalmed remainder was to have its blackening extremities and bloating skin and flesh beneath eaten and broken down by thirsty burrowing insects; this was followed by frequent visits from intrepid, pecking, hungry birds within the next eight. The rest of the unfortunate

Maltese detective was left in peace to rot away in the daily heat before the rotten fat and muscles tissue holding his bones together in his ragged clothes would get washed away in the rains. Over the course of a 45-year period, his final bones would also fall to the ground only to be scattered by animals and flash floods over an area larger than his beloved Malta. Only his belt, service revolver, his wallet and the rags of his trousers were ever recovered. The mystery of his whereabouts solved without energy, almost 50 years later. His face in the newspaper - no one cared.

One Hundred and Eighteen

1995 - Mr Madonna

Let No Man Put Asunder

When Mr Madonna got wind of Vella's freak death, he threw a party at his tiny apartment. The only guests were his on-off older boyfriend Len, and his pet teacup terrier, Ryan.

One Hundred and Nineteen

1991 - Glenn

Gentle November

It's early. Very early, down at the marina, Glenn can sense the offshore southerly rising. The shackles and guide ropes start to bang out a louder drunken rhythm on their various props and masts. Flags and loose sail covers whip and contort in the wind, an irritated, tethered dance. The water is turning black as the sun spectacularly fails to rise. The slate-coloured sky is not good for the cracking. Our bright star has not seen fit to grace the ensuing day instead heralding a wind, and a messy swell; all body, no apex.

Glenn reasons that trouble awaits them over the horizon, so he squares up to the fact that him and Robbie will not be going down the coast in his speedboat to a 'sweet' fishing spot beyond the passage men long dead had dynamited through the coral and rocks. About ten nautical miles south there's a sand atoll called Zulu Bank, miles of sea bird colonies, noise and the smell of dead fish and guano everywhere. *"Stinks like fuck, but it is gorgeous out there. You've been I'm sure of it."*

"Wasn't with me."

*

The clouds eventually separate to reveal a calm sea, smooth and quartz. The speedboat, Sea Cow, is launched momentarily as they skim across the bommie on their way out. Robbie whoops, laughing. Getting past the bombara always made him cheer, like he was escaping everybody in Dewie. The bloke loved the sea. Didn't they all? But Robbie was into boats, wanted to be a marine engineer but would settle for being a local and well-respected boat mechanic with a good business down on Cook Street later in life.

About 40 minutes out, they drop anchor, and the ocean shivers, the sun replicated on the water's surface a million times in the small waves. Robbie dashes overboard with his spear gun and he's already 4 metres down below by the time Glenn had gotten a single flipper safely on his foot.

Looking down to the limestone and sandy bottom Glenn sees a swirl of pomfret, the odd breaksea cod, and other species he doesn't know the name of. Robbie knows every fish or so he thought. With the flippers now installed he was just about ready to plunge below the surface when Robbie resurfaces, with a grin on his chops. He clambers into the boat on his belly and begins to frantically reel in a large fish he'd speared through the head.

"What is it?"

"Dunno, never seen one. Have to look him up later," huffs Robbie, merrily. *"Let's put him in the hold."*

They pop open a compartment in the base of the boat and throw the unidentified golden fish below and put the lid back on.

"Again?" Robbie doesn't wait for a reply and probably hadn't even noticed that Glenn hadn't even been 'in' yet.

One the horizon, Glenn can make out a Japanese cargo ship,
the name on the side is undecipherable. He sits back down
and kicks his flippers off. Glenn removes the compartment lid
and looks at the dead fish. The calm water laps the hull of the
boat.

*"Tons of fox fish, bream, cod, all sorts down here mate…
come on. Come see."* Robbie disappears again.

*

About an hour later they head out for Zulu Bank to stretch
their legs. Glenn would think about Nicole, wondering where
she was. What had prompted her absence for days on end?
Had he done something to provoke her, put her off him? And
now Jocasta. He shouldn't have fucked her. It was just mates.
A trip out for some ice cream and a half-good film had been
the idea. 'Some time' they'd said but that had evolved into
later the same day after he ran into her at the servo. Was she
seriously making a play for him? All they did was misunder-
stand one another, whilst him and Nicole just glided along
together like the fish he'd just been with that day. It was
just easy with her. But now she'd been avoiding him. And it
had only taken him three days for him to stray, to sleep with
someone else.

*

Robbie didn't ask and Glenn didn't volunteer info on what
had happened the night before. The storm had threatened to
break, a wind had shook the palm fronds in the front garden
as he lay on his bed, he listened to the wooden house creak
around them - Jocasta fast asleep next to him. Glenn had crept
out of bed. They'd done it twice. Once right away, and the
second time in lieu of conversation - an avoidance of asking

where, if anywhere, all this would lead. She didn't stir, even when he kissed her on the shoulder before he left the bedroom to meet Robbie at the marina. The inauspicious last kiss.

*

"Were you in that lesson, ages ago when Ballbags was talking about an alien spaceship trapped in the Earth's orbit?"

"No Robbie... Maybe."

"He didn't get very far, cos some dickheads were talking shit and he threw us all out. But I went back and asked him stuff... and he said that there's some people reckon that this object known as The Black Knight has been up there in our orbit for over 10,000 years. 10,000 years mate."

"It's an asteroid, I reckon..."

"No it's a spaceship. Top secret. You can even see it on a clear night through a telescope. Next time you're over mine I'll show you..."

"Imagine if a spaceship, came down right now, here on Zulu Bank... No one would believe us. How would we prove it...? We could just go back now and say, 'Hey we saw a spaceship."

"What would you get out of making up such bullshit?"

"That's my point... Why does this spaceship caught in our orbit have to be bullshit..? It's a fact, why would people make something like that up?"

One Hundred and Twenty

1994 - Pete

O For The Wings Of A Dove

In the Ted Hughes poem 'The Moors' he describes the Peak District as, *"...a stage for the performance of heaven."* Pete Wilson's mother was transfigured by poetry. Her books were her 'escape' as she put it. She'd squirrel a small volume into her handbag and quietly read some verse on her lunch breaks at Coles. He found a green covered notebook amongst her things after her death, it was full of passages she'd noted from books she'd read, lines of poetry; purple prose from novels. He hadn't heard of many of them beyond seeing their names on the spines of his mother's small collection as he was growing up. Similarly in the books themselves, passages had been underlined or the corners of pages folded over. The underlined sections usually pertained to a description of the divine, or a light, a wide-open space, the wild sea, a dark forest... On the front she'd written the words, 'All heaven breaking loose'.

Above the TV was a giant print of a black and white photograph, a panorama of a rocky mountain range with a pine forest on its steppes - a cheap print of an Ansel Adams effort. Against the white peaks and you could discern the falling snow if you took the time to look closely at it. Pete had kept her notebook but everything else got scattered to the four winds, he didn't want any of it. The small book was all he wanted, his Mother's delicate handwriting and those other worldly word confections that you could never hope to utter in the real world. Not here anyway.

Up on the moors, God's real estate, the fog wasn't clearing
and Pete watched his footing carefully. After an age he stood
at the edge of a vehicle track that wound further up the hill.
Perhaps this was part of one of the national walking paths. He
knew he had to be nearing the highest point of the Roaches
because he'd been climbing for a long time yet the fog had
still to burn off. All he could see was the trail's ascent and
loads of animal shit.

Pete stopped walking, partly to rest, partly to listen. It was so
quiet all he heard was the rustle of material on his weather
inappropriate coat. He did think to bring his Akubra hat to
England with him and this gave him some protection from the
elements today.

Only in the wilderness is man made pure again.

Pete watched the fog blow across the headland like gun
smoke on a civil war battlefield. Fucking England and its sun
that gives no warmth.

Adrift in a cloud, O'Little Lamb, Who Made Thee?

One Hundred and Twenty One

1980 - Glenn

Horses, Horses, Horses

I can remember this kind music teacher I had in primary school, a Pommie fella called Tony Morton. We'd all congregate in the school hall and the curtains were drawn so that the light was dim. The session was called 'Music and Movement' and us nippers just loved it. In our vests and undies, we'd imagine ourselves to be whatever Mr Morton told us we were in his booming voice. The whole class would run rings around the outside of the hall with our teacher at the centre.

About 15 years ago a memory came back to me, I'd heard this forgotten song in a café in Brisbane. The urgent chorus and the desperate energy coming from the singer as she orated, "Horses, Horses, Horses."

I had to know what it was as it was one of the songs we'd gallop in circles to in our sessions. Whinnying and shaking our heads, leaping over imaginary hedges or dead fall. "Horses, Horses, Horses."

The man in the café looked at me incredulously, "Mate, its Patti Smith's 'Horses.' You don't know this?"

But I did and for the next half an hour as I nursed my coffee on that cold morning I journeyed back. The next time I was in the city I looked for a record store and bought the CD. I think of the people we became, all the boyhood chatter, the playground politics.

When I was a very small boy, very small boys talked to me.

One Hundred and Twenty Two

1991 - Mark

You Got To Pray Just To Make It Today

The record shop, 'Marks', was very small and sat at the corner of a tiny indoor mall that inversely cut the corner of Seeley and Bourke Street, kind of dog legging around the back of a larger surf clothing shop called Pratts. The owner, Mark, was only just catching on to the fact that vinyl was being replaced with CDs. So long-boxed CDs mingled with the stock of records. A lot of the kids came in to buy the pop stuff and the older boys had a penchant for gangster rap. Mums & pops still visited to get their Johnny Cash and Charley Pride box-sets too. The stream of customers was the quiet side of steady with a peak around an hour after school broke out, so he closed up about five to half five.

Kerry 'the sleaze' would come in to buy stuff, probably his best customer, but it was an irritation how he'd lean on the shelves and hang over the teenagers like he was one of them, asking the girls leading questions and being over 'matey' with the lads. A lot of the boys humoured him yet they couldn't relax or let their guard down because they never knew what he wanted from them. They knew he liked girls and wasn't a bum feeler - yet he was over-sincere, a bit too nice to be the genuine article. He'd hassle Nicole Wexler no end. Putting his hand on hers, touching her arse ever so slightly with the back of his hand as she flicked through the racks. She never moved away or said all that much though. Nicole would only buy cassettes, cassette singles mainly or compilations.

"Do you like MC Hammer, Nicole?"

"No...not really."

"Oh, I thought I heard you playing Pray in your car the other morning..."

"It might have been the radio?"

Fucking Kerry, licking his lips like a lizard. Mark wished he had an excuse to throw him the fuck out.

One Hundred and Twenty Three

2019 - Roo

When I Was A Child, I Thought As A Child

Roo Stamper wasn't a bad bloke. He'd just had the mantle of being the town arsehole thrust upon him. You know those films where you're meant to back an honourable criminal, you make allowances for them because he's 'less' bad than the other baddies and you have faith that he'll come good and redeem himself, either by helping a dame or a man-child with learning difficulties. Perhaps this was taking things a bit too far in Roo's case, but there were expectations. His family were rich, they could trace their lineage all the way back to England and the very first white settlers in the Dewhurst region, the ones that had done deals with the local Yuibera people, of which, today, there were no trace. His father, Lionel Stamper, had donated some diaries to a local trust, one of which was written by one of their ancestors detailing some of the earliest information about the area and the settlement of Dewhurst. Roo had never forgotten a short chapter he'd read when he'd been allowed to handle the books one day. It recounted how his distant dead relative had chased and hunted kangaroos through the bush with packs of dogs. Roo had shuddered involuntarily at the account with its cold prose and matter of fact manner.

Roo's progress from a young boy had been watched avidly by Dewhurst's older generations who had grown up with his grandfather, grandmother, mother and father and all in all he'd lived up to it. When he began to realise that the respect

that other children had shown had been inherited rather
than earned on his own merits, he'd then push them to see
how much he could get away with. Giving them a thump if
they touched his toys and other acts of tiny tyranny, but as
he grew older, he began to learn that unlike other kids, he
wasn't forced to tow the line by adults. His schoolteachers
and parents would scold him briefly in passing and move on
swiftly. He had a circle of protectors, even amongst kids his
age. Children of locals that were trying to curry favour with
his parents. This was because his mother and father were both
city councillors and on virtually every committee to approve
new builds, grants, and government loans (details).

With the death of his beloved dog Sarah came a turning point.
Loads of his goons 'raised up' and wanted to punish that
accidental killer and girl-beating brute Glenn Pearce. The
vet's bill had come to hundreds of dollars, just for putting her
down, but that's not what irked him. This prick was unapolo-
getic, he never came to the house to say he was sorry, he just
went and holed up at Dean Wexler's or down at Motel 501
serving drinks in that scummy club. Some people play the
victim their whole life without knowing it.

Poor dog, he'd since missed being awoken every morning,
about 6:30, by her. She would nose his leg and sit at the
side of the bed until he got up to walk her along the beach.
Depending on the time of year, they caught the sunrise. The
last morning he walked her, a gigantic oil tanker was out
beyond in open waters beyond the estuary. It was dropping
anchor and he noticed the low, rapid rumble of its colossal
chain as its links plunged below the surface, a bassy 'toi toi
toi' echo off the water's back. Sarah would bark at the birds
as she ran along the shore. She would often run in a huge arc

around him, kicking up sand as she took a corner. Racing the kite-surfers through the shallows was one of his all-time favourite things to watch. The uncut joy of a dog at play - few things could make him happier.

After confronting Glenn at Johnny Pearce's funeral and the fight had broken out he'd been put in the cooler by one of the younger cops. With an abrupt change, comes a rethink. His first time in a cell. This cop didn't care for the local form of just letting him out with a few cursory words and a tipped wink. Bloke's name was Brett Coulson and you could tell he was a dedicated cop and wasn't one for talking. He was rough too. So, no dog, and an afternoon in a lock up.

*

Years later, Roo had become known as Mr Stamper, headmaster of North Dewhurst High and an national advocate against bullying in all its forms, a staunch feminist, pro-active on equal rights for disabled students and a spokesman on tribal land rights - a real stand up guy. He never left Dewhurst and he successfully turned himself around from being a lout for the first 22 years of his life into somebody that was worthy of the following he had automatically enjoyed back then. People all over town would stop and talk to him and old people would joke that they knew he'd grow up into a good bloke one day.

Roo celebrated his retirement by buying himself a launch that he would name Sarah and he was never short of fishing buddies. He never married.

One Hundred and Twenty Four

1994 - Ari

Some Songs Catch Me Out, Sometimes

Wasn't it Ari that had demanded that Vella apply for a transfer? She'd had a terrible time fitting in with all the other women her age in Dewhurst. *"Get in where you fit in…"* the unofficial town motto had put her at odds with the 'school run mums', the dessert clubs, the book reading circles. Her interest in classical music, world cinema, interesting wines and tasteful fashion had singled her out as one to be a bit wary of, *"She's a bit up herself that one…"*

There was nothing to talk about with the majority of them beyond the latest 'news' on who had left their husband, whose daughter had won the junior literature prize for an awful ditty about a naughty kangaroo, who had won the local fruit pie bake off, and that whoever was out of hearing range was a complete bitch, a prick tease, a bad mother or a moron. Where did all these bogans-with-money come from? All their kids had made up names like Boden, Dax, Zuckuss, Kugan and Brontay too; all these names were for villains in a 1970s space-soap opera or a hard-surface floor cleaner. There was almost a culture in their lack of culture. Ari truly hated feeling like a snob but what option did she have when she'd been dragged out of a life of relative comfort to this empty and endless corridor of tropical blandness? Dewhurst - what distinguished, fuckwit pioneer decided it was a good idea to put a flag in the map and establish a city right here?

Their children liked Dewhurst though and had made lots of friends at school. Luca, who was eight, had slotted in at the top of his set and was a hit with the other boys, who loved a bit of name calling and rough and tumble. Anyone who wasn't blonde or ginger was called a fob, or a pinoy sh*t, chink or wog. Luca had set them straight by telling these poisonous little lambs that his father was the new sheriff and had the keys to many jails - also that race hate made you the lowest of the low. She had been worried about racism moving so far out, but luckily none of the 'mums' had said anything in her earshot yet.

Maria, who was six, made a few little friends here and there, as opposed to being the 'big hit' her son was back then. They were always at each other's houses and they loved to play 'make believe' or scribbling felt-tip drawings that often featured family members. Ari would secretly laugh at the colourful portraits of Marcos with a circular body, an outsized baldhead, a jazzy shirt and a gap-toothed grin. When he would see these drawings he would chase Maria around the house saying that he would eat her up if she didn't make him look like Charlie Sheen.

Ari thought it would be a shame to pull Luca and Maria out of school again, but the good, humorous relationship she usually enjoyed with her Marcos had begun to fray.

"You are even more beautiful than Gina Lollobrigida." he used to whisper in her ear. *"I want to slurp your pussy up like a milkshake."*

One Hundred and Twenty Five

1994 - Glenn

Let Me Live By Your Side Everyday

Looking down over the Marina from his borrowed apartment Glenn witnessed a bag snatch. A girl in the surfer's 'uniform' - tanned, blonde hair, Oakleys, long-sleeved loose cardigan, shorts, thongs - lifted a designer shopping bag off the back of a another woman's chair. The font on the side of the bag looked upmarket. The owner never noticed. From this elevation he followed the girl as she worked her way through a crowd of dorks. Within seconds the girl had turned a corner and he could no longer see her. When he looked back to the table, the victim had already left the table and was heading indoors to pay for her lunch, oblivious. Nobody really knew he was in the apartment because nobody ever looked up in Dewhurst.

Glenn's vigil was disturbed by a letter dropping through the mailbox. It had 'by hand' written on the front. Clearly some flunky didn't have time to put it right in his hand and instead just dropped it here at Ed's cousin's / mate's.

The letter was confirmation of what his father had left him in the will, which was nothing. Everything had been left to the Queensland Police Service. The house was to be used for young police families, new to the area and the rent to go into generating a budget for rehabilitation courses for high-spirited youths and rat bags, etcetera. There was also short note scribbled on police issue notepaper from his Dad - he'd already seen it at the lawyers.

"Dear Son,

I hope you enjoyed your time in jail, I've left you fuck all in my will but these written words.

Love, Dad."

The note is now framed and hanging above the guest toilet at Glenn's apartment in Brisbane. It's not been left there for sentimental reasons.

One hundred and Twenty Six

1994 - Ari

Between 'The Nowheres' And 'The Nothing Out Theres'

Marcos' endless shifts and Ari's depleted contact with her beloved community in Sorrento began to take their toll. She began to take long drives in the family 4x4 and would park at Slade Point staring out across the ocean. Ari would enjoy a salad lunch at the Eimeo Pub, one of the oldest establishments in the area, or an extra long sojourn out to Eungella. One weekend, she planned to take a longer drive. She also called on one of her so-called friends to allow Luca and Maria to have a sleepover with her children at the last minute and trusted them to be happy. So off Ari went into the empty places. The blank spaces. As the bush thinned out and the landscapes grew hard and red, the sky seemed larger, whiter, and sometimes bluer. Somehow the road had spirited her away - on and on and on, further away from her responsibilities.

II

Ari is driving west of Charters Towers along the highway and she spots the white expanses of what she correctly thinks is a dried up lake. Here and there along the roadside are clusters of derelict metal and wooden boats that had been stranded no longer within sight of any water. Jilted. What a sad place, Ari thinks. There is no radio signal out this far and she'd play her pop cassette inside out, some old hits from a few years earlier;

now she's got 'The Horses' by Daryl thingy in her head.
"That's the way it's gonna be little darling."

Had there been a drought? She vaguely remembers reading
about it sometime recently.

*

The far off hills, that never seemed to get any closer. Ari's
4X4 now spun past acres of unused, unwanted cranes, large
vehicles with tracks or wheels that were at least 12 feet in
diameter. All these road revenants rusting patiently in the
unrelenting sun scoured desert like a decommissioned army.
There had to be a town all the way out here. So many depleted
opal mines, abandoned pits so large that they could swallow
most Queensland cities whole; the remnants of big industry
littered this country, leaving in their wake broken machinery
and vehicles too expensive to haul across the land to the next
pit or hole in the ground. This stretch reminded her of Coober
Pedy without the PR. Yet there were advertising hoardings
ahead, was she at the edge of a city? Ari didn't know.

Sat in the shade of one of the hoardings she spotted a figure.
Probably a hitchhiker, Ari had heard the stories but she still
slowed down to take a further look. The hitchhiker was a
woman, and she was holding a large cardboard placard. Ari
only managed to read the first bit before the girl was left far
behind. It read, 'I'm thirsty! Take me onwards!' Ahead is a
road sign, **Winton 23 kilometres**. She'd never heard of it,
but it is the very least she could do was to take the girl some
water. It is about a kilometre before Ari found a wide spot to
turn around in, but she did so, returning to see if the woman
was still there. Ari estimated the woman to be in her early 30s.

*

"I'm heading through Winton, would you like a ride?"

"Yes, please."

That's when Ari spots the dog – a black and white patchy mongrel. Amongst the woman's bags; a rucksack and two smaller bags, it had been lying down in the shade next to a bowl of water. The dog stands up and gives her a friendly woof.

"Is the dog gonna be OK?"

"Sure, he'll behave if you don't mind having him in the back."

Ari manages to get a good look at the woman as they haul the bags into the rear of the car. She has dark hair, is healthy and tanned, and looks younger now. Ari wonders if this woman is running away from somebody, somewhere, but perhaps she's just projecting… As the hitcher gets into the car, she offers Ari a fleeting smile of gratitude. The dog hops through the gap in between the two front seats before Ari gets a chance to open one of the back doors to allow it clear access.

"Manners, Geoff! Now lie down." Dani reaches back and pats the dog on the side and it sits down obediently on the back seat. *"Sorry about that, he's friendly enough. He won't jump any more."*

Ari smiles and starts the car. She doesn't mind dogs at all. And this one seems personable.

"I was grateful of that shade back there, else I'd have cooked

by now."

"Yes, we underestimate the desert don't we? How dangerous it can be out here… I'm not lecturing, but I think we all forget. I was hot, even with the air conditioning blasting."

"Well thanks for stopping."

"I have some water, if you can reach on the back seat. Take a bottle please."

Dani has already reached back and is drinking, gulping, water spilling down her front, onto the car's upholstery… Ari watches, and wonders how long this woman had been out on this lonely stretch of highway. She starts the car and sets off back towards Winton.

"I'm Dani."

"Ariadne. I'm going through Winton, you can get out there, at least you'll be out of harm's way there."

"I just came from Winton but my last lift ended up coming back the way I've just come from. I think he was confused. Anyway, I asked him if he was heading west, but he ended up coming this way back east, towards the coast."

"Where are you headed, Dani?"

"Broome. I've got a job over there but I don't start for another two weeks so I thought I'd hitchhike across. A way bigger undertaking than I thought it'd be so it turns out."

Chatter fades to silence quickly, the sun is beginning to cast long shadows along the ground. Silhouettes come out to play, the shadow of the car shimmers on the rock and sand along the highway.

"I don't want to pry, but since I'm giving you a lift, I want to make sure that you're OK. It's awfully lonely out here on the highway, and you never know."

"I'm 36."

"OK. But you know, even I wouldn't take this kind of risk."

"That's probably because you're rich, oops that sounded aggressive, but."

"Maybe, maybe not. OK I'll drop it. Anyway what's this new job, if you don't mind my asking."

"I'm going to be a senior nurse. I was at Dewhurst City General but I fancied a change of scene. Dewie's too concrete jungle for a country girl like me."

"Wow, I actually think the opposite. I moved there a few months ago from Melbourne and I think its Dewhurst that's a one-horse town."

"Funny."

Dani looks out of the window. The sun has dropped behind a hill range, leaving an orange corona around the peak of one of the hills.

After about 15 minutes they come to a level crossing; its red lights are pulsing. A freight train has stalled and for as far as the eye can see in the fast diminishing daylight there seems to be no end to its string of carriages. The two women wait for a sign of movement but the train is silent, as is the bell at the level crossing that usually tolls as a train passes through.

"The driver must have a problem, no?"

"He might be asleep."

"I wonder if I should backtrack."

"It's about 100 kilometres to go back the other way via the highway. And that's a rough guess."

"He could be here for the night, that's all I'm thinking."

"What a stupid place to stop, maybe he doesn't know his tail is blocking a road."

"I can turn around, let's go."

"I got an idea, 'cos as soon as we turn around this train will start up, Murphy's law right?"

"I have some food, let's eat and then decide."

"You don't mind sharing?"

"It's nothing special, just some cold cuts and salad, in that esky in the back."

Dani hops out of the car and walks around to the rear of the car.

At that moment the level crossing bell begins to ring startling Geoff, who squeezes out from behind Ari's and Dani's seat and bounds out the car. Ari is just short of catching his lead but it slips her grasp and the dog has gone, hurtling off into the blackening desert.

"Fuck, why'd you let him go?"

The train shudders to life, creaking and clanking as it builds up to its funereal pace. Ari jumps out of the car.

"I'm sorry Dani. He was so fast."

Dani shakes her head and shrugs. *"He won't be far. We'll be alright."*

Dani runs off after the dog, calling out in hope that the dog will stop in its shoes or turn back to her. About 50 yards ahead there is a bend in the track and the pair disappear in the same direction as the freight train was travelling. She's not sure but she thinks she can hear Geoff barking as if he's on the trail of something tasty. Within minutes, Dani and Geoff are obscured by the rumbling train as it continues to roll past her 4x4. Car after car trundles onwards – 50, 60, 70. Minutes pass and as night falls, there's no sign of Dani or Geoff at all. Ari returns to the car, and decides to wait for them there. She parks the car a few yards off to the side of the road.

The next thing she knows, it's the morning.

*

The train has gone: its hypnotic, loud rhythm had sent her into a deep sleep. Like counting sheep the passing cars had been a potent substitute. Ari had fallen asleep before eating, but her growling stomach was the least of her worries. Dani's rucksack and bags were still where they'd been left in the back of the car. As Ari goes to check on them, she scans the bare landscape for Dani and her dog. All she can see are the empty tracks disappearing into the parched wastes. There's nothing on the road ahead or back in the direction she came from. The heat is oppressive already and the sun isn't even all that high in the sky. It's 7:15am.

Ari shouts their names but there's no reply. It's as if the desert had swallowed them up without a trace. There's no shade out here. Nowhere to hide, how could they survive here, especially the dog. Ari contemplates driving her 4x4 alongside the tracks for a few miles but the ground is too uneven and even if her car were good enough, what if she got into trouble? No, her best course of action was to drive to Winton and tell the local police what had happened. She wasn't really abandoning them, she was finding help. It was only 10 kilometres away so help was less than ten minutes away, she loosely calculated.

So that's what Ari did. She drove to Winton promptly finding its single-storey police station. When she arrived in the tiny car park she saw that Dani was waiting outside sat beneath a palm tree with Geoff. Waving cheerfully. Ari felt a flush of anger.

"We've been waiting for you!"

"I've been looking for you! I thought you'd both been hit by

the train or died of heatstroke."

"No, we're fine. We've been right here. We thought we'd wait here for you because it's the most logical place for you to come. You look honest and I figured you'd drop our bags here and explain to the cops what you saw."

"What did I see?"

"Well Geoff, ran after the train, followed it all the way into town, it's that slow, and I followed Geoff. It was too far to walk back out to you, and we were both knackered so I figured I'd find the cop shop first of all and hang out here. If you hadn't shown up by, say, half eight, I'd have gotten a lift to come and find you."

"This is crazy."

"You've still got my bags haven't you?"

"Yes, they're in the back." Ari is still dazed and confused by Dani's logic.

"Can I have them?"

"Help yourself."

Dani goes to the car and pulls her bag out. Ari's Esky fall out on to the car park too and lands on to its roof. *"Shit, I'm sorry."*

Ari crouches down to retrieve the plastic food cooler and turns it upright. On opening it she sees a mash of squashed cherry tomatoes, ham, water, wet bread and a burst yoghurt pot. Ari looks on hopelessly.

Dani puts her hand gently on her shoulder - Ari stands and folds into her, the women dovetail into a long hug. And that's when it happens, Ari begins to cry, sobbing uncontrollably, as she sniffs and wipes tears from her eyes a young police man comes out onto the lot and looks on. He pets Geoff gently on the head then crouches down to stroke his back.

One Hundred and Twenty Seven

2009 - Nick

There But For The Grace of God Go I

The blood-curdling scream came from about halfway down the coach. Nick thought, at first that it was some dickheads playing a joke on a sleeping mate. But there was continued commotion - a lot of screeching and hollering. There was nowhere to stop out on this section of highway, if they were to stop, even with hazards on they could be shunted by a mini-road train or anything. It was pitch black out and they were still 50 kilometres south of Dewhurst.

An abnormally tall, middle-aged fella with a totally baldhead came down to the front said quite economically, without panic, and almost as if he expected common or garden coach drivers to be trained for this kind of thing, *"There's a fella back there who's dead. Could we, perhaps, pullover?"*

For the record, it's a once in a lifetime occurrence. You'd have to be living a cursed life for it to happen twice, Nick thought.

"Pullover!"

"Stop the bus."

"Call the fucking cops," suggested a cacophony of voices.

Nick only just noticed the middle-aged baldy was wearing sunnies as he staggered back to his seats. *"I'm sat with him,"* he said dryly before he made the return trip back up the aisle.

If Nick did a U-turn and went back to Sarina, life would be made a whole lot simpler but that was much further and this was a dead body they were all dealing with now. Fucking Dewie.

One hundred and Twenty Eight

1991 - Jocasta

Pringles

Jocasta began dating a third year medical student the week
after her night with Glenn. Like a hawk, she'd seen something
she wanted, flew in, took it and then moved on. She may
have had thoughts to herself but why waste energy on a
bloke like Glenn who was mooning after that repulsive and
selfish flake, Nicole Wexler. In a way, if he'd come across,
they would most probably have gone through the procession
of occasions that were the general standard for any young
couple. Barbecues at Black's Beach with other kids; groping
in cars; fucking in bedrooms when the parents are downstairs
watching *Family Feud* – his hand clamped over her mouth so
she didn't get busted for making too much noise; trying not
to pick the same university so that she could hopefully sneak
in a few sly roots with other boys; break up over the phone or
by letter; get back together in the summer break; stay together
through graduation; then break up forever when she would
decide it's time to live a little. Move to one of the bigger
cities; meet the love of her life; get dumped; sleep around a
lot; hit her magic number; and then find out that one of her
casual 'go-tos' could just be the one. Get married to them,
go on a few holidays, a stint living and working in Mother
England; buy a dog; have an ugly big-eared kid; have another
kid twice as ugly; fuck someone else to alleviate the tedium of
suburban 'celliutude' – u still got it - u go girl, discover that
even fucking someone behind her beloved's back is a chore;
realise that she doesn't even like sex anymore; she begins to

hate her selfish prick children and the slow realisation that her legacy of femi-freedom was one inherited from her grandparent's generation. Nothing new under the sun but amnesia. There were no new frontiers for women, or men. The illusion of free will was as useful to her as a banjo-playing ball bag puppet.

Jocasta reaches for another handful of Pringles.

Last night, Medical Marc with a 'c' asked her to try a sex position with him called a reverse cowgirl. She's supposed to bronco up and down on his thing whilst all she gets to see are his toes. She admitted to him that it made her feel hot whilst doing it in front of a mirror - she had a full-length one in her bedroom at home.

"Nah, let's just do it here," Marc barked.

Although Marc was pretty short and showed signs of getting fat, he had no shortage of nurses running around after him at work. One day he suggested a threesome with another girl called Simone in the summerhouse at the end of his garden. She was tempted but just couldn't bring herself to do it with another girl.

"We're not all into it," she said flatly.

Soon-to-be junior doctor Marc didn't stick around for all that long as it happens. He got a job on graduation and transferred upstate, Vella-style. The love of Jocasta's life, the one who would fill her with babies and name a jet-ski after her would be one of her former teenage detractors - the reliable, quiet and generally well-liked ginger, freckle monster Robbie Diaz.

She rarely sits down to think about the past, people like Glenn Pearce became little more than a footnote to the cavalcade of normality that was to come her way. Was she one of the lucky ones or one of the damned? Why fight it, why fight the days?

She hear's the front door open downstairs - Robbie's singing, 'Drive' by The Cars, *"Who's gonna tell you when, its tooooo late?"*

One Hundred and Twenty Nine

1994 - Vella

The Secrets Of Us

One day, Mindy Ward's dog, a poodle called Pat, dug up a human skull. Pat had plopped the muddy cranium in her lap whilst she sat reading Thomas Harris' *Silence of the Lambs* out on the deck at the rear of her opulent new house.

This bizarre episode prompted Vella to order a further excavation that had unearthed even more bones. He entertained thoughts that these were the remains of the 'runaway' Nicole Wexler but they weren't. Turned out the bones were about 150-years old and had belonged to a native Aborigine girl - the scientists called her Myrtle Slate for the newspapers and for posterity's sake. The cause of death couldn't be established, but it got the local press and a few of the locals excited, as it was the biggest historical news event to have happened in the Whitsundays region in decades.

Word got around that a body had been found up amongst 'The Soft and Hard' at the back of the Tit Hills. The yellow police tape around the wooded boundary and the SOCO tent in the dell behind the house were enough to start tongues wagging and eyes squinting.

It had always been assumed that the land was too rocky, yet boggy, up there to build houses. But where there's a will there's a way and four large properties on sturdy stilts with decks and concrete platforms were flung up, Beverly

Hills-style. They stood empty for a few months and then the asking price came down as the developers realised there was no aristocracy in Dewhurst, no celebrity set - nobody. The people that moved in were the property developers themselves. Calling in favours, using an angle to bag one of the snazziest, jazziest houses within city limits. Awesome.

One Hundred and Thirty

2009 - Nick

The Answer Must Be In The Attempt

This kind of holdover was the worst kind and Nick was never in Dewhurst longer than was needed. It wasn't a transport hub, it wasn't a place for a 'driver switch' or a long tea break. The drivers could often choose where a good roadhouse was for them to stop and have a coffee and a bite to eat halfway through the night (provided they weren't breaking maximum wheel-time). Nick didn't like having any kind of run-ins with the police in this city.

Turned out the dead passenger had died from secondary drowning. He had been swimming in the sea and had gotten into trouble, caught in a rip, gone under. Luckily he'd fucked up at a popular beach and had gotten rescued by a lifeguard who'd then revived him with the kiss of life. Knowing that he had a coach to catch the dead man gave the ambulance men the slip at the hospital and went to the travel hub. Unbeknownst to him, he still had seawater in his lungs, pretty much signing his own death warrant the next time he slept. A Renee Kathod (the bald man with shades perched on his shiny head) had alerted other passengers by taking the pulse of the deceased. Another passenger, a Frances Dodds, who sat across the aisle from Kathod, had spotted that he was trying to take the dead man's pulse from the wrong place - he had rolled up the sleeve half way and had two fingers places on nowhere near a prominent vein. Dodds asked if the man needed help, to which Kathod answered bluntly, *"No he doesn't. He's dead."*

This prompted the blood-curdling scream from a young
woman called Do'reece Carter and the resulting kerfuffle. The
dry, drowned dead man was a Mono Shergolt from Canada, a
young lawyer on sabbatical, travelling the world. On deeper
examination he lead a clean healthy life, no history of medical
difficulties and was basically a friendly nobody - whose death
would inadvertently bring about the resolution of a separate
mystery virtually nobody had hung around long enough to
learn.

One Hundred and Thirty One

1980 - Glenn

I Am Here

That Mr Morton would use his soft drum beaters to play a roll on this gigantic gong he had, so big that it had to be ferried around on circular a frame on castors - the stencil painted block words 'Phoenix' emblazoned on the rear side.
He'd say to all of us kids lying on our backs on the assembled crash mats, "Everybody close your eyes and listen as the sun rises up over the horizon..."

Then the sound would slowly summon up a vision of the sun in our heads; the gentle splashes layering over the deep, shimmering metallic noise conjured up with his cloth-covered beaters. When he eventually told us to open our eyes once more, other teachers had opened the curtains and we found ourselves stood reborn, resplendent in the golden dazzle of the school hall, squinting at each other - bathed and renewed in light.

"Now embrace the air above your heads and around you like this and turn around in circles and shout these words as loud as you can on the count of three, "I am here! I am here!" again and again until I say stop."

We'd all reached up, into the air and did as Mr Morton had asked as he continued to play the gong with his two beaters, the songs of our young lives.

"I am here. I am here. I am -"

One Hundred and Thirty Two

2019 - Glenn

The Incomplete Kiss

Whenever I get asked about my family, it's easier to tell them about Mum - how she buggered off down to Sydney when I was 15 and that nowadays she lives happily with her second family close to Randwick Racecourse. There's more to tell than just that (obviously) but I figured whoever I'm telling isn't really all that interested anyway - it's just small talk right?

These days, Mum volunteers at a care centre for the elderly; she also meets her friends for a strolls along Coogee Beach on a Wednesday morning before the sun gets too high in the hot sky. Her harmless yet endless quest to find new traces of the mark of Eternity in the old neighbourhoods gradually began to take up more and more of her time too. Mum confessed to me that she once even wrote the one-word sermon on the wall in a public toilet stall at Sydney Central Station - scraping it into the paintwork with a key. She left her name, Aggie, etched there alongside it.

Mum never misses an ANZAC parade in the city - we argue over whether or not it's the right time or platform for indigenous Australians to protest about land rights and past treatment by our white government - it's a sore subject.

For Dad, I've made up an elaborate fiction; I deny Johnny Pearce, and the listener, his true story. A hard life for some

*is a like a badge of honour - they'll sing their tales of woe
verbatim to any old sod, but he doesn't deserve a breath
let alone a word; his essence is a putrid enigma with a
permanence I cannot rinse off. Talking about him makes him
real again. For those that go on to dig deeper, I wheel out
the following tawdry, melodramatic fantasy, in that he was
a flying doctor and that, one day, he flew out to a remote
farmstead never to return. No mayday, no wreckage, a
thug-version of Amelia Earhart, lost in a plume of snapped off
sky; a curtain of blackness drawn behind him to never again
to be re-opened. This is how I live with what he did but it
doesn't wash out. Never will.*

*I occasionally picture his fictionalised white Cesna parked on
an outcropping red sandstone plateau, a dusty backdrop. My
father's obscured shape, sat beneath the shade of the wings,
drinking bottles of medicine for fluid sustenance - this is what
doubles for the unresolved truth. Johnny Pearce is somewhere
no one could ever find him - where everything I can no longer
bear to see has been banished to.*

*

*Perhaps it was inevitable that it was to be Nicole that reached
out from the past to pull me back into the maw - I don't know
why it had come as a complete surprise to me either. The
internet - if you're online they'll find you somehow. It took
Nicole until about a month ago to come out of the woodwork.*

*When a Nick Bootman sent me a friend request on Facebook
I was confused, I didn't think I knew any hefty, rosy-cheeked
women who dressed like German backpackers - yet there she
was, it was Nicole.*

We arranged to meet at a riverside bar in Townsville just over a week later. A 2 hour flight was nothing, although if I'd have waited another week I could have met her closer to Brisbane but I guess she assumed I was still in Dewie.

A long distance coach driver for McCaffreys for over 20 years, Nicole had based herself in Southport, in the Gold Coast's gay enclave, Lime Hill, and led a relatively well-insulated life, tucked away in a protective community; a different world from the one she'd grew up in. On the surface, it seemed to me like she had adjusted to a new life on the Gold Coast, where it was assumed that if you didn't want to talk about your past you weren't pressed. It was understood that it was ok to have a history - blissful forgetfulness and recovery were welcomed and par for the course for the many who lived there.

*

Nicole confessed to how she'd travelled through Dewhurst behind the wheel of a McCaffrey's bus about twice a week since she'd gotten the job as a driver. These days Nicole owned a crash pad in Townsville as well as her place down south.

We expressed regret at how much time we'd let pass before meeting up again but it seemed crass and in the worst taste as soon as we heard ourselves say the words.

After all these years her smile was the same - the mangled phantom of a smirk that now turned into a yard of false teeth, their brilliant whiteness betraying their inauthenticity.

The reason for her re-emergence wasn't so much to recount

*the past as to try and give herself some overdue closure,
that's what she told me, but everything we spoke about was a
mere chapter heading compared to what we were feeling and
already knew.*

*I was the loose piece in the jigsaw in her extensive rebuild, all
these fortifications. Nicole had come to let me know that the
scar on her face, the jagged split lip that made her look like a
fat hare, wasn't all that had changed her heart and her ways
a long time ago - the nature of the betrayal that befell her. It
was wrong of me to dwell on her looks, her transformation,
this was just the window dressing to the unknowable, and
the result of a brave recovery - the return to a normal life.
In a single night, all her easy beauty had been smashed and
ground down to nothing but it was still her - I could see her.
This was the girl I'd walk any line for, here with me, over 25
years later.*

*

*We talked about Dean. Nicole goes to his grave whenever her
shifts allow for a stop over in Dewie. She then explained that
Dean had successfully hidden his past from her and that she
knew nothing of his life before he came to Australia (neither
did I). And her 'disappearance' had accidentally balanced
this out in some warped way - a mystery for a mystery -
heartbreak with a shared dual mechanism. I couldn't really
understand how she could justify it that way but I didn't push
her for answers to anything.*

*Nicole wasn't present to empty Dean's house, her old home.
Uli and his son Pawel cleared the place of its contents in the
end – she only learnt about his death when a lawyer tracked
her down to discuss the contents of his will in which he'd*

left her everything except the scrapped cars. She returned to Dewhurst for the first time after the incident in 1996 and took a cab up past the old house. She half-expected to see Dean sat in his recliner up on the veranda looking down over the street like he would always do of an evening but he wasn't there - no trace of anything from those days remained. A new lick of paint, a new lawn, a repaved driveway, a jungle of acacia, tamed melaleucas and big red was all that was needed to delete the days and years.

She had arranged to stay overnight with Uli and Pawel. Uli had kept a couple of crates of her things back for her from the house clearance. They left her alone to pore through them but she couldn't bring herself to look at them. Nicole had the rest of her life to grieve, but there she was with a box of props from a time she had sworn off - age hadn't withered what was hidden inside them, hosts of inanimate objects, UXBs waiting in the dark, primed to tear her apart. It would be months before she'd venture in. Nicole needed to disappear inside the crates in her own surroundings when she was sure she'd be stronger - four crates for four ghosts: Johnny, Pete, Glenn, Dean.

The only pleasant surprise awaiting her in Dewhurst was seeing her old dog, Betsy, on a walk with the kindly neighbours that must have taken her in after Dean's passing. It was as if the dog had been waiting for her to come back. Betsy jumped up and sniffed at her and licked her face, her coat shiny and living a healthy life - the hot buttered toast smell of dog fur. Her friend had returned; Nicole had been remembered, the love of an elderly dog, "She never gave up on me."

When it was time to open the crates, months later, Nicole found a box of notebooks filled with some puzzling repetitious content in amongst Dean's belongings. Page after page contained a different day's date next to a list of four names: Pavla Sapielak, Jiri Sapielak, Marta Sapielak, Piotr Sapielak. Were these the names of his family? There were books to span every year covering every day until just before he died, dozens of assorted coloured, dog-earred lined books of all shapes and sizes - decade's worth. There was virtually nothing else left from his life, and zero dating further back than his arrival in Australia. Most of Dean's personal effects were put into a storage unit, but the mould-damaged stuff was burnt in the fire pit, Uli had told her. A hidden life. So many secrets. Horrors best left buried. "Did you know he was Polish? Yet he gave me a German surname."

Photos of her mum, Jeanne; photos of herself at Yalbarroo with her grandparents Val and Amanda; polaroids of school friends - names forgotten - and a school blouse they'd all signed for her; her teenage poems; music tapes; a videotape of 'The Man from Snowy River'; Stephen King's 'It', and a forlorn rabbit she'd had since birth that she'd named Whiffy Will, which is the only artefact from the crates on show in either of her apartments, "Hello Will."

Nicole confessed earnestly that she was sorry that she'd run away - that she'd failed to speak up for me - to tell the truth. Her world had dropped down a hole. And she was petrified, alone, physically broken and mentally paralysed with shock. It had taken almost 20 years to repair the rips in the very fabric of her being. She'd had counselling, psychotherapy, along with slowly letting new friends and lovers in, step by step. An apology was unexpected. Why was she sorry, sorry to me?

Pete Wilson had battered her within an inch of her life for sport. My father had looked on and viewed the proceedings, and she was the one saying sorry, asking for forgiveness? I don't think I'll ever come close to finding a reason why any of this happened to us - I'll never know. I glimpse at his legacy - where did all that hate come from?

"All I could do as he hit me again and again was look at you locked in the back of the police car, hammering your fists on the windows to get out. Shouting. Kicking. I know you'd have saved me," Nicole said gravely. Her eyes searching the opposite river bank for nobody.

Nicole had her bright young life replaced by one filled with fear. This remarkable ghost told me that she still experienced extreme pain from her jaw that had never fully reset, and had to wear gel-saturated bandages to numb the sensation almost daily. Uli and Dean had taken her to a house in Sarina to recover with the help of a nurse friend and then she was taken to Brisbane to stay with someone Uli knew, an old girlfriend. She didn't want any news from home and when she was well enough her new life, whatever it was to be, could begin to be put together, piece by piece.

And what about Pete? The question had hung in mid-air. Nicole's stare became harder. Then she slowly shook her head and returned her gaze to me. There were no words. That evil fucker was out there, walking around somewhere, most probably unchanged, leading a normal life, his past a safely locked room. Maybe he would he reach all the way out from the nightmare days used up to seal our fates once and for all. The three of us and the dead were all linked together forever;

*did Nicole haunt him, like he did us? Are we in control of our
ghosts, do we see what they see?*

*

*We had at least five 'one for the road' drinks as the two of us
became pathetically scared that we'd never see each other
again. And that was the truth of the matter, we both knew that
once we parted ways that night, that was our ending. What
would replace the years of not knowing, the years of dark
doubt?*

*When the last bar in the centre of Townsville closed for the
evening, we staggered to a bench at a nearby taxi rank.
It was around 4 or 5 AM. With nothing left to say I kissed
her ravaged lips - a long, drunken, yet strangely familiar
version of the old version, at first desperate, then tender, then
hungry, then sad. After our lips parted, we sat in silence. The
astonishing sun was coming back again to sweep the moon
and all the night stars back into their bright daytime hiding
places. And the magpies would lift the sky with a stick.*

THE END

Acknowledgements

I would like to thank my wife Rose, my parents Jacqueline and Alan Roberts, my sister Colette Roberts. I would also like to thank my personal editors Jayne Miller, Samantha Thomas and Joanna Gibbs for their considered, expert and very welcome help and guidance during the early (Jo) and late (Sam) drafts. Each of you has given me that extra boost of confidence to see this project through to the end. Words of thanks to Chris Smekel – my unofficial Australian dialogue consultant. Mark McDonald @getmarktodoit for the stunning first edition jacket design and license to reproduce 'OVERREVS' for my front cover image. Also, gratitude to Steve Taylor and Trond-Vegard Odergarden for the alternative jacket designs to consider. Hanna Lambert for her typesetting skills. Ula Markowicz for her help with the Polish language excerpts. Andy Rous and James Starkey of The Travel Chapter for my author profile photo.

Hello and thank you to the following for encouragement, support and advice throughout the creative period: Adam Lacey, my niece & nephew: Erin & Samuel Lacey, Sue & Graham Ashley, Liz Ashley & Gav D, Giles Kent (for feedback on the very first scribbles), Matt Usher, Tom Putnam, Auntie Mary & Cousin Kenny Wood (Queensland family), Antony Valenti, Matt & Edith Fassnidge, Graham Holden, Hannah Jury, Kate Williams, Marilyn Medina Ribeiros, Ben Manning, Trudi Clarke, Fraser Jansen, Jon Woolcott (Little Toller Books), Dan Wallis, Paul Tanter, Steven 'Aqua Melon Records' Nash, Neequaye 'Dreph' Dsane, Richard Jones, Roger Balfour, Amin el Eshaiker, Brad & Mandy Eagle, Jon Simmonds, Paul & Mel Toller, Richard & Michelle Fielden, Collins A. Leysayth (RIP), Benjamin Elam, Victoria Machin, Maggie Ellis, Kimberley Wind-Manning, Tim Brading, Kenneth Ofosu, Dave 'Huggy' Williams, Eric J Drysdale, Clare Willcocks. Dan Horrigan, Graham Hawkins, Galley Beggar Books (for inspiration), Pam Holstein, Sandra Borg Wood, family: Carol, Tony, Karen, Paula, Angela, Debbie, George, Helen, Kim, Brant, Robbie, John, Anne, Jay, Liam, Stasia, Tracey, Alex, Ollie, Bernie, Peter, Sue, Anthony, Jason,

Jim, Pamela and my lovely Aunty Madge (RIP). Jon Powell, Mark Stanyer, Mark 'Wiganovsky' Williams, Patricio Carpo. Also, my lovely dog, Flossie. To my late Nan, Eva Beamer and Aunty Eva Pugh (RIP), I miss you.

Tiny excerpts of song lyrics and quotes misquoted and sprinkled in for context:

All lyrics have been quoted, paraphrased, misquoted and used in context of the narrative in observance of 'fair use' practices in step with current UK copyright laws at the time of writing/editing. This has been done with respect and admiration of the original art and has not been perverted or exploited to further our own ends. Very short excerpts of lyrics and literary quotes contained in 'The Magpie' by Alan Edward Roberts are as follows:

'In a Lonely Place' by Andrew P Solt & Edmund H North (paraphrased)
'A Christmas Carol' by Charles Dickens
'Strictly Ballroom' by Baz Luhrmann
'All Out of Love' by Air Supply
'OG: Original Gangster' – by Ice T
'Wonderful Tonight' – Eric Clapton
'Horses' – Patti Smith
'Pray' – MC Hammer
'True Faith' – New Order
'Horses' by Daryl Braithwaite
'Superwoman' by Karyn White
'Gangsta Gangsta' by NWA
'It Was a Good Day' by Ice Cube
The Holy Bible

All these songs are available for download and streaming on iTunes / Spotify and other online platforms.

Please contact www.roadsongbooks.com to discuss any issues.